THE
IDOL OF PARIS

SARAH BERNHARDT

1st WORLD
LIBRARY
Literary Society

The Idol of Paris

Sarah Bernhardt

© 1st World Library – Literary Society, 2005
PO Box 2211
Fairfield, IA 52556
www.1stworldlibrary.org
First Edition

LCCN: 2004195671

Softcover ISBN: 1-4218-0486-7
Hardcover ISBN: 1-4218-0386-0
eBook ISBN: 1-4218-0586-3

Purchase *"The Idol of Paris"*
as a traditional bound book at:
www.1stWorldLibrary.org/purchase.asp?ISBN=1-4218-0486-7

1st World Library Literary Society is a nonprofit
organization dedicated to promoting literacy by:

- Creating a free internet library accessible from any
  computer worldwide.
- Hosting writing competitions and offering book
  publishing scholarships.

Readers interested in supporting literacy
through sponsorship, donations or
membership please contact:
literacy@1stworldlibrary.org
Check us out at: www.1stworldlibrary.ORG
and start downloading free ebooks today.

The Idol of Paris
contributed by Tim, Ed & Rodney
in support of
1st World Library Literary Society

PART I. PARIS

CHAPTER I

In the dining-room of a fine house on the Boulevard Raspail all the Darbois family were gathered together about the round table, on which a white oil cloth bordered with gold-medallioned portraits of the line of French kings served as table cover at family meals.

The Darbois family consisted of François Darbois, professor of philosophy, a scholar of eminence and distinction; of Madame Darbois, his wife, a charming gentle little creature, without any pretentions; of Philippe Renaud, brother of Madame Darbois, an honest and able business man; of his son, Maurice Renaud, twenty-two and a painter, a fine youth filled with confidence because of the success he had just achieved at the last Salon; of a distant cousin, the family counsellor, a tyrannical landlord and self-centered bachelor, Adhemar Meydieux, and the child of whom he was godfather, and around whom all this particular little world revolved.

Esperance Darbois, the only daughter of the philosopher, was fifteen years old. She was long and slim without being angular. The flower head that crowned this slender stem was exquisitely fair, with the fairness of a little child, soft pale-gold, fair. Her face had, indeed, no strictly sculptural beauty; her long flax-coloured eyes were not large, her nose had no special character; only her sensitive and clear-cut nostrils gave the pretty face its suggestion of ancient lineage. Her mouth was a little large, and her full red lips opened on singularly white teeth as even as almonds; while a low Grecian forehead and a neck graceful in every curve gave Esperance a total effect of aristocratic distinction that was beyond dispute. Her low vibrant voice produced an impression that was almost physical on those who heard it. Quite without intention, she introduced into every word she spoke several inflections which made her manner of pronounciation peculiarly her own.

Esperance was kneeling on a chair, leaning upon her arms on the table. Her blue dress, cut like a blouse, was held in at the waist by a narrow girdle knotted loosely. Although the child was arguing vigorously, with intense animation, there was such grace in her gestures, such charming vibrations in her voice, that it was impossible to resent her combative attitude.

"Papa, my dear papa," she was asserting to François Darbois, "You are saying to-day just the opposite of what you were saying the other day to mother at dinner."

Her father raised his head. Her mother, on the contrary, dropped hers a little. "Pray Heaven," she was saying to herself, "that François does not get angry with her!"

The godfather moved his chair forward; Philippe Renaud laughed; Maurice looked at his cousin with amazement.

"What are you saying?" asked François Darbois.

Esperance gazed at him tenderly. "You remember my godfather was dining with us and there had been a lot of talk; my godfather was against allowing any liberty to women, and he maintained that children have no right to choose their own careers, but must, without reasoning, give way to their parents, who alone are to decide their fates."

Adhemar wished to take the floor and cleared his throat in preparation, but François Darbois, evidently a little nonplused, muttered, "And then after that - what are you coming to?"

"To what you answered, papa."

Her father looked at her a little anxiously, but she met his glance calmly and continued: "You said to my godfather, 'My dear Meydieux, you are absolutely mistaken. It is the right and the duty of everyone to select and to construct his future for himself.'"

Darbois attempted to speak....

"You even told mama, who had never known it, that grandfather wanted to place you in business, and that you rebelled."

"Ah! rebelled," murmured Darbois, with a slight shrug.

"Yes, rebelled. And you added, 'My father cut off my allowance for a year, but I stuck to it; I tutored poor students who couldn't get through their examinations, I lived from hand to mouth, but I did live, and I was able to continue my studies in philosophy.'"

Uncle Renaud was openly nodding encouragement. Adhemar Meydieux rose heavily, and straightening up with a succession of jerky movements, caught himself squarely on his heels, and then, with great conviction, said: "See here, child, if I were your father, I should take you by the ear and put you out of the room."

Esperance turned purple.

"I repeat, children should obey without question!"

"I hope to prove to my daughter by reasoning that she is probably wrong," said M. Darbois very quietly.

"Not at all. You must order, not persuade."

"Now, M. Meydieux," exclaimed the young painter, "it seems to me that you are going a little too far. Children should respect their parents' wishes as far as possible; but when it is a question of their own future, they have a right to present their side of the case. If my uncle Darbois's father had had his way, my uncle Darbois would probably now be a mediocre engineer, instead of the brilliant philosopher who is admired and recognized by the entire world."

Gentle little Madame Darbois sat up proudly, and Esperance looked at her father with a world of tenderness in her eyes.

"But, my lad," pursued Adhemar, swelling with conviction, "your uncle might well have made a fortune at machinery, while, as it is, he has just managed to exist."

"We are very happy" - Madame Darbois slipped in

her word.

Esperance had bounded out of her chair, and from behind her father encircled his head with her arms. "Oh! yes, very happy," she murmured in a low voice, "and you would not, darling papa, spoil the harmony of our life together?"

"Remember, my dear little Esperance, what I said to your mother concerned only men - now we are considering the future of a young girl, and that is a graver matter!"

"Why?"

"Because men are better armed against the struggle, and life is, alas, one eternal combat."

"The armour of the intellect is the same for a young girl as for a young man."

Adhemar shook his shoulders impatiently. Seeing that he was getting angry and was like to explode, Esperance cried out, "Wait, godfather, you must let me try to convince my parents. Suppose, father, that I had chosen the same career as Maurice. What different armour should I need?"

François listened to his daughter affectionately, drawing her closer to him. "Understand me, my dearie. I am not denying your wish as a proof of my parental authority. No, remember this is the second time that you have expressed your will in the matter of the choice of your career. The first time I asked you to consider it for six months: The six months having passed, you now place me under the obligation of -"

"Oh! papa, what a horrid word!"

"But that is it," he went on, playing with her pretty hair, "you have put me under the obligation of answering you definitely; and I have called this family council because I have not the courage, nor, perhaps, the right, to stand in your way - the way you wish to go."

Adhemar made a violent effort to leap to his feet, declaiming in his heavy voice, "Yes, François, you must try and prevent her from going this way, the most evil, the most perilous above all, for a woman."

Esperance began to tremble, but she stood resolutely away from her father, holding herself rigid with her arms hanging straight at her sides. The rose tint of her cheeks had disappeared and her blue eyes were dimmed with shadows.

Maurice hastily made a number of sketches of her; never before had he found his cousin so interesting.

Adhemar continued, "Pray allow me to proceed with what I have to say, my dear child. I have come from the country for this purpose, in answer to your father's summons. I wish to offer my experience for your protection. Your parents know nothing of life. François breathes the ether of a world peopled only by philosophers - whether dead or living, it makes little difference; your mother lives only for you two. I expressed at once my horror at the career that you have chosen, I expatiated upon all the dangers! You seem to have understood nothing, and your father, thanks to his philosophy, that least trustworthy of guides, continues futilely reasoning, for ever reasoning!"

His harangue was cut short. Esperance's clear voice broke in, "I do not wish to hear you speak in this manner of my father, godfather," she said coldly. "My father lives for my mother and me. He is good and generous. It is you who are the egoist, godfather!"

François started as if to check his daughter, but she continued, "When mama was so sick, six years ago, papa sent me with Marguerite, our maid, to take a letter to you. I did so want to read that letter, it must have been so splendid.... You answered...."

Adhemar tried to get in a word. Esperance in exasperation tapped the floor with her foot and rushed on, "You answered, 'Little one, you must tell your papa that I will give him all the advice he wants to help him out of this trouble, but it is a principle of mine never to lend money, above all to my good friends, for that always leads to a quarrel.' Then I left you and went to my Uncle Renaud, who gave me a great deal more even than we needed for mama."

Big Renaud looked hot and uncomfortable. His son pressed his hand so affectionately under the table that the good man's eyes grew wet.

"Ever since then, godfather, I have not cared for you any more."

The atmosphere of the little room seemed suddenly to congeal. The silence was intense. Adhemar himself remained thunderstruck in his chair, his tongue dry, his thoughts chaotic, unable to form a reply to the child's virulent attack. For the sake of breaking up this general paralysis, Maurice Renaud finally suggested that they should vote upon the decision to be given to his brave little cousin.

They gathered together around the table and began to talk in low tones. Esperance had sunk into a chair. Her face was very pale and great blue circles had appeared around her eyes. The discussion seemed to be once more in full swing when Maurice startled everyone by crying, "My God, Esperance is ill!"

The child had fainted, and her head hung limply back. Her golden hair made an aureola of light around the colourless face with its dead white lips.

Maurice raised the child in his arms, and Madame Darbois led him quickly to Esperance's little room where he laid the light form on its little bed. François Darbois moistened her temples quickly with Eau de Cologne. Madame Darbois supported Esperance's head, holding a little ether to her nose. As Maurice looked about the little room, as fresh, as white, as the two pots of marguerites on the mantel-shelf, an indefinable sentiment swelled up within him. Was it a kind of adoration for so much purity? Philippe Renaud had remained in the dining-room where he succeeded in keeping Adhemar, in spite of his efforts to follow the Darbois.

Esperance opened her eyes and seeing beside her only her father and mother, those two beings whom she loved so deeply, so tenderly, she reached out her arms and drew close to her their beloved heads. Maurice had slipped out very quietly. "Papa dearie, Mama beloved, forgive me, it is not my fault," she sobbed.

"Don't cry, my child, now, not a tear," cried Darbois, bending over his little girl. "It is settled, you shall be...." and the word was lost in her little ear.

She went suddenly pink, and raising herself towards him, whispered her reply, "Oh! I thank you! How I love you both! Thank you! Thank you!"

CHAPTER II

Esperance, left alone with her mother, drank the tea this tender parent brought to her, and the look of health began to come back to her face.

"Then to-morrow, mother dearest, we must go and be registered for the examinations that are soon to be held at the Conservatoire."

"You want to go to-morrow?"

"Yes, to-day we must stay with papa, mustn't we? He is so kind!"

The two - mother and daughter - were silent a moment, occupied with the same tender thoughts.

"And now we will persuade him to go out with us, shan't we, mother dear?"

"That will be the very best thing for both of you," agreed Madame Darbois, and she went to make her preparations.

Left alone, Esperance cast aside her blue dress and surveyed herself in the long mirror. Her eyes were asking the questions that perplexed her whole being. She raised herself lightly on her little feet. "Oh! yes, surely I am going to be tall. I am only fifteen, and I am quite tall for my age. Oh! yes, I shall be tall." She came very close to the mirror and examined herself closely, hypnotizing herself little by little. She beheld herself under a million different aspects. Her whole life seemed passing before her, shadowy figures came and went - one of them, the most persistent, seemed to keep stretching towards her long appealing arms. She shivered, recoiled abruptly, and passing her hand across her forehead, dispelled the dizzy visions that were gathering there.

When her mother returned she found her quietly reading Victor Hugo, studying "*Dona Sol*" in *Hernani*. She had not heard the opening of the door, and she started at finding her mother close beside her.

"You see, I am not going to lose any time," she said, closing the book. "Ah! mama, how happy I am, how happy!"

"Quick," said her mother, her finger to her lips. "Your father is waiting for us, ready to go out."

Esperance seized her hat and coat quickly and ran to join her father. He was sitting as if thinking, his head resting in his hands. She understood the struggle between love and reason in his soul, and her upright little soul suffered with his. Bending gently beside him she murmured, "Do not be unhappy, papa. You know that I can never suffer as long as I have you two. If I am quite mistaken, if life doesn't bring me any of the things that I expect, I shall find comfort in your love."

François Darbois raised his head and looked deep into the lovely eyes, "God keep you, my little daughter!"

Next morning Esperance was ready to go to the Conservatoire long before the appointed hour. M. Darbois was already in his study with one of his pupils, so she ran to her mother's room and found her busy with some papers.

"You have my birth certificate?"

"Yes, yes."

"And papa's written consent?"

"Yes, yes," sighed Madame Darbois.

"He hesitated to give it to you?"

"Oh! no, you know your father! His word is sacred, but it cost him a great deal. My dear little girl, never let him regret it."

Esperance put her finger across her mother's lips. "Mama, you know that I am honest and honourable, how can I help it when I am the child of two darlings as good as you and papa? My longing for the theatre is stronger than I can tell. I believe that if papa had refused his permission, it would have made me unhappy and that I should have fallen ill and pined away. You remember how, about a year ago, I almost died of anaemia and consumption. Really, mother dear, my illness was simply caused by my overstrung nerves. I had often heard papa express his disapproval of the theatre; and you, you remember, said one day, in reference to the suicide of a well-known actress, 'Ah, her poor mother, God keep me from seeing my daughter on the stage!'"

Madame Darbois was silent for a moment; then two tears rolled quietly from beneath her eyelids and a little sob escaped her.

"Ah! mama, mama," cried Esperance, "have pity, don't let me see you suffer so. I feared it; I did not want to be sure of it. I am an ungrateful daughter. You love me so much! You have indulged me so! I ought to give in. I can not, and your grief will kill me. I suffered so yesterday, out driving, feeling papa so far away. I kept feeling as if he were holding himself aloof in an effort to forget, and now you are crying.... Mama, it is terrible! I must make myself give you back your happiness - at least your peace of mind. Alas! - I can not give you back your happiness, for I think that I shall die if I cannot have my way."

Madame Darbois trembled. She was familiar with her daughter's nervous, high-strung temperament. In a tone of more authority than Esperance had ever heard her use, "Come, child, be quick, we are losing time," she said, "I have all the necessary papers, come."

They found at the Conservatoire several women, who had arrived before them, waiting to have their daughters entered for the course. Four youths were standing in a separate group, staring at the young girls beside their mothers. In a corner of the room was a little office, where the official, charged with receiving applications, was ensconced. He was a man of fifty, gruff, jaundiced from liver trouble, looking down superciliously at the girls whose names he had just received. When Madame Darbois entered with Esperance, the distinguished manner of the two ladies caused a little stir. The group of young men drew nearer. Madame Darbois looked about, and seeing an empty bench near a window, went towards it with her daughter. The sun, falling upon Esperance's blonde hair, turned it suddenly into an aureola of gold. A murmur as of admiration broke from the spectators.

"Now there is someone," murmured a big fat woman with her hands stuffed into white cotton gloves, "who may be sure of her future!"

The official raised his head, dazzled by the radiant vision. Forgetting the lack of courtesy he had shown those who had preceded her, he advanced towards Madame Darbois and, raising his black velvet cap, "Do you wish to register for the entrance examinations?" he said to Esperance.

She indicated her mother with an impatient movement of her little head. "Yes," said Madame Darbois, "but I come after these other people. I will wait my turn."

The man shrugged his shoulders with an air of assurance. "Please follow me, ladies."

They rose. A sound of discontent was audible.

"Silence," cried the official in fury. "If I hear any more noise, I will turn you all out."

Silence descended again. Many of these women had come a long way. A little dressmaker had left her workshop to bring her daughter. A big chambermaid had obtained the morning's leave from the bourgeois house where she worked. Her daughter stood beside her, a beautiful child of sixteen with colourless hair, impudent as a magpie. A music teacher with well-worn boots had excused herself from her pupils. Her two daughters flanked her to right and left, Parisian blossoms, pale and anaemic. Both wished to pass the entrance examinations, the one as an ingenue in comedy, the other in tragedy. They were neither comic nor tragic, but modest and charming. There was also a small shop-keeper, covered with jewels. She sat very rigid, far forward on the bench, compressed into a terrible corset which forced her breast and back into the humps of a punchinello; her legs hanging just short of the floor. Her daughter paced up and down the long room like a colt snorting impatiently to be put through its paces. She had the beauty of a classic type, without spot or blemish, but her joints looked too heavy and her neck was thrust without grace between her large shoulders. Anyone who looked into the future would have been able to predict for her, with some certainty, an honourable career as a tragedian in the provinces.

Madame Darbois seated herself on the only chair in the little office. When the official had read Esperance's birth certificate, he exclaimed, "What! Mademoiselle is the daughter of the famous professor of philosophy?'"

The two women looked at each other with amazement.

"Why, ladies," went on the official, radiantly, "my son is taking courses with M. Darbois at the Sorbonne. What a pleasure it is to meet you - but how does it happen that M. Darbois has allowed...?" His sentence died in his throat. Madame Darbois had become very pale and her daughter's nostrils quivered. The official finished with his papers, returned them politely to Madame Darbois, and said in a low tone, "Have no anxiety, Madame, the little lady has a wonderful future before her."

The two ladies thanked the official and made their way toward the door. The group of young men bowed to the young girl, and she inclined her head ever so slightly.

"Oh, la-la," screamed the big chamber-maid.

Esperance stopped on the threshold and looked directly at the woman, who blushed, and said nothing more.

"Ho, ho," jeered one of the youths, "she settled you finely that time, didn't she?"

An argument ensued instantly, but Esperance had gone her way, trembling with happiness. Everything in life seemed opening for her. For the first time she was aware of her own individuality; for the first time she recognized in herself a force: would that force work for creation or destruction? The child pressed her hands against her fluttering heart.

M. Darbois was waiting at the window. At sight of him, Esperance jumped from the carriage before it stopped. "What a little creature of extremes!" mused the professor.

When she threw her arms about him to thank him, he loosed her hands quickly. "Come, come, we haven't time to talk of that. We must sit down at once. Marguerite is scolding because the dinner is going to be spoiled."

To Esperance the dinner was of less than no importance, but she threw aside her hat obediently, pulled forward her father's chair, and sat down between the two beings whom she adored, but whom she was

forced to see suffer if she lived in her own joy - and
that she could not, and would not, hide.

CHAPTER III

The weeks before the long-expected day of the examination went by all too slowly to suit Esperance. She had chosen, for the comedy test to study a scene from *Les Femmes Savantes* (the rôle of "*Henriette*"), and in tragedy a scene from *Iphygenia*. Adhemar Meydieux often came to inquire about his god-daughter's studies. He wished to hear her recite, to give her advice; but Esperance refused energetically, still remembering his former opposition against him. She would let no one hear her recitations, but her mother. Madame Darbois put all her heart into her efforts to help her daughter. Every morning she went through her work with Esperance. To her the rôle of "*Henriette*" was inexplicable. She consulted her husband, who replied, "'*Henriette*' is a little philosopheress with plenty of sense. Esperance is right to have chosen this scene from *Les Femmes Savantes*. Molière's genius has never exhibited finer raillery than in this play." And he enlarged upon the psychology of "*Henriette's*" character until Madame Darbois realized with surprise that her daughter was completely in accord with the ideas laid down by her father as to the interpretation of this rôle. Esperance was so young it seemed impossible that she could yet understand all the double subtleties....

Esperance had taken her first communion when she

was eleven, and after her religious studies ended, she had thought of nothing but poetry, and had even tried to compose some verses. Her father had encouraged her, and procured her a professor of literature. From that time the child had given herself completely to the art of the drama, learning by heart and reciting aloud the most beautiful parts of French literature. Her parents, listening with pleasure to her recitations of Ronsard or Victor Hugo, little guessing that the child was already dreaming of the theatre. Often since then, Madame Darbois had reproached herself for having foreseen so little, but her husband, whose wisdom recognized the uselessness of vain regrets, would calm her, saying with a shake of his head, "You can prevent nothing, my dear wife, destiny is a force against which all is impotent! We can but remove the stumbling-blocks from the path which Esperance must follow. We must be patient!"

At last the day arrived! Never had the young girl been more charming. François Darbois had been working arduously on the correction of a book he was about to publish, when he saw her coming into his library. He turned towards her and, regarding her there in the doorway, seemed to see the archangel of victory - such radiance emanated from this frail little body.

"I wanted to kiss you, father, before going ... there. Pardon me for having disturbed you." He pressed her close against his heart without speaking, unwilling to pronounce the words of regret that mounted to his lips.

Esperance was silent for an instant before her father's grief: then with an exaltation of her whole being she flung herself on her father's neck: "Oh, father, dear father, I am so happy that you must not suffer; you love me so much that you must be happy in this happiness I owe to you; to-morrow, perhaps, will bring me tears. Let us live for to-day."

The professor gently stroked his daughter's velvet cheek. "Go, my darling, go and return triumphant."

In the reception-room Esperance and Madame Darbois went to the same bench, where they had sat upon their former visit. Some fifty people were assembled.

The same official came to speak to them, and, consulting the list which he was holding ostentatiously, "There are still five pupils before you, Mademoiselle, two boys and three young ladies. Whom have you chosen to give you your cues?"

Esperance looked at him with amazement. "I don't understand," she said, Madame Darbois was perturbed.

"But," answered the man, "you must have an '*Armande*' for *Les Femmes Savantes*, an '*Agememnon*' and a '*Clytemnestra*' for *Iphygenia*."

"But we did not know that," stammered Madame Darbois.

The official smiled and assumed still more importance. "Wait just a moment, ladies." Soon he returned, leading a tall, young girl with a dignified bearing, and a young man of evident refinement. "Here is Mlle. Hardouin, who is willing to give you the cues for '*Armande*' and '*Clytemnestra*,' and M. Jean Perliez, who will do the '*Agememnon*.' Only, I believe," he added, "you will have to rehearse with them. I will take all four of you into my little office where no one can disturb you."

Mlle. Hardouin was a beautiful, modest young girl of eighteen, with charming manners. She was an orphan and lived with a sister ten years older, who had been a mother to her. They adored each other. The older sister had established a good trade for herself as a dressmaker; both sisters were respected and loved.

Jean Perliez was the son of a chemist. His father had been unwilling that he should choose a theatrical career until he should have completed his studies at college. He had obeyed, graduated brilliantly, and was now presenting himself for the entrance examination as a tragedian.

The three young people went over the two scenes Esperance had chosen together.

"What a pretty voice you have, Mademoiselle," said Genevieve Hardouin timidly.

After the rehearsal of *Les Femmes Savantes*, when they finished the scene of *Iphygenia*, Jean Perliez turned to Madame Darbois and inquired the name of Esperance's instructor.

"Why, she had none. My daughter has worked alone; I have given her the cues." She smiled that benevolent smile, which always lighted her features with a charm of true goodness and distinction.

"That is indeed remarkable," murmured Jean Perliez, as he looked at the young girl. Then bending towards Madame Darbois, "May I be permitted, Madame, to ask your daughter to give me the cues of '*Junia*' in

Britannicus? The young lady who was to have played it is ill."

Madame Darbois hesitated to reply and looked towards Esperance.

"Oh! yes, mama, of course you will let me," said that young lady, in great spirits. And without more ado, "We must rehearse, must we not? Let us begin at once."

The young man offered her the lines. "I don't need them," she said laughing, "I know '*Junia*' by heart." And, indeed, the rehearsal passed off without a slip, and the little cast separated after exchanging the most enthusiastic expressions of pleasure.

A comrade asked Perliez, "Is she any good, that pretty little blonde?"

"Very good," Perliez replied curtly.

Everything went well for Esperance. Her appearance on the miniature stage where the examinations were held caused a little sensation among the professor-judges.

"What a heavenly child!" exclaimed Victorien Sardou.

"Here is truly the beauty of a noble race," murmured Delaunay, the well-known member of the Comedie-Française.

The musical purity of Esperance's voice roused the assembly immediately out of its torpor. The judges, no longer bored and indifferent, followed her words with breathless attention, and when she stopped a low murmur of admiration was wafted to her.

"Scene from *Iphygenia*," rasped the voice of the man whose duty it was to make announcements. There was a sound of chairs being dragged forward, and the members of the jury settling themselves to the best advantage for listening. Here in itself was a miniature triumph, repressed by the dignity assumed by all the judges, but which Esperance appreciated none the less. She bowed with the sensitive grace characteristic of her. Genevieve Hardouin and Jean Perliez congratulated her with hearty pressures of the hand.

As she was leaving Sardou stopped her in the vestibule. "Tell me, please, Mademoiselle, are you related to the professor of philosophy?"

"He is my father," the girl answered very proudly.

Delaunay had arisen. "You are the daughter of François Darbois! We are, indeed, proud to be able to present our compliments to you. You have an extraordinary father. Please tell him that his daughter has won every vote."

Esperance read so much respect and sincerity in his expression that she curtsied as she replied, "My father will be very happy that these words have been spoken by anyone whom he admires as sincerely as M. Delaunay."

Then she went quickly on her way.

As soon as they were back on the Boulevard Raspail and home, Esperance and her mother moved towards the library. Marguerite, the maid, stopped them. "Monsieur has gone out. He was so restless. Is Mademoiselle satisfied?"

"I was; but I am not any more, Marguerite, since papa is not here. Was he feeling badly?"

"Well, he was not very cheerful, Mademoiselle, but I should not say that there was anything really the matter with him."

Mother and daughter started. Someone was coming upstairs. Esperance ran to the door and fell into the arms of that dearly-loved parent. He kissed her tenderly. His eyes were damp.

"Come, come, dear, that I may tell you...."

"Your lunch is ready," announced Marguerite.

"Thank you," replied Esperance; "papa, mama, and I, we are all dying of hunger."

Madame Darbois gently removed her daughter's hat.

"Please, dear papa, I want to tell you everything."

"Too late, dear child, I know everything!"

The two ladies seemed surprised. "But - ? How?"

"Through my friend, Victor Perliez, the chemist; who is, like me, a father who feels deeply about his child's choice of a career."

Esperance made a little move.

"No, little girl," went on François Darbois, "I do not want to cause you the least regret. Every now and then my innermost thoughts may escape me; but that will pass.... I know that you showed unusual simplicity as '*Henriette*,' and emotion as '*Iphygenia*.' Perliez's son, whom I used to know when he was no higher than that," he said, stretching out his hand, "was enthusiastic? He is, furthermore, a clever boy, who might have made something uncommon out of himself as a lawyer, perhaps. But -"

"But, father dear, he will make a fine lawyer; he will have an influence in the theatre that will be more direct, more beneficial, more far-reaching, than at the Bar. Oh! but yes! You remember, don't you, mama, how disturbed you were by M. Dubare's plea on behalf of the assassin of Jeanne Verdier? Well, is it not noble to defend the poets, and introduce to the public all the new scientific and political ideas?"

"Often wrong ideas," remarked Darbois.

"That is perhaps true, but what of it? Have you not said a thousand times that discussion is the necessary soil for the development of new ideas?"

The professor of philosophy looked at his daughter, realizing that every word he had spoken in her hearing, all the seed that he had cast to the wind, had taken root in her young mind.

"But," inquired Madame Darbois, "where did you see M. Perliez?"

The professor began to smile. "Outside the Conservatoire. Perliez and I ran into each other, both impelled by the same extreme anxiety towards the scene of our sacrifice. It is not really necessary to consult all the philosophical authorities on this subject of inanition of will," he added, wearily.

"Oh! chocolate custard," cried out Esperance with rapture, "Marguerite is giving us a treat."

"Yes, Mademoiselle, I knew very well...."

A ring at the front door bell cut short her words. They listened silently, and heard the door open, and someone come in. Then the maid entered with a card.

François Darbois rose at once. "I will see him in the salon," he said.

He handed the card to his wife and went to meet his visitor. Esperance leaned towards her mother and read with her the celebrated name, "Victorien Sardou." Together they questioned the import of this visit, without being able to find any satisfactory explanation.

When François entered the salon, Sardou was standing, his hands clasped behind him, examining through half-closed eyes a delicate pastel, signed Chaplain - a portrait of Madame Darbois at twenty. At the professor's entry, he turned round and exclaimed with the engaging friendliness that was one of his special charms, "What a very pretty thing, and what superb colour!"

Then advancing, "It is to M. François Darbois that I have the pleasure of speaking, is it not?"

He had not missed the formality in the surprise evinced

by the professor as, without speaking, the professor bowed him towards a chair.

"Let me say to begin with, my dear professor, that I am one of your most fervent followers. Your last book, *Philosophy is not Indifference*, is, in my opinion, a work of real beauty. Your doctrine does not discourage youth, and after reading your book, I decided to send my sons to your lectures."

François Darbois thanked the great author. The ice was broken. They discussed Plato, Aristotle, Montaigne, Schaupenhauer, etc. Victorien Sardou heard the clock strike; he had lunched hastily and had to be back at the Conservatoire by two o'clock, as the jury still had to hear eleven pupils. He began laughing and talking very fast, in his habitual manner: "I must tell you, however, why I have come; your daughter, who passed her examination this morning, is very excellent. She has the making of a real artist; the voice, the smile, the grace, the distinction, the manner, the rhythm. This child of fifteen has every gift! I am now arranging a play for the Vaudeville. The principal rôle is that of a very young girl. Just at present there are only well-worn professionals in the theatre."

He rose. "Will you trust your daughter to me? I promise her a good part, an engagement only for my play, and I assure you of her success."

M. Darbois, in his amazement and in spite of the impatience of the academician, withheld his answer. "Pray permit me," he said, touching the bell, "to send for my daughter. It is with great anxiety, I admit to you, that I have given her permission to follow a theatrical career, so now I must consult her, while still trying to advise."

Then to the maid, "Ask Madame and Mademoiselle to come here."

Sardou came up to the professor and pressed his hand gratefully. "You are consistent with your principles. I congratulate you; that is very rare," he said.

The two ladies came in.

"Ah," he continued, glancing toward the pastel, after he had greeted Madame Darbois, "Here is the model of this beautiful portrait."

The gracious lady flushed, a little embarrassed, but flattered. After the introduction, Sardou repeated his proposal to Esperance, who, with visible excitement, looked questioningly at her father.

"It seems to me," said Madame Darbois, timidly, "that this is rather premature. Do you feel able to play so soon in a real theatre, before so many people?"

"I feel ready for anything," said the radiant girl quickly, in a clear voice.

Sardou raised his head and looked at her.

"If you think, M. Sardou, that I can play the character, I shall be only too happy to try; the chance you give me seems to come from destiny. I must endeavour as soon as possible to appease my dear father for his regret for having given me my own way."

François would have spoken, but she prevented him,

drawing closer to him. "Oh, dear papa, in spite of yourself, I see this depression comes back to you. I want to succeed, and so drive away your heavy thoughts."

"Then," said Sardou quickly, to relieve them all of the emotion they were feeling, "it is quite agreed." Turning to Madame Darbois, who was trembling, "Do not be alarmed, dear Madame; we still have six or eight months before the plan will be ready for realization, which I feel sure will be satisfactory to all of us. I see that you are ready to go out; are you returning to the Conservatoire?"

"Yes," said Esperance, "I promised to give '*Junia's*' cues to M. Jean Perliez."

"The son of another learned man! The Conservatoire is favoured to-day," said Sardou. "I shall be pleased to escort you, Madame," he added, bowing politely to Madame Darbois, "and this child shall unfold to me on the way her ideas on the drama: they must be well worth hearing."

It was already late. The two gentlemen shook hands, anticipating that, henceforth, they would meet as friends.

When they had left him, François looked at the pastel, which he had not examined for a long time. The young girl smiled at him with that smile that had first charmed him. He saw himself asking M. de Gossec, a rich merchant, for the hand of his daughter Germaine. He brushed his hand across his forehead as if to remove the memory of the refusal he had received on that occasion: then he smiled at the new vision which rose before his imagination. He saw himself in the church of St. Germain des Pres, kneeling beside Germaine de Gossec, trembling with emotion and happiness. A cloud of sadness passed over his face: now he was following the hearse of his father-in-law, who had committed suicide, leaving behind him a load of debt. The philosopher's expression grew proud and fierce. The first thirteen years of his marriage had been devoted to paying off this debt: then came the death of the sister of M. de Gossec, leaving her niece eight hundred thousand francs, five hundred thousand of which had served to pay the debt. For the last four years the family had been living in this comfortable apartment on the Boulevard Raspail, very happy and without material worries: but how cruel those first thirteen years had been for this young woman! He gazed at the pastel for a long time, his eyes filling with tears. "Oh, my dear, dear wife!"

In the carriage on the way to the Conservatoire the conversation was very animated. The dramatic author was listening with great interest while the young girl explained her theories on art and life. "What a strange little being," he thought, and his penetrating glance tried in vain to discover what weakness was most likely to attack this little creature who seemed so perfect.

The carriage stopped at the Conservatoire. Jean Perliez was waiting at the foot of the stairs. At sight of them his face lighted up. "I was afraid that you had forgotten me in the joy of your success."

The girl looked at him in amazement. "How could I forget when I had given my word?"

"You know Victorien Sardou?"

"Only to-day," said Esperance laughing; "yesterday we did not know him."

They were back in the reception-room which was only a little less noisy than it was in the morning. Many candidates believed that they had been accepted; several had even received encouraging applause; others, who had been received in frigid silence, comforted themselves with the reflection that they had at least been allowed to finish.

When Jean Perliez and Esperance entered the auditorium there was a flattering stir, as much in pleasure at seeing the young girl again, as in welcome to the future actor.

"Scene from *Britannicus*, M. Jean Perliez, '*Nero*'; Mlle. Esperance Darbois, '*Junia*,'" proclaimed the usher.

The scene was so very well enacted that a "Bravo" broke from the learned group around the table. Which one of the judges had not been able to contain his admiration? The young actors could not decide. Each one believed sincerely the success was due to the other. They congratulated each other with charming expressions of delight, and took each other by the hand.

"We shall be good friends, shall we not, M. Perliez?" said Esperance.

The young man turned quite red, and when Madame Darbois held out her hand to him, he kissed it politely, with the kiss he had not dared to give to Esperance.

CHAPTER IV

Esperance having chosen the stage as her career, the whole household was more or less thrown into confusion. It became necessary to make several new arrangements. As François Darbois was not willing that his wife should accompany Esperance every day to the Conservatoire, it became quite a problem to find a suitable person to undertake this duty.

For the first time in her life Madame Darbois had to endure humiliating refusals. The young widow of an officer was directed by a friend of the family to apply. She seemed a promising person.

"You will have to be here every morning by nine," Madame Darbois said to her, "and you will be free every afternoon by four. The course is given in the morning, but twice a week there are classes also in the afternoon; on those days you will lunch with us."

"And Sundays?"

"Your Sundays will be your own. The Conservatoire has no classes on Sunday."

"So I understand that you would employ me only to accompany your daughter to the Conservatoire, Madame!" said the officer's widow, dryly. "I shall be compelled to refuse your offer. I am unfortunately forced to work to support my two children, but I owe some respect to the name I bear. The Conservatoire is a place of perdition, and I am astonished," she added, "that the professor, who is so universally esteemed and respected, could have been able...."

Madame Darbois rose to her feet. She was very pale. "It is not necessary for you to judge the actions of my husband, Madame. That is enough."

When she was left alone Madame Darbois reflected sadly upon the narrow-mindedness of her fellow creatures. Then she reproached herself with her own inexperience that put her at the mercy of the first stupid prude she encountered. She was well aware that the Conservatoire was not supposed to be a centre of culture and education, but she had already observed the modesty and independence of several of the young girls there: the well-informed minds of most of the young men. Nevertheless, she had had her lesson, and was careful not to lay herself open to any new affront. After some consideration, she engaged a charming old lady, named Eleanore Frahender, who had been companion in a Russian family, and was now living in a convent in the Faubourg Saint-Germain, where only trustworthy guests could be received. The old lady loved art and poetry, and as soon as she had met Esperance, was full of enthusiasm for her new duties. The young girl and she agreed in many tastes, and very soon they were great friends.

M. Darbois was quite contented with the arrangement, and could now attend to his work with complete tranquillity. Every morning the family gathered in the dining-room at half-past eight to take their coffee together. Esperance would recount all the little events of the day before and her studies for the day to come. Whenever she felt any doubt about an ambiguous phrase, she went at once to get her father's advice upon it. Sometimes Genevieve Hardouin would drop in to talk with her and Mlle. Frahender. Esperance adored Racine and refused to study Corneille, before whom Genevieve bowed in enthusiastic admiration.

"He is superhuman," she exclaimed, fervently.

"That is just what I reproach him for," returned Esperance. "Racine is human, that is why I love him. None of Corneille's heroines move me at all, and I loathe the sorrows of '*Phaedre*.'"

"And '*Chimene*'?" asked Genevieve Hardouin.

"'*Chimene*' has no interest for me. She never does as she wishes."

"How feminine!" said the professor, gently.

"Oh! you may be right, father dear, but grief is one and indivisible. Her father, cruelly killed by her lover, must kill her love for the lover, or else she does not love her father: and, that being the case, she doesn't interest me at all. She is a horrid girl." Tenderly she embraced her father, who could easily pardon her revolt against Corneille, because he shared her weakness for Racine.

Several months after Esperance's most encouraging admission to the Conservatoire, Victorien Sardou wrote a note to François Darbois, with whom he had come to be warm friends, warning him that he was soon coming to lunch with them, to read his new play to the family. Esperance was wild with excitement. The time of waiting for the event seemed interminable to her. Her father tried in vain to calm her with philosophical reflections. Creature of feeling and impulse that she was, nothing could control her excitement.

Sardou had also asked François Darbois to invite Mlle. Frahender, whose generous spirit and whose tact and judgment he much esteemed. The old lady arrived, carrying as usual the little box with the lace cap which she donned as soon as her bonnet was laid aside. On this great day the little cap was embellished by a mauve satin ribbon, contrasting charmingly with the silver of her hair.

All through lunch Esperance was delightful. Her quick responses to Sardou's questions were amazing in their logic. The extreme purity of this young soul seeking self-expression so courageously, struck the two men with particular emphasis.

The reading was a great success. The part intended for Esperance, the young girl's part, the heroine of the piece, had become of primary importance. Sardou had been able to study Esperance's qualifications during the months he had been a frequent visitor at the Darbois's home, and he had made the most of his prescience.

Lack of experience of the theatre, so natural in a child of sixteen, suggested several scenes of pure comedy. Then, as the drama developed, the author had heightened the intensity of the rôle by several scenes of real pathos, relying completely on Esperance to interpret them for him. Quite overcome by the death of the heroine she was to impersonate, she thanked the author, with tears streaming down her cheeks, her hands icy, her heart beating so furiously that the linen of her white blouse rose and fell.

"It is rather I who shall be thanking you the day of the first production," said Sardou much touched, as he wrapped round his neck the large, white square he always wore. "I believe that to-day has not been wasted."

The rehearsals began. Sardou had asked for and obtained from the Conservatoire six months leave for his young protégée, but Esperance would on no account consent to give up her classes. The only concession she would make was to give up the after-noon classes twice a week.

The press began to notice this infant prodigy, who wished to remain quite unheralded until her debut. François Darbois, in spite of his friendship with several journalists, could not make them adhere to their promises of silence, and when he complained bitterly to the head of a great daily, "But, my friend," the editor rejoined, "that daughter of yours is particularly fascinating, and certainly when you launched her into this whirlpool, you should have remembered that the only exits are triumph or despair!"

The philosopher grew pale.

"I believe," went on his friend, "that this child will vanquish every obstacle by the force of her will, will stifle all jealousies by the grace of her purity, and she already belongs to the public, while the fame of your name has simply served for a stepping-stone. You, in your wisdom, have been able to impart true wisdom to your child. But before the public has ever seen her she is famous, and Sardou affirms that the day after her appearance she will be the idol of all Paris. I owe it to the profession of journalism to write her up in my paper, and I am doing it, you must admit, with the utmost reserve."

CHAPTER V

And so at last the day of the performance came. Esperance, who was so easily shaken by the ordinary events of life, met any danger or great event quite calmly. For this young girl, so delicately fair, so frail of frame, possessed the soul of a warrior.

The sale of tickets had opened eight days in advance. The agents had realized big profits. The first night always creates a sensation in Paris. All the social celebrities were in the audience: and, what is less usual, many "intellectuals." They wished to testify by their presence their friendship for François Darbois, and to protest against certain journalists, who had not hesitated to say in print that such a furore about an actress (poor Esperance) was prejudicial to the dignity of philosophy.

In a box was the Minister of Belgium, who had been married lately, and wanted to show his young wife a "first night" in Paris. The First Secretary of the Legation was sitting behind the Minister's wife.

"Look there, that is Count Albert Styvens," said a journalist, pointing out the Secretary to his neighbour, a young beauty in a very *decolletée* gown.

The neighbour laughed. "Is he as reserved and as

Sarah Bernhardt

serious as he looks?" she inquired.

"So they say."

"Poor fellow," answered the pretty woman, with affected pity, examining him through her opera glasses.

Sardou, behind the scenes, was coming and going, arranging a chair, changing the position of a table, catching his foot in a carpet, swearing, nervous in the extreme. He made a hundred suggestions to the manager, which were received with weariness. He entered into conversation with the firemen. "Watch and listen, won't you, so that you can give me your impression after the first act?" For Sardou always preferred the spontaneous expressions of workmen and common people to the compliments of his own *confrères*.

The distant skurry in the wings that always precedes the raising of the curtain was audible on the stage. This rattling of properties is very noticeable to actors new to the theatre, though it is quite unsuspected by the general public.

The first act began. The audience was sympathetic, but impatient. However, the author knew his public, knew when to spring his surprises, how to hold the emotion in reserve until a climax of applause at the final triumph.

Esperance made her first entrance, laughing and graceful, as her rôle demanded. A murmur of admiration mounted from the orchestra to the balcony. Hers was such startling, such radiant fairness! Her musical, fluting voice acted like as a strange enchantment on the astonished audience. From the first moment the public was hers. The critic touched his neighbour's elbow. "Look at Count Albert, he seems stunned!"

As the Count leaned forward to watch more intently: "Great Heavens, do you suppose he will fall in love with her, do you believe he will really care for that little thing?" murmured the woman, mockingly.

The curtain fell amidst a shower of "Bravos." Esperance had to return three times before the public, which continued to applaud her unstintedly, as she smiled and blushed under her make-up. In spite of fifteen minutes' waiting, the intermission did not seem long. The occupants of the boxes were busy exchanging calls.

"She is perfectly adorable, she takes your breath. Just think of it, only sixteen and a half!"

"Do you think it is a wig?"

"Oh! no, that is her own hair - but what a revelation of loveliness! And what a carriage!"

"But her voice above all! I do not think that I have ever heard such declamation!"

"She is still at the Conservatoire?"

"Yes."

"The Theatre-Française ought to engage her immediately. They would find it would at once increase their subscription list."

"They say that her father is very much distressed to see her in the theatre. Why there they are, the Darbois. Don't you see them, in that box far back? They are looking very pleased."

A tall, pale man passed by.

"Ah! there goes Count Styvens. Have you read the article he wrote in the *Debats* this morning?"

"No, he puts me to sleep."

"I read it; it was rather unusual."

"What about?"

"About the fecundity of the pollen of flowers."

The chatter ceased. The count was within hearing.

"What have you to say about Esperance Darbois?" inquired a young lady.

The count blushed vividly, an unaccustomed light gleaming in his clear eyes. "It is too soon to pass judgment yet," he said, losing himself in the throng again.

In the Darbois's box there was a constant coming and going of friends. Jean Perliez joined them, his face betraying a conflict of emotions that were not lost on the father of Esperance.

"Did you see my daughter?"

"Yes. I just went to congratulate her."

"How did you find her?"

"Amazing! She is splendid, but not vain. She seems sure of herself and at the same time shows a little stage fright, a special variety which makes her hands like ice, and tightens her throat, as you must have noticed from the strain in her first speeches."

"Indeed I noticed it, and was a little frightened," said Mlle. Frahender.

"I know," said Jean Perliez, "but we need not be worried. It does not affect her powers and the force of her decision. She is invincible."

He heaved a deep sigh and withdrew into a corner to hide the emotion which was choking him. François Darbois had divined the fervent love this youth felt for his daughter, and understood the sufferings of this timid love which dared not declare itself lest it be repulsed. However, the chemist, the father of this young man, occupied a respected position as a well-to-do man, with an unblemished reputation. Why should he not declare himself, or at least try to find some encouragement? François Darbois would have been well contented with this marriage. Esperance was still too young, but, once engaged, they could wait awhile. He secretly took cognizance of Jean Perliez's sufferings, and a wave of pity surged up in his heart. "I will have to speak to him myself," he thought.

The curtain went up, disclosing Esperance, a book in her hand, her back to the public. She was not reading. That was evident from the weary droop of her body, from the rigid gaze into space. A coming storm was heralded by her quick motion, when she sprang up, threw aside her book, shook the pretty head to drive away the black butterflies in her brain, and ran to kiss her stage mother, who was playing Bridge with the villainess of the piece. There was such spontaneity in her movements that the sympathetic audience cried out, "Bravo!"

In the course of the act, Esperance secured several salvos of applause. The sustained emotion of the grief that overwhelmed her and the spasm of weeping which closed the act gave the young artist complete assurance of the public's earnest approval.

Sardou had dropped into the box of the Minister Plenipotentiary. He hid himself from the public, but sought the opinion of his great friend.

"Will you," asked the Minister, "present me to your young heroine?"

"Oh! let me come with you," besought his wife.

The Belgian Prince looked questioningly at Sardou, and at his nod of acquiescence they prepared to go and salute the new star just risen in the Parisian firmament.

"Come with us, my dear Count."

Albert Styvens became livid, a cold sweat broke out on his forehead, a polite phrase died in his throat. He rose to his feet and followed the Prince of Bernecourt.

The little reception-room next to Esperance's dressing-room was full of flowers, but no one was there. The manager and author had agreed that no stranger should approach the young artist. Only the family, Jean Perliez and Mlle. Frahender were allowed to enter. This good old soul was with Esperance now, as was Marguerite, who was not willing to leave her young mistress.

Sardou knocked. "Let me know, my dear child, when you are ready."

The door opened almost immediately, and the young girl rushed joyfully out into the little room. She stopped short upon seeing three strangers, and her eyes sought Sardou's, full of startled surprise.

"I have taken the liberty of disturbing you, little friend.... I want to present you to the Princess de Bernecourt."

Esperance curtsied with pretty grace. The Minister-Prince complimented her graciously; he was a dilettante, who could express himself most charmingly, in well chosen, artistic terms.

"Your Excellency overcomes me," said the young actress. "I shall do my best to deserve your kindness."

With a quick movement she re-adjusted her tulle scarf on her shoulders and blushed a little. The Minister turned and saw Albert Styvens standing with nervous interest - gazing like one bewitched at the enchanting maiden.

"Let me present to you Count Albert Styvens."

Esperance inclined her head a little and drew instinctively nearer to Mlle. Frahender.

The Count had not moved. The Prince led him away as soon as he had made his adieux to the young girl and the elder lady.

"Are you ill or insane?" he asked his Secretary.

"Insane, yes; I think I must be going insane," murmured the young man in a choking voice.

The play was in four acts, there were still two to come. The audience seemed to watch in a delirium of delight, and when the last curtain dropped, they called Esperance back eight times, and demanded the author.

In spite of all the talent displayed by Sardou as author, there was much enthusiasm and an unconscious gratitude in him as the discoverer of a new sensation.... No comet acclaimed by astronomers as capable of doubling the harvest would have moved the populace as did the description in all the papers of this new star in Paris.

CHAPTER VI

The family found itself back on the Boulevard Raspail. The Darbois had not cared to leave their box. After every act, Mlle. Frahender carried their comments and tender messages to Esperance. François Darbois had great difficulty in constraining himself to remain in the noisy vestibule. He suffered too acutely at seeing his daughter, that pure and delicate child, the focus of every lorgnette, the subject of every conversation. Several phrases he had overheard from a group of men had brought him to his feet in a frenzy; then he fell back in his place like one stunned. Nevertheless there had not been one offensive word. It was all praise.

The philosopher held his daughter in his arms, pressed close against his heart, and tears ran down his cheeks.

"It is the first time, and shall be the last, that I wish to see you on the stage, dear little daughter. It is too painful for me, and what is worst of all I fear it will take you away from me."

Esperance replied trembling, "Pardon me, Oh! pardon me, it is such a force that impels me. I am sorry you suffer so. Oh! don't give way, I beg of you!"

She fell on her knees before her father, sobbing and kissing his hands.

Sarah Bernhardt

Sardou, who was expected, came in just then, and his exuberance was dashed to the ground when he witnessed the trouble the family were in.

"Come, this is foolishness," he said, helping Esperance to her feet.

Then turning to the old Mademoiselle, "Here, dear lady, take this child away to compose herself, wash the tears off her poor little face, and hurry back, for I am dying of hunger."

Madame Darbois remembered that she was the hostess, and disappeared to see if everything was ready in the dining-room.

As soon as he was left alone with the philosopher, the author exclaimed, "In the name of God, man, is this where philosophy leads you? You are torturing that child whom you adore! Oh! yes, you are distressed, I know. The public has this evening taken possession of your daughter, but you are powerless to prevent it, and now is the time for you to apply to yourself your magnetic maxims. Esperance is one of those creatures who are only born once in a hundred years or so; some come as preservers, like Joan of Arc; others serve as instruments of vengeance of some occult power" (Sardou was an ardent believer in the occult). "Your child is a force of nature, and nothing can prevent her destiny. The fact that you have seen her brilliant development in spite of the grey environment of her first sixteen years, should convince you of the uselessness of your protests or regrets. The career that she has chosen is bristling with dangers, and full of disillusions, and gives free rein to a pitiless horde of calumniators. That cannot be helped. Your task, my friend," he added more calmly, "is to protect your daughter, and above all to assure her of a refuge of tenderness, and love and understanding."

Esperance came back, followed by her mother and the old Mademoiselle. Her father held out his arms to her and whispered, "You were wonderful, darling; I am happy to...."

He could not go on, and put his hot lips against her beautiful pure forehead to avoid the embarrassment that distressed him so powerfully.

Thanks to Sardou's gifts as a *raconteur*, the supper passed off pleasantly enough. This great man could unfold the varied pages of his mind with disconcerting ease. He knew everything, and could talk and act with inimitable vivacity. His anecdotes were always instructive, drawn from his manifold sources of knowledge in art or science. Mlle. Frahender was stupified by so much eclecticism, the philosopher forgot his grief, Madame Darbois realized for the first time that there might exist a brain worthy of comparison with her husband's. As to Esperance, she was living in a dream of what the future would unfold. One evening had sufficed for her to conquer Paris, to capture the provinces, and arouse the foreigner, frequently so indifferent to great artistic achievements.

The young pupil pursued her courses at the Conservatoire, in spite of Sardou's remonstrances that she would find it fatiguing. The modesty and simplicity of her return to the midst of her comrades restored her to the popularity her triumph had endangered.

"She is, you know, quite a 'sport,'" pronounced a sharp young person, who was destined to take the parts of the aggressive modern female.

A tall young man, with a grave face and settled manner, approaching baldness, in spite of his twenty-three years, pressed Jean Perliez's hand affectionately. "Don't give in, old fellow, keep up hope. You never know!"

Jean smiled sadly, shaking his head. He looked at Esperance, who was lovelier than ever. He had waited for her at the foot of the stairway, for the intimacy of the two families gave him a chance to know when to expect his glorious little friend.

"Why, how pale you are, Jean!" she exclaimed at sight of him. "What is the matter with you?"

"What is the matter with me?" he murmured.

"What is the matter with him?" echoed several of the students.

Esperance alone was not aware what was the matter with him, poor fellow, for, in spite of the encouragement of François Darbois, Jean would say nothing. He realized the shock that it would be to Esperance. She liked him so much as a friend! On the long walks they took, with Genevieve Hardouin and Mlle. Frahender, she had very often frankly confided to him that she did not want to think about getting married for years and years!

"I want to live for my art," she would say, "and I will never marry an artist!"

He had then thought very seriously of giving up the theatre and becoming a barrister, as his father had always wished him to do, but that would mean that he would lose the chance of seeing Esperance so often.

Jean Perliez had become great friends with Maurice Renaud, the girl's cousin. They both talked of her and loved her, but Maurice's love was more selfish, less deeply rooted. He was not jealous of Perliez; he was sorry for him and counselled him to speak up, since his uncle, the professor, was in sympathy with him.

"No," said Jean, "she is really too young to understand."

Maurice shrugged his shoulders. "It is true that Esperance is not yet seventeen, but her intelligence has always been ahead of her years. At twelve she could outdo me by the logic of her reasoning on the mysteries of religion. We both adore, my dear Jean, a very extraordinary little person. I will get out of your way gracefully, if you succeed; but I have a presentiment that neither you nor I will be the lucky fellow. I shall console myself, but you, take care!"

Esperance suspected nothing of the different emotions she was causing. Her youth guarded her against any betrayal of the senses. She thought that love was the natural result of marriage. The great passions as the poets sang them exalted her spirit, made her heart beat faster, but for her they remained in the realms of the ideal.

CHAPTER VII

A horrible catastrophe occurred in Belgium, leaving the inhabitants of the lower quarter of Brussels without shelter or clothing. Relief was organized on all sides, and the Theatre-Française announced a great representation of *Hernani* to be given as a benefit for the sufferers in the Royal Theatre de la Monnaie in Brussels. The star who had undertaken "*Dona Sol*" fell ill ten days before the performance was due. The Comedie was much embarrassed, for the usual understudy of the indisposed actress was an amiable echo, with little talent. Mounet-Sully thought immediately of Esperance and obtained permission to make whatever arrangements he could with her. His arrival at the Darbois home occasioned great excitement.

"I claim your indulgence in the name of charity, Monsieur," he said to François. "The Comedie-Française finds itself in the most awkward quandary. We have prepared a big gala performance at La Monnaie, to raise money for all those poor Belgian sufferers."

"Oh! I have seen the notices," said Esperance, "with artistes of the Comedie, even in the smaller rôles. What would I not give to see that production!"

Mounet-Sully smiled. "If your father will give his

permission, Mademoiselle, you can certainly see it; for I have come to ask you to take part therein."

"What do you mean?" asked M. Darbois curiously.

"Our '*Dona Sol*' is sick, very sick, and her understudy is not equal to such an occasion. The last examination you passed in *Hernani* delighted us with your manner of interpreting the rôle. We will give you all the rehearsals you need at the Comedie; you will be assisting at a work of charity, and you will be recompensed for whatever outlay or expense that you may incur."

Esperance drew herself up. "If my father will give his consent for me to make my own reply...."

"Yes," said the professor simply.

"Then I will say ... thank you, father dear," she said, tremulously, "I will say that I am happier than I can possibly tell you, at the great honour you have done me, but that I do not want any recompense."

Mounet-Sully started to speak.

"Oh! no, I beg you, do not spoil my joy."

"Then, we will take care of your travelling expenses, and those of your party."

She contracted her beautiful eyebrows a little. "Oh! M. Mounet-Sully, I am rich just now, think of all the money that I have made these four months that we have been giving Victorien Sardou's play. I don't want anything, I am glad, so glad...."

She kissed her father and her mother impulsively, and also the astonished old Mademoiselle.

"What about me?" asked Mounet-Sully gaily; "do I not get my reward?"

She held up her forehead for a salutation from the artist, who took leave of the family, glowing with delight at the good news he had to carry back to the Comedie.

"To-morrow you will get a schedule of rehearsals," he called from the doorway.

Madame Darbois was worried about the journey, and Mlle. Frahender agreed to accompany Esperance. It was decided that Marguerite should go to look after them. The faithful soul had practically brought up the child; her zeal and devotion were unfailing.

But M. Darbois raised the objection, "You should have a man with you."

The door bell rang, then they heard a voice, "In the salon? Don't bother to announce me, I'll go up!"

Maurice Renaud entered immediately, followed by Jean Perliez.

"Well, my boy," said François Darbois to his nephew, "you are quite a stranger; it must be a month since we saw you last. You are most welcome."

He shook hands cordially with both young men. He was struck by Jean's sad expression and hollow cheeks. "You are not looking like yourself, my friend."

Jean did not hear this, he was gazing at Esperance, so pretty in her feather toque.

"We are come, uncle, expressly to ask your permission to accompany my cousin to Brussels. We were told of the project yesterday by Mounet-Sully, and if you approve...."

"On my word, my dear fellow," cried out the professor, delightedly, "you will do me a real service, I was just considering about writing to Esperance's godfather!"

"What a narrow escape! papa darling, and what a horrid surprise you were plotting without giving any sign!"

"Then you prefer this arrangement? You accept Maurice and Jean as your knights-errant? I am delighted with the arrangement, and I hope that Mlle. Frahender will raise no objection."

The gentle old lady smiled at them all. She was very fond of Jean Perliez, and Maurice Renaud's high spirits delighted her.

It was decided that Jean, as most responsible, should be in charge of all the details of the journey. François Darbois led him into the library and entrusted him with a goodly sum of money.

"This should cover your expenses. I count upon you, my young friend, and I thank you."

He paused a moment, then asked affectionately, "Have you no hope?"

"None," replied Jean, simply, "but what does it matter, but to-day, at least, I am quite happy!"

Two days after this visit, the notice of the first rehearsals was received. Esperance was at the theatre long before the hour required, and went at once towards the stage. The curtain had just been raised, and the lamp of the servant dusting served only to lighten the gloom. Followed by Mlle. Frahender, the young girl traversed the corridor ornamented with marble busts and pictures of the famous artists who had made the house of Molière more illustrious by their talent. With beating heart, she descended the four steps that led to the stage.

There she stopped shivering. She seemed to see shadows drawing near her, and her hand clenched that of the old Mademoiselle.

"What is it, Esperance?"

"Nothing, nothing."

"Was that not Talma, down there, and Mlle. Clairon and Mlle. Mars, and Rachel, that magnificent, expressive masque there ... look?"

Mounet-Sully came in. Esperance still seemed in a dream.

"Your pardon, master, the atmosphere of glory that one breathes here has intoxicated me a little."

During the rehearsal the music of the voice of the new "*Dona Sol*" blended charmingly with the powerful accents of the great actor, so that all the artists listened with emotion and delight.

In the final act, when "*Dona Sol*," beside herself, raises her poignard to "*Don Ruy Gomez*," saying, "I am of the family, uncle," there was an outburst of "Bravos" for Esperance, who, erect and trembling, shoulders thrown back, had just sobbed these words in a vibrant voice between clenched teeth. With her pale face and out-stretched arm, she might have been the statue of despair struggling with destiny.

Madame Darbois was heavy hearted to have her go. It was the first time that she had been parted from her daughter for even a few days. She often looked at her husband, hoping that he would understand her anxiety and urge her not to go, too. Jean and Maurice came to escort Esperance, who had been ready for a long time. Mlle. Frahender was carrying a cardboard box, containing two bonnets and a light cloth, in which to wrap her hat in in the train. All the rest of her belongings were contained in a little attaché case of grey duck, so flat that it seemed impossible that it could contain anything.

When Madame Darbois saw them drive away, she was filled with distress, and as there was maternal anxiety in the mother's breast, so was there foreboding of evil in the father's mind.

"I hope nothing bad will happen," thought the good woman, "but railway accidents are so common nowadays."

"Who will she be seeing while she is away? What is destiny providing for her? My child is not armed against adventure," the philosopher was thinking.

The two looked at each other, divining the miserable anxiety to which the other was prey.

The rough, strident notes of Adhemar Meydieux's voice suddenly broke upon this atmosphere of gentle melancholy - "Well! what is this I hear? Esperance has gone; it is madness! I read in my paper this morning that she is going to play '*Dona Sol*' at Brussels! So I have come to escort her."

François wrung his hand without saying a word.

"What is the matter with you," went on Adhemar, "you seem to have changed into pillars of salt. I know very well that the theatre is Sodom and Gomorrah in one, but wait a little before you give way entirely! Who is going with my goddaughter?"

"Mlle. Frahender, Marguerite, Maurice Renaud and Jean Perliez," the poor mother hastened to say.

"And what an escort," jeered Adhemar. "The old mademoiselle will be open-mouthed before her pupil, she knows nothing of life. Provided that Esperance obeys the commandments of the Church and does not miss Mass on Sunday, she will be satisfied. Her piety and her sudden love of the theatre coincide with her attempt to save a soul; but I tell you that she cannot see farther than the end of her nose, which, though long enough in all conscience, doesn't furnish elevation for much view. And," he continued, pleased with his wit, "Maurice Rcnaud, that wild rascal, is he apt to inspire respect for Esperance? As to Jean Perliez, the poor little ninny is head over heels in love with her. I don't suppose that you have noticed it?"

"Not only noticed it, but encouraged the young man," said François, "and he would be a very honourable and desirable son-in-law."

"My poor friend, my good fellow," and Adhemar collapsed in a chair and rubbed his hands together; "my poor dear friend, and you believe that Esperance...?"

He laughed aloud.

"I will thank you to drop that tone of irony which is offensive both to my wife and to myself," said the professor rising. "If it pleases you to follow your goddaughter to Brussels, do so. I must leave you; I have some proofs to correct. *Au revoir*, Meydieux!"

The old blunderer began to realize that he had overstepped the limits of decorum.

"But why did she go this morning, instead of by the train with all the other artists this evening?"

"Esperance," explained Madame Darbois, "left early in order to have time to see Brussels, which everyone says is a charming city. I think it is quite natural, my dear Meydieux, that you want to join your goddaughter! I will telegraph to her at once!"

"No, no," replied Meydieux, very hurriedly. "I would much rather surprise her. I beg you not to warn her."

"As you will then. I shall not interfere."

PART II. BRUSSELS

CHAPTER VIII

Meantime seated in the Brussels express, Esperance had fixed her attention on the constantly changing horizon, and was giving herself up to myriad impressions as they went fleeting by. The great plains rolling interminably out of sight pleased her; the light mist rising from the earth seemed to her the breath of the shivering tall grasses, offering the sun the drops of dew which glinted at the summit of their slender stems. She too, on this beautiful autumn morning, felt herself expanding towards the sky. Her fresh lips were offering themselves to the kisses of life. She was at that moment a vision of the radiance of youth. Maurice was so struck by her beauty that he drew a little sketch, and resolved to do her portrait, just as she was at that moment. No love entered into this admiration; he saw as a painter, he dreamed as an artist! Jean Perliez looked at the sketch, then at the model, and was left dazzled and dolorous. Finally magnetized by the looks fixed upon her, Esperance turned her head away with a little cry of surprise. Mlle. Frahender, who had been asleep, opened her eyes, and straightened the angle of her bonnet. Esperance shook her pretty head laughing, while Maurice exhibited his sketch and announced to his cousin his desire to paint her portrait.

"How pleased my father will be," she cried. "I thank you in advance for the joy that you will give him."

The conversation became general, animated, merry, just what was to be expected at their happy age. Soon after the train stopped; they had arrived at Brussels.

Jean Perliez jumped lightly on to the platform. Mlle. Frahender adjusted her hat, after having carefully folded up her bonnet, and Maurice helped Marguerite to count the pieces of luggage. Just as Esperance was getting out to help her old companion, she had a feeling of reaction, her face grew pale with fright at an impression she could not define: two long arms were stretched towards her. And she recalled the hallucination or vision she had seen in her own mirror at home, on the day when she had tried to interrogate destiny.

Count Albert Styvens was standing on the platform before her, holding out his arms, his hands open. Totally dazed without understanding herself why it should be so, the young girl closed her eyes. She felt herself lifted, and set down upon the ground. Although the movement had been one of perfect respect, she felt angry with this man for having imposed his will upon her. When she looked at him he was already speaking to Mlle. Frahender, whom he recollected having seen in Esperance's room at the Vaudeville.

"Will you not both take my mother's carriage?" he asked.

His voice, slow, correct, a little distant, fell on the ear of the young actress.

"But," Jean objected quickly, "I have engaged the landau from the Grand Hotel."

"Very well, we three can go in that," said the Count, as he guided the old lady and the young one towards a perfectly appointed *coupé*, drawn by two magnificent sorrels.

Esperance, who had been brimful of joy, not ten minutes before, at finding herself in Brussels, now felt a cloud upon her spirits. The manner, almost the authority, of this tall, young man of distinction, but of no beauty, of no magnetism, depressed her. She did not wish to have him take it upon himself to conduct her small affairs, and she stepped into the Countess Styvens's beautiful carriage with the feeling that she was leaving her liberty behind.

Albert Styvens got into the hotel landau with the two other young men. They knew the Count very slightly, and regarded him with some curiosity. Although but twenty-seven, he had a reputation for austerity most unusual for one of his age.

As the carriage drew up at the hotel, all three young men jumped lightly out to be ready to help the girl. Mlle. Frahender was received on the Count's arm. At the same instant Esperance had bounded out of the other door, pleased to have escaped the obligation of thanking the Legation Secretary.

When she entered the suite that had been reserved, she stopped a moment in silent astonishment before the flowering vases and ribbon-bedecked baskets that filled the reception-room with their rich colours and delicate perfumes. All that for her! She threw her hat quickly on a chair and ran from vase to basket, from basket to vase. The first card she drew out said Jean Perliez. She looked for him to thank him, but he had slipped away to hide his confusion. For he had taken such pains to order that bouquet through the hotel manager, never foreseeing that others might have had the same idea! A pretty basket of azaleas came from the Director of the Monnaie. In the middle of the room, on a marble table with protruding golden feet, stood a huge basket of orchids of every shade - this orgy of rare flowers was an attention from the Count. The girl grew red as she raised her eyes to thank him. He was looking at her so strangely that she stammered and fled into the next room, where she had seen Mlle. Frahender disappear.

"That man frightens me," she whispered, pressing close to her old friend.

"Who frightens you, dear child?"

"Count Styvens."

"That gentlemanly young man, who is so considerate?"

Esperance did not dare to speak her thought. "That is not the way that others look at me." She was ashamed to entertain such an idea!

The *maître d'hôtel* knocked discreetly to announce lunch.

"Oh! let us begin at once, so that we shall not lose any time in seeing Brussels!"

They set out in great spirits, following wherever the

caprice of Esperance led them. "Already a famous woman, and what a child she is," Maurice observed aside to Jean. They had a long ramble, zigzagging extravagantly about the city. The adorable little artist appreciated the beauty of the lovely capital, and the church of Saint Gudule delighted her. They took a cab to go to the Bois de la Cambre. Esperance was much affected by the horses, who led a hard life up and down the little streets, which were so picturesque in their unevenness.

The little expedition was not over until half-past seven. Visitors' cards attracted Mlle. Frahender's attention. They were from the Minister Prince de Bernecourt and the Count Albert Styvens, Secretary of the Legation. Feeling that she would not see the Count gave the young artist the sensation of relief comparable to that of a prisoner walking straight out of his jail into freedom.

During dinner Esperance was quite exuberant and proposed a hand at *trente-et-un* as soon as dessert was finished. "After that, we will go to bed very early, to have our best looks ready for to-morrow, will we not, my little lady?" she said, placing her slender hand on the wrinkled fingers of Mlle. Frahender. "My little lady" was the pet name Esperance often gave her.

Maurice was only moderately receptive of the idea of a game of *trente-et-un*, but after consulting the clock, he was reassured. "By ten o'clock I shall be free."

CHAPTER IX

The next morning Marguerite had some difficulty in waking her young mistress, who was sleeping soundly. Esperance enquired as soon as her own eyes were well opened, what kind of night her chaperone had passed. "Deliciously restful, and you, my dear child, how did you sleep?"

"I never woke once. Oh! what a sun. Have you seen what a glorious day it is?"

"It is the forerunner of good news," Jean cried out from the next room.

"Who knows?" said Esperance.

The telephone at her bedside rung. Marguerite picked up the receiver, and announced dejectedly, "M. Meydieux wishes to speak to Mademoiselle."

"My godfather in Brussels!... You see, Jean, that I was right to doubt your omen."

The young people burst out laughing.

"Really," continued Esperance, "I feel that he is going to spoil my trip here. I don't like him, and his advice never coincides with that of my father, whom I love so much."

Meantime M. Meydieux was getting impatient on the telephone.

"Tell him that I am not up yet, and ask him to lunch with us at twelve-thirty. Then," she explained to Mlle. Frahender, who had just come into her room, all powdered, all pinned and bonneted for the morning, "he will not dare to bother me when everybody else is present."

Marguerite was still answering M. Meydieux's excited questions: "What! at half-past nine not up, that is shameful! I must talk to her ... I will come to lunch, oh yes! but above all I must talk to her."

Esperance was motioning violently to Marguerite to hang up the receiver, but Mlle. Frahender objected to this lack of courtesy, so the young girl giving way to her remonstrance yielded gracefully. She even re-requested Marguerite, who knew her godfather's culinary preferences, to order a lunch that he would like. Then she dressed in haste to allow herself plenty of time to write to her family. They had already exchanged telegrams, but she knew that her father would like to have a long letter, giving him the minutes, so to speak, of herself. A tender gratitude swelled up in her, and her eyes were wet as she evoked the image of these two beloved beings reading her letter, commenting upon it, and entering completely for those moments into the life of their child. As soon as the letter was finished, she asked Mlle. Frahender to go with her to post it, so that she could herself speed it on its way to them. She had a strong desire to get out-doors, even if only for a half-hour.

As they turned into the square, Esperance stopped, clutching her aged friend by the arm. "Look there," she said.

There were two men side by side in deep conversation. Esperance had instantly recognized Count Albert and her godfather. How did Adhemar Meydieux happen to know the Secretary of the Legation?

They had just passed the post-office, so Esperance posted her letter without being seen by either of them, and returned to the hotel. Lunch time brought together all the guests except the godfather, who would not enter until the exact minute, if he had to wait in the corridor.... He thought it witty to behave so. His hateful, stupid mind flattered itself on being original. Therefore as the half-hour began to strike he was pompously ushered in, watch in hand.

"I am here, you see, to the tick," he said noisily, kissing the forehead his goddaughter pressed forward to him. Then, turning to the waiter, "You can serve without delay," he said. "I like my food hot."

Mlle. Frahender, although she was well acquainted with the abrupt ways of the godfather, frowned at him with disapprobation. Nevertheless, thanks to Maurice, who made a point of laughing at everything Adhemar said, they had a gay luncheon, and Adhemar himself, appreciating the consideration shown for his palate, cast aside his ill humour and enjoyed with full indulgence the present hour, the savoury food and the plentiful wine.

At the end of the meal he examined the room. "On my word, my girl, they have given you the royal suite: that must come pretty expensive."

"M. Darbois," said Jean Perliez, "gave me a very liberal sum of money, with instructions to spare nothing for our little queen."

"There you have it, if that is not the exaggeration of a lover! Little Queen! You are pouring poison in continuous doses into this little head, which is already full of nonsense. Esperance will end by taking herself seriously; she is already far too dictatorial for a child of seventeen." He added to himself, "She must be corrected, I will do it myself!"

Esperance raised her eyelids, and her clear blue eyes seemed to pierce the eyeballs of the foolish blunderer, until he fluttered his lashes and closed his eyes to escape the powerful silent denial of his authority.

"Very well," he said, succeeding in half opening his eyes, "look at me as much as you like, that does not keep me from distrusting you, my child. You are nice-looking, you have a pretty voice, you may some day develop some talent; but you know, your inexperience is obvious, and I am very anxious to know how you will pull through to-night."

"Do not disturb yourself, M. Meydieux, Esperance had a triumph at the last rehearsal at the Française." (Mlle. Frahender nodded agreement.) "I believe," Jean continued, "that she is going to receive a perfect ovation this evening."

"I believe it too," added the old lady, "and permit me to state, my dear sir, that you judge my young pupil very unfairly. She is just as modest, just as gentle, as she was a year ago, and those who love her may be well reassured of that fact. Since you are among them," she went on boldly, "you should realize it and rejoice in it."

Adhemar shrugged his shoulders. "They are all mad, even the old saint!"

They left the table. He stopped before a basket of flowers. "Who sent you those, my child?"

"Count Albert Styvens," replied Jean.

"Ah! He does things well," commented Adhemar, but he did not breathe a word concerning his conversation with the Count that morning.

Before there was time for a reply a waiter entered with a card. "M. Mounet-Sully would like to come up."

"Oh! yes," cried out the young artist with delight.

A little startled at finding five people in the room, Mounet-Sully regained his assurance as he recognized Jean and Maurice.

"My dear child, we rehearse at two-thirty," he said to Esperance, "so be prompt, because we have heard that the Queen will be there, though you may not see her. She is not well enough to come out in the evening."

The young girl blushed with excitement. "It is fortunate that I shall not see her, I think that I should be paralyzed!"

"Perhaps she will send for you after the rehearsal,"

returned the tragedian. "She is a patroness of art, and very kind to artists."

"Will His Majesty, King Leopold, come this evening?" demanded Meydieux, with great interest.

"Certainly," Mounet-Sully assured him.

Then, as he was about to go, he turned, "Have you received your invitation for...?"

The door opened. Count Albert, being introduced by the *maître d'hôtel*, had heard the last words.

"I am just delivering it myself," he said, handing Mlle. Frahender a card which she read to Esperance - "His Excellence, the Count de Bernecourt, Minister of Belgium to France, and the Princess, hope that Mlle. Frahender and Mlle. Esperance Darbois will join them for supper after the play, at midnight, at their house."

"But I cannot accept without the permission of my father," said Esperance.

The raucous and heavy voice of the godfather pronounced, "I will assume the responsibility. Your mother encouraged me to watch over you. I consider that this is an honour which you should not decline."

"Especially as His Majesty the King will have you presented," replied the Count.

"Nevertheless," said Esperance, "I want my father's approval. I will go down and telephone to Paris."

"I will accompany you," said the diplomat quickly.

She stopped short, and her expression implied distress. Jean went forward at once. "I will go and secure the connection for you," he said; "I will wait for you downstairs."

The Count made a scarcely perceptible gesture, as if to stop him; but he restrained himself and followed the girl in silence out of the room. He rang, the lift stopped before them, empty. Albert Styvens went forward, but Esperance drew back, and then she said, quickly, "I will go down by the stairs."

And light as a breath, she was gone.

Alone in the lift, the young Count felt for a moment abashed, but he speedily recovered himself, and when Esperance reached the bottom of the stairs she found him waiting for her.

As she leaped down the last step, she again felt herself lifted and deposited upon her feet.

"What are you doing?" she cried angrily, startled and offended.

The rapid half-embrace had been almost brutal. Esperance could still feel on her delicate skin the pressure of the man's strong fingers.

He apologized, and was sincerely repentant. He had acted without reflection; he had forgotten his great strength which had this time served him ill. He was violently attracted by this charming little creature, with whom he admitted to himself that he was deeply in love; he, who up to this time had always avoided women as if he feared them.

The telephonic communication was lengthy. François Darbois gave his consent to his daughter to attend the supper. Madame Darbois was distracted, and must find out what dress Esperance would wear.

"I will keep on my costume from the last act of *Hernani*," she answered, and after a gentle farewell, Esperance hastened to the theatre for the rehearsal.

The Director of the Monnaie announced that Her Majesty had come and that they could begin. Hugo's masterpiece was magnificently presented. The greatest artists filled even minor rôles. Mounet-Sully surpassed himself, and Esperance drew cries of admiration from that select but critical audience.

Count Albert was seated in the orchestra stalls with his mother. The Countess Styvens, widowed after five years, had bestowed upon her son all the affection she had cherished for her husband. She had never left him, but had had him educated under her own supervision, giving him at the age of nine, as tutor, a Jesuit who was one of the most austere, if also one of the most learned, of the Order. The young man was a perfect pupil, studious, ever disdaining the pleasures of his age. His childhood passed in the grey and pious atmosphere in which his mother steeped herself. His youth developed under the rule of his preceptor, a pale youth, without laughter, without aspirations. The physicians had never been able to persuade the Countess to let her son have the joy of travel of sea and mountain, so he had to be satisfied with the physical exercises she permitted. So he gave himself up to gymnastics with enthusiasm, expending his youthful vigour against his drill professor, and the Japanese who taught him jiu-jitsu. The boy's strength became quite remarkable. But his pale face, disproportionately long arms, and reputation for austerity, had made him the mark, from the very first days of his diplomatic career, for the gossips, ballad makers, and authors of questionable cabaret skits.

The day he heard that he was serving as Turk's head in a Brussels music-hall, he went instantly behind the scenes of the theatre and demanded to see the Director, who was in conversation with the author of the piece. He went right up to them. "I," he said, raising his hat politely, "am Count Albert Styvens. I shall be very glad to have you suppress the scene, which, I understand, is intended to caricature me."

The Manager, a prosperous brewer, who had become proprietor of a theatre for the pleasure of producing revues, which if not witty were certainly vulgar, shrugged his heavy shoulders.

"You expect me to lose money! That act is one of the best we have got."

"And you, sir?" Albert turned on the author, a man of doubtful reputation, always on the alert for any occasion of scandal in others.

"Oh! of course I am sorry to offend you, but I can't take off the piece."

The last word was not out of his mouth when the Count grabbed both of them by the napes of their necks and knocked their heads together till the blood spurted from their surprised faces. Their cries were heard even by the audience. Reporters came running to witness this unbilled spectacle. The stage hands tried to

Sarah Bernhardt

free the Manager, but desisted when one received a terrible smash from the Count's fist, and another a kick that sent him through space. When the two men were reduced to rags, Albert held them upright and addressed them:

"I am going into the hall to see the show. I advise you to withdraw the scene we spoke of and to which I object."

Then he quietly re-arranged his clothes and went into the auditorium where the audience were very noisy and laughing at the news the journalists had reported. Count Albert was one of the best known figures about Brussels, where his father had played a very important part in the foreign affairs of the country, and enjoyed, for more than twenty years, the confidence of King Leopold. When he died his wife was still a young and very beautiful woman, and his great fortune had made the only heir of the family already famous. The Count was astonished at the clamorous ovation that received him. He would have liked to impose silence on the people, but he was a poor orator, and very timid; he kept silence and wont to his seat. He was popular from that day, and greatly respected.

At the Monnaie, as soon as the rehearsal was over, the Queen sent for Esperance and Mounet-Sully. The Queen assured the tragedian of the admiration that she had long felt for him, for Mounet-Sully played almost every year in Brussels; but all her kindly enthusiasm was directed towards Esperance.

"What a perfectly delicious voice!" she said. "How old are you?"

"Seventeen, Madame."

The Queen undid a bracelet from her arm.

"Accept this modest souvenir of your first appearance in our city, Mademoiselle."

The young girl trembled with emotion. After she had kissed the royal hand, she tried to clasp upon her wrist the jewel she had just received. The Countess Styvens, who had just approached, helped her gently.

"My mother admired you very much," said the Count, joining them.

Esperance raised her eyes and looked at the mother of the young man. She was dressed in mauve; her temples, prematurely grey, accentuated the delicacy of her complexion. Her whole person breathed constant goodness, sacrifice without regret. The young artist loved at sight this woman she was beholding for the first time, and at the same time she had a presentiment that this charming and elegant lady would not remain a stranger to her during her life.

The Queen desired Count Styvens to accompany the young girl, who was forced to take his arm to her dressing-room. She walked quickly, in a hurry to rid herself of her strange cavalier, who pretended to be oblivious of her nervous haste. Esperance requested him to convey to the Countess, his mother, her gratitude for her kindness. Albert Styvens bowed without speaking, and left her in a glow of delight.

At the hotel there was no topic except the rehearsal and the reception the Queen had given Esperance. The godfather examined the bracelet set with sapphires and diamonds. He put on his glasses, counted the stones, shook his head and grunted, "It is a superb bracelet, do you realize that, child?"

"I realize that it is superb because it is a testimony of good will offered by this kind Sovereign. That is what makes it so valuable to me."

"What a haughty child!"

And Adhemar began to laugh, the laugh with which realism strives to destroy dreams. Mlle. Frahender gently removed the bracelet from the hands of the objectionable old meddler.

"You must rest and avoid excitement, dear, dear child," she said, leading Esperance to her room, after bowing to Adhemar. Maurice and Jean, who had witnessed the godfather's want of tact, reasoned with him.

"In my opinion, M. Meydieux, you annoy my cousin too much, and for no reason. You forget that she has created for herself a position beyond her years, and you treat her like a child not out of the school-room."

"Well, isn't it all for her good?" screamed out Adhemar in a fury. "The rest of you burn incense before her; she will be destroyed by pride and that will be your fault!"

"No such thing," returned Maurice with equal energy. "She is adorable in her simplicity and has remained as really childlike, as trusting and light-hearted as anyone in the world. You cast a gloom on her spirits, you try to curb her spontaneity, you want her bourgeoisie like yourself, but you will never succeed, I give you my word for it, and that is a blessing."

"Oh!" retorted Adhemar, stung to the quick, "What do you mean by that, you fine painter fellow? You are glad enough to have these bourgeoisie that you scorn pay for your pictures!"

"If I make pictures and anybody buys them, that is proof enough that they are idiots. But my hatred of the bourgeoisie only extends to the category to which you belong; those who, ever since they were born, have found their food ready under their noses; those who, never using their ten fingers, never using their brains, live only to increase inherited incomes; hearts locked by greed, narrow minds unwilling to hear the just claims of the humble, of those who work and suffer for them; enemies of progress, enemies of their country."

"Oh! oh! oh!" screamed Meydieux.

"Yes, refusing to perform the sole function the State expects of them."

"And that is?"

"To become a husband, a father, a parent."

"You are insolent! It is not worth my while to reply to you. You may tell my goddaughter...."

The door opened, and Esperance, who had been kept awake by the noise of their voices, appeared to know what was the matter!

"Ah! there you are. I will say good-bye! Your cavaliers annoy me."

He threw a furious glance towards Jean, who had not spoken a word. It is a fact that the majority of people cherish more rancour against the witness of an insult than against the insulter himself.

"I will not be present at your triumph - as they call it. I am going to your father and shall tell him everything."

"My father, godfather, knows that I always tell the truth; he will await my return to judge my actions and those of my dear comrades."

Adhemar pulled on his hat and stormed out of the room, swelling with wounded dignity.

Esperance blew a kiss to the two young men.

"Now I am going to sleep until dinner time. I have just three-quarters of an hour. Do not forget, my loyal attendants, that we dine at six-thirty," she added with a sweeping courtesy, and disappeared, light of heart at the departure of her godfather.

CHAPTER X

The performance was an unparalleled triumph for the players and little "*Dona Sol*" received the most flattering part of the success. The King, knowing that the Queen had already favoured this delightful child, would not be outdone in generosity, and sent to the dressing-room of the new star a very beautiful ring, set with a magnificent pearl and two diamonds. Esperance, who had never had any jewellery except a gold chain that her mother's aunt had left her and the little ring her father had given her for her first communion, found herself, in one day, possessor of two ornaments which the most fastidious worldling would not have disdained. She put the ring immediately on her first finger, since it was a little loose for the ring finger, and looked at herself in the glass, arranging a lock of hair with the ringed hand, raising an eyebrow and laughing delightedly to see the effect produced by the ring. Count Albert watched her from the neighbouring room where he was waiting. His face was of a livid pallor. His heart beat so fast that he felt weak, and was forced to sit down. He was out of his senses. All the frenzy of youth, repressed so long, mounted in a wave to his brain.

Marguerite, coming to dress her mistress, announced that the gentlemen were waiting. She quickly threw on a cloak, saying, "I am ready."

Mounet-Sully and Count Albert entered together. The Count offered his arm to the old Mademoiselle, and Esperance, free of the contact that disturbed her, joyfully accepted the tragedian's assistance.

The supper was charming, and proved to the young girl that the feasts of artists and men of the world do not end in the orgies described by the odious godfather. The young girl was at the right of the Prince with Mounet-Sully opposite, at the right of the Princess. None of the guests could help noticing the Count's agitation. The Military Aide, representing King Leopold, Baron von Berger, was an old friend of the Styvens's family. He was uneasy, and when he saw the young Count preparing to take the ladies home, "No, no, my boy," he said to him in a low tone, "You are not yourself - you are distraught. I am afraid that you have been hard hit."

"You are not mistaken," replied the young man, "I burn like a devil, and at the same time I am as happy as a god."

"Well, now I am going to escort these ladies, and to-morrow I will have a talk with you."

Esperance slept badly and woke late. The old Mademoiselle was sitting beside her, spectacles across her nose, reading the papers. Her kind face was beaming. She was cutting out and putting aside certain articles, then she pinned them in order, all ready to send to M. and Madame Darbois.

The young girl was touched, and raising herself in bed, flung her arms about the old lady.

"What a dear you are, and how I love you!"

Mlle. Frahender at that moment had her reward for all the little sacrifices she had made for her pupil.

The critics were dithyrambic in their discourses concerning the new "Dona Sol," but the casual reporters were, as always, indiscreet, and disguised the truth under little prevarications, fantastic and suggestive. After having read two or three of the articles, Esperance pushed them all aside. She took the name of all the critics, and wrote them little notes of thanks, while Mlle. Frahender added the addresses. In the neighbouring room a discussion was going on between her knight-attendants. Esperance did not gather its cause, although certain phrases were audible.

"No, I tell you," Maurice was saying, "if it is worth while at all, I must be the one."

"I could always demand a correction," replied Jean.

"Correction of what? It is simply one of those ambiguous phrases which are used every day. Why notice it?"

The sound of Esperance's voice cut short their discussion.

"What are you talking about?" she called out.

"Nothing at all," returned Maurice, "that is, only stupid things you would not understand."

"That is not a very gallant morning greeting, cousin, but you have not forgotten your promise to lake me to the Museum this morning, I hope."

"Yes, my dear, we will go to the Museum in a very little while."

She heard the door close.

"Are you still there, Jean?" she called.

"And at your service," he replied.

"There is nothing I need, thank you. I just want to know what correction you were talking about."

"It is a private affair of Maurice's," stammered the young actor.

"I see, thank you."

After lunch the travellers set out for the Museum. Maurice was surprised and delighted by the instinct that guided his cousin towards the best that was in the pictures. He explained to her in the language affected by painters the reason for certain unreal shadows in a certain picture, and the necessity for them, the tact a painter must use in managing his light, the difficulty of foreshortening. He told her the well-known anecdote of Delacroix replying to the professor who objected that he had put a full face eye in a profile, "But, my dear master, I have tried everything and that is the only eye that gives the profile its proper value." And the professor of the great painter-to-be, after several sketches on the transparent paper over his pupil's canvas, said to him, "You are entirely right. Keep that full face eye."

They left the Museum, animated by different feelings. The more that Maurice discovered his cousin's noble qualities, the delicacy of her feelings, the strength of her loyalty, the more he felt of protective affection for this child who was so pure, so free, and who had made her entry so bravely into the whirlpool where things are generally turbulent, and most brutal in the brutal side of Parisian life. The admiration of his twenty years, for Esperance's alluring beauty, was purified into a friendship which he felt growing deeper and stronger. As to Jean Perliez, he had become more and more resigned that his love should remain forever in the shade, unlimited devotion for all time, all his being offered in sacrifice to the frail idol, who went her way star-gazing, unsuspecting all the time that she was trampling upon hearts under her foot.

Sarah Bernhardt

CHAPTER XI

M. and Madame Darbois had received the telegram announcing the return of their daughter, and were at the station to meet her. Esperance saw them and would have jumped out before the train had fully slopped. Maurice held her just in time.

"No foolishness there, little cousin. Your bodyguards must return you intact to your family's four arms. One more moment of patience. What a hurry you are in to be rid of us."

She held out her little hands to the two young men. "Oh, naughty Maurice! You know very well that I shall never forget these three days we have passed together, when you have been so good to me and taught me so very much."

Maurice kissed her boldly; Jean put his lips very respectfully to the warm, soft little hand.

The train stopped and the Darbois family were in an instant reunited. Mlle. Frahender declined escort to her convent. François Darbois installed her in a landau, and after he had thanked her heartily for her kindness to his daughter, gave the address to the coachman, who drove away with the old lady holding her inevitable little package on her lap, and steadying her old-fashioned little attaché case on the seat opposite.

The Darbois family took their places in another carriage. Esperance must sit between her father and mother, leaning close to them, caressing them endlessly, and dropping her little blonde head on her mother's shoulder.

"Oh! how long it seems since I have seen you," she kept repeating.

She held her father's hand and pressed it against her heart. It seemed to her suddenly as if she had suffered from that absence of three days, and yet she could not specify at what moment she had wished herself back with them. She recounted all the little events that had taken place during the three eventful days.

"You know," she explained to her father, "I am bringing you all the newspaper articles. Then I have the letter from the President of the Committee, and the beautiful presents from the King and Queen."

The carriage stopped at the Boulevard Raspail. The *concierge* came forward.

"I am sure I hope that Mademoiselle has had a success."

Esperance looked at her with astonishment, but the woman's husband came up with a newspaper in his hand, which he unfolded to display the picture of Esperance just beneath the headlines.

"Oh!" she exclaimed, "they will make me odious to the public. Mounet-Sully was so wonderful. Worms so fine in his monologue...."

Sadness overcame her.

She was still sad when she entered her own room. She touched all the familiar little objects, and kissed the feet of the ivory Virgin upon her mantel-piece with great emotion. She thanked her mother with a look when she saw the fresh marguerites in the two enamel vases. In comparison with the luxury of her apartment at the Grand Hotel in Brussels, the simple surroundings of her own room charmed her anew. She swayed for a moment in her rocking-chair, sat down on her low stool, knelt upon her bed to straighten the branch of box beneath the silver crucifix her mother had given her when she was seventeen.

Marguerite came in with the trunk and luggage.

"What is that?" asked Esperance, spying a big box fastened with nails.

"I don't know anything about it, Mademoiselle. They gave it to me at the hotel saying it was for you."

The box on being opened displayed a magnificent basket of orchids. Attached by a white ribbon was a card - "Countess Styvens."

Esperance grew pale; she took the card from her mother's hands, fearing that she might be mistaken. It was indeed the Countess and not the Count. She breathed again! Marguerite and the maid carried the basket into the salon; then the young girl went into the library with her mother. The newspaper clippings were spread out on the table, and the two famous trinkets had been taken from their cases. Madame Darbois clasped and unclasped her hands.

"Oh! but they are too beautiful, simply too beautiful!" she said.

And the philosopher, half in indignation, half in indulgence, exclaimed, "My poor child, you can not possibly wear such jewels at your age!"

"Ah!" said Esperance with disappointment, "I cannot wear them?"

"Why, no, it is out of the question."

"You will be able to wear them in a play, at the theatre," said Madame Darbois, but her tone lacked assurance, for she did not know whether that would be possible either.

M. Darbois had turned his attention to the notices, having pushed aside the descriptive paragraphs. He read them and gave them to his wife.

"Your godfather came to complain to us of Maurice, of Jean Perliez, and of yourself. You all displeased him; tell us just what happened?"

Esperance recounted the happenings with perfect impartiality, adding honestly that she had done nothing to try to persuade her godfather to remain. The philosopher smiled.

"Very well, let us forget all that. We will take up our happy life again, that has been interrupted by your triumphs," he added sadly. And then, as the women were preparing to leave the library, "Tell me, Esperance, who is the Countess Styvens?"

"A great lady at court, and oh! so charming."

"Is Count Albert Styvens of the Legation any relation of hers?"

"Yes, father, he is her son. But why do you ask that?"

"Your godfather spoke to me of this young man, who, it seems, wants to complete his studies in philosophy."

The poor little star trembled. She was on the point of confessing all her presentiments, her terrors, to her father.... But he had just sat down to his desk and seemed already indifferent to what was going on around him. She went softly out of the library, following her mother, who was bearing away the newspaper excerpts and the royal jewel cases.

In the beautiful house which Countess Styvens occupied with her son, an animated discussion was taking place at the same moment between Baron von Berger and Count Albert.

"I advise you, my boy," the Baron was saying brusquely, "to ask for another post. You, so sensible, too sensible, for a man of your age, in fact it's a little ridiculous...."

"That has nothing to do with it," returned the younger man coolly.

"All very well, but my quasi-paternal duty is to stop you before certain danger. You admit that you adore this young star of seventeen, the daughter of a philosopher of high standing. You do not intend, I suppose, to make her your mistress?"

Albert Styvens felt the blood run into his temples, but he did not answer.

The Baron continued, more determinedly, "You do not intend to propose her as a daughter-in-law to your mother?"

For an instant a vertigo froze the young man's being. His heart stopped beating, his throat contracted with a terrific pressure of blood. He did not answer a word.

"In God's name," cried the Baron violently, "am I in the presence of a woman or a man?"

"A man," said Count Albert, getting to his feet. "A man whose anger is held in check by his respect, but who can endure no more," he added, throwing back his arms to allow his chest to dilate still farther. "I am going to answer you; please listen without interruption."

Then, after a moment more of silence, he declared, "Yes, I am desperately in love with this young girl, and I am going to try everything, not to make her love me, for that she probably never will - but that she will let herself be loved. What will come of it, I have not the least idea. I want her and no one else. I will commit no disloyal act, I give you my word for that. If she should become my wife, it would be with my mother's full permission. I beg you now, my dear Baron, to say nothing further about it; I am old enough to regulate my life, as much as the divine guiding force which you call 'Destiny' permits."

He came up to the Baron, clasped his hand in a firm grasp, and reaching for his hat, added, "I want to get out in the air. Shall we go together?"

The Baron recognized the opposition of an unchangeable will to his own, which no discussion could influence.

CHAPTER XII

Life had resumed its regular course in the apartment on the Boulevard Raspail, but an important relationship was developing in Esperance's life. Count Albert Styvens came three times a week to pursue his philosophic studies with Professor Darbois. This arrangement had been contrived by the hypocrite, Adhemar Meydieux. He did not mistake the Count's infatuation for his goddaughter. A marriage of such wealth and aristocratic connections flattered his foolish egoism, and he was sworn to attempt everything that would bring about such a magnificent consummation.

A friend of the family, Doctor Bertaud, noticed alarming symptoms in the girl, most prevalent between five and seven o'clock each evening. He could not ascertain the cause, but persuaded the philosopher to take her to Doctor Potain, a celebrated heart specialist. Madame Darbois took Esperance for an examination.

François was perfectly amazed by the deep culture of the Count, who at first sight seemed of only average intelligence. When the family gathered together for dinner, he commented on his impressions to his wife and daughter.

"This young man is a very remarkable personality," he said, "very difficult to penetrate, yet nevertheless very sincere. I do not believe that the slightest untruth has ever crossed his lips. I enjoy working with him. Ah! that reminds me, I have invited him to dine with us on Thursday. He is very anxious to be presented to you, and Esperance already knows him, so I thought you would find it agreeable."

The young girl trembled. Her blood seemed to stop in her veins. Her hand pressed against her heart felt no movement there. Her father, noticing the change in her, exclaimed, "Bertaud is quite right, you are sometimes abnormally pale; do you feel ill?"

"No, father, it is nothing; I felt dizzy for a moment."

"All the same we must hurry Bertaud with his examination."

Back in her own room the young girl began to weep. "I shall never escape that man, never, never."

Her eyes invoked the Virgin of ivory. Her two arms extended, implored her, but it seemed to Esperance that they were opened also to whatever discouragement Destiny might have in store. She fell asleep in her chair, worn out by self-hypnosis on the holy image.

A horrible nightmare unfolded in her brain. She found herself on a great map of the world, with a voice calling to her, "Why are you frozen there, why don't you move? You are free as the air of this great globe." Then she began to walk, but at once she saw the earth open and long tentacles, like arms, emerge to clutch her. She recoiled quickly and started in another direction but the same phenomenon occurred again. After that she determined to climb on to a great plain that she saw ahead. She thought she was safe when all at once she saw arising on every side the frightful tentacles which crept along her hiding-place, viscous and black, nearer, near enough to touch her. An indescribable terror brought her to her feet with a cry for help! Mile. Frahender and Marguerite came running in. They found her pale and bathed in perspiration. Her lips were trembling, stammering. It was five minutes before she recovered herself. She described her dream, and the old Mademoiselle prescribed a little walk in the air. The child followed her chaperon with nervous docility.

It was the day after the next when Albert Styvens was to come to dinner. Esperance had thought of saying that she was ill, but her heart misgave her at the thought of the anxiety she would occasion her mother, and then ... and then ... the dinner would be postponed, and "This man will have what he will have, and I am the prey of his dream," she said with a sigh of resignation.

The dinner was arranged for seven-thirty. The young Count presented himself at seven-fifteen, having been preceded by two great bunches of flowers, for Madame Darbois and Esperance, who was at the piano when he came into the room. The Count entered with Madame Darbois, whom her husband had just presented to her, and they stopped silent to listen to Mendelssohn's beautiful nocturne, "Song of a Summer Night." When the last echoes of the last phrase had died away, discreet applause was wafted to her. She swung quickly on her stool and found herself before the young man who was bowing, and taking the hand she held out to him. She had not yet overcome that terror he inspired in her, and was surprised to find him so much at ease. After dinner they talked of music, and Esperance, praising a magnificent duet of Liszt, from the symphony of Orpheus, was overcome when the young man rose, took her hand and led her towards the piano.

"Come, let us try to play it together." He looked towards François Darbois and received his nod of acquiescence from the depths of the arm-chair where the professor sat clasping his long, fine hands.

The Count was intoxicated by the light perfume of Esperance's body there so near him that he seemed almost to touch her. His strong hands rose and fell beside her delicate fingers, making the young girl think of a great hawk fluttering over white pigeons, at the farm of Penhouet in Brittany, where for years she had spent her holidays. The fragment was executed brilliantly, for these two persons, united in their enthusiasm for art, although so different in personal reactions, gave the two auditors of this musical treat a magnificent interpretation of Liszt's genius. François Darbois and his wife, both distinguished in their appreciation of the beautiful, could not sufficiently thank the Count, dividing his praises with congratulations to their daughter.

"You surpassed yourself, my dear," said the philosopher, "but then I admit that you have never before had such a partner. It was really remarkable."

When the young man had left, Esperance excused herself, saying that she was tired. She kissed her parents tenderly, although for the first time she felt an unjust and unfounded resentment against them. She was aggrieved that they should see nothing of Count

Styvens's manoeuvres.

The maid, helping her to undress, exclaimed, "How grand it was this evening, Mademoiselle, and what a fine young gentleman!"

Esperance shrugged her shoulders disdainfully. Marguerite, coming in to see that the young mistress whom she adored wanted nothing, could not help saying, "Ah! Mademoiselle, what talent he has, that young Count! How well you two did look, your backs, sitting side by side! I just said to myself...."

Esperance shivered, guessing what was coming, and interrupted the good woman quickly, "Don't talk to me Marguerite, to-night. I am tired and I must go to sleep."

But she did not sleep.

CHAPTER XIII

The last presentation of Sardou's play was a veritable ovation for Esperance. Flowers were presented to her on the stage. Two baskets attracted special attention, one overflowing with white orchids; the other, with gardenias, so powerful in their sweetness that even the first rows of the orchestra felt their strength. It was rumoured in the boxes that the white orchids were sent by the Countess Styvens and her son Albert, who were sitting in a stall in the auditorium. As to the gardenias, the card attached to the green ribbons of the basket revealed the name of the most elegant clubman of Paris, the Duke Charles de Morlay-La-Branche. He was a handsome man of thirty-two, very wealthy, adored by women, popular with men. A ripple ran through the audience.

"You know the Duke, they say that he is very much taken...."

"They know each other?"

"No, he has never been presented."

"No, look out for the love of the immaculate Albert," said mockingly a beautiful woman with bold eyes, glancing toward the stall occupied by Albert and his mother; but her eyes widened at seeing the Duke enter to present his compliments to the Countess Styvens. A few minutes later he was seen to go out with Count Albert. He was going to be presented to the young artist.

Count Styvens's love was known to all Paris, as was also the respect with which he surrounded his idol. It was also known that the young girl did not return this love; likewise that the son of the chemist Perliez was devoting his life to Esperance. But what would be the end of these two gallants, both so timid, so full of silent ardour? But now had entered upon the scene a rival possessed of beauty, of confidence, one who had toyed lightly with women's hearts, until he had wearied of the facile love his physical charm and wit attracted.

"That should be good sport to watch," said an old beau. "I am betting on the Duke."

A newly married bride turned towards him, "I am betting on the young girl."

A journalist, thin, blonde, very young, just beginning his career, had followed the Duke and the Count behind the scenes. He accompanied them into Esperance's little room and described what happened us follows: -

"She was holding the two cards, there in the midst of the overpowering odour of gardenias. She blushed when she heard the name of the Duke, Albert Styvens was presenting to her. She thanked them both very prettily, but without showing any preference for either. The Duke began complimentary speeches without making any impression. When they took leave, he wanted to kiss Esperance's hand, but she withdrew it

Sarah Bernhardt

looking very much surprised. This rather confused the Duke. As soon as these gentlemen departed I was presented, and her manner was just as charming. Jean Perliez came in just then to tell her that the curtain would go up in three minutes. He brought her a bunch of Parma violets, and she took them from him and put them in her girdle; you will see her wearing them on the stage. Perliez is desperately in love with her, and he grew very pale. He went out without a word. I think he must have gone to cry out his emotion in a corner. That is all," concluded the rising journalist.

He repeated his story twenty times, and by next morning all Paris knew that the Duke de Morlay-La-Branche had been received by Esperance like any other gentleman, that Count Albert Styvens had been noncommittal, and that Jean Perliez had been overcome. The young journalist wrote a very suggestive article concerning this little scene, highly ornamented with phrases that would attract attention; but unfortunately the editor refused to print it. The Duke did not care for notoriety, and was, moreover, a renowned fencer, so the editor exercised his discretion. Count Styvens belonged to the foreign diplomacy and was very particular, and no one had infringed on his privacy since the little affair in the Brussels music hall. That left only Jean Perliez, who was merely sincere and pathetic; the public did not want to read that kind of thing! So much for the little journalist.

Countess Styvens was spending a month in Paris, staying at the Legation with the Princess de Berne-court, who always had a suite ready for her. There was to be a grand opening ceremony of the Opera season, and for many years the Styvens had never missed the first nights of the Opera or the Comedie-Française.

One evening at dinner the conversation turned upon music, and a guest regretted the mechanical performance of the musical prodigies at the Conservatoire.

"It gives them a certain amount of cleverness, or technique, or whatever you like to call it, but there is no flair of the ideal, and often no important personality."

"I know a young artist," said Albert Styvens, "who plays with her whole soul, and I, who really love music, find her far ahead of all your prodigies."

Almost a sensation was produced among the guests.

The Countess said with her sweet smile, "I see that they tease you here as well as at Brussels."

"That does not affect me, mother, you see; I remain faithful to my ideal."

"Never mind, tell us the name of this new discovery."

"Her name is Esperance Darbois," said Albert rising, resting his two hands on the table. Then, having produced his effect, he sat down again.

"What! she is a good musician too?"

"Excellent," replied Albert, "and I will wager that whoever hears her will agree with me.

"How is it possible to hear her? She does not play at the concerts. But tell us how did you contrive to hear her?" demanded the Princess.

Sarah Bernhardt

"I study with her father, François Darbois, so I have become a friend of the family. They asked me to dinner once, and I was early enough to hear Mlle. Esperance play. After dinner we played a very difficult duet together. She had absolute command of her execution and her emotion."

A young attaché murmured to an amiable dowager, "I am afraid that they have completely taken him in."

Count Albert sprang to his feet.

"I am not willing that you should try to belittle this family whom you do not know. François Darbois, the philosopher, is a fine character, of unparalleled honour and integrity: his wife has never frequented the world where people are 'taken in,' as you say, and as for Mlle. Esperance ... so much the better if you do not know her?"

The Duke de Morlay-La-Branche, sitting beside the Princess, said to her, loud enough for all to hear, "Albert Styvens is entirely right: they are people of a very different order. They are a very refreshing trio for Parisian society."

Everyone kept quiet and listened to what the Duke had to say. It was well known that he was attracted by Esperance's beauty and talent, and it was also known that he was a sceptic, a railer, not easy for anyone to "take in." The attaché, not knowing how to back out of his awkward position, apologized for having spoken in jest. He had heard ... but the world is so unjust ... etc., etc. No one listened.

"For my part," said the Princess, "I see only one way to

put to the proof the statements of the Duke de Morlay-La-Branche and Count Albert, and that is to ask the Darbois family to dinner. Afterwards, Albert must undertake to persuade this adorable little comedian to reveal her ability as a musician."

The Minister was most agreeable and said, "All our guests this evening must be present at the dinner."

Albert Styvens was consumed with joy. And the Duke did not attempt to conceal his satisfaction.

The only difficulty was to find a suitable excuse for inviting the Darbois. Chance proved itself the Count's accomplice. In conversation with the professor the next day the Count was told that there would be no lesson on the following Tuesday, because the professor was to deliver an address on the question of the hour - "Can philosophy and religion evolve without danger in the same mind?" The conference was to be held at the home of Madame Lamarre, the wife of a fashionable painter. Albert knew that his mother was a great friend of this lady. He told the Countess and the Princess, and it was agreed that they should both go to this conference. When the Professor was presented it would be easy for the Princess to say that Countess Styvens was anxious to meet again her little friend of Brussels, then the invitation could easily follow. Everything happened according to the Count's plans.

François Darbois had a great success; the Catholic party owed him recognition for his noble dissertation on the rôle of philosophy in religion. He was a fervent follower of the author of "The Genius of Christianity."

The Princess de Bernecourt presented sincere

compliments to the affable philosopher. The Countess Styvens presented herself to Madame Darbois, who thanked her for her special kindness to Esperance, who regretted that she had not herself been able to thank her sufficiently.

"Now won't you," said the charming Princess, "do us the honour to come to dinner at the Legation next week? That will give the Countess and myself a chance to renew our acquaintance with your adorable daughter."

François, being appealed to, accepted the invitation for the following Tuesday.

"My husband will be delighted, dear M. Darbois, to meet you; he is one of your most faithful readers," said the Princess.

On their return the Darbois found Esperance very anxious to learn the result of the conference. François said very simply as he kissed his daughter, "You would have been satisfied...."

But Madame Darbois, made loquacious by her husband's success, recounted everything at length and the triumph obtained by her husband in every detail.

The invitation to dine at the Belgian Minister's rather dismayed, in truth distressed, Esperance. Her joy in her father's success was diminished by this prospect. Count Styvens was certainly not unaware of this unexpected invitation.

"You are quite right, little daughter," went on Madame Darbois, "the mother of the young Count is perfectly delightful. She is especially anxious to see you again."

Esperance breathed deeply, as if to draw more strength from within. She knew her parents were flattered at the idea that the attentions of the young Count could only end in an offer of marriage. They were not ignorant that she did not love him, but they hoped that she would in time be touched by his respectful affection. The philosopher and his wife had often talked of this prospect with each other. They did not want to cause any pain to their cherished daughter. M. Darbois had already had to give up all idea of Jean Perliez, for he had begged him not to speak of him to Esperance. She was his goddess; he adored her but felt unworthy of her. With resignation François charged his wife to find out Esperance's state of mind, but these were futile efforts. Madame Darbois could never approach the burning question; she hovered round it with such uncertainty that Esperance never for an instant suspected her mother's real motive in the long talks they had together.

CHAPTER XIV

A radiant sun woke Esperance on the following Tuesday. Her thoughts, always on the future, refused to be subjugated by the confused anguish she felt which almost stifled her. Yet this evening was sure to be one of importance in her young life! Had the Count said anything to her mother? She rejected the idea that he could think of her as capable of becoming his mistress.... Then, his wife? She would not give up the theatre.... "No, nothing in the world could make up for that, far rather death." And she smiled at the idea that she might perhaps become a victim of the great art. She saw herself struggling against all hardships and dying as an adored victim of circumstances, regretted and wept by the many who loved her.

Her imaginative speculations were rudely interrupted by Marguerite bringing in her chocolate. On the tray was a card with a little present for the evening. Esperance read the card, and taking the bouquet looked at it for a long time until tears veiled her pretty eyes.

"Poor fellow," she said, "I did not think of his side of it."

For the first time Esperance absented herself from the Conservatoire voluntarily. She had so much to do! She wanted to look beautiful, "perfectly beautiful," she confided to Mlle. Frahender.

"I feel that something great is in store for me in the early coming days."

She took particular pains with her toilette, and looking at herself in the tall glass of her wardrobe, reflected, "I do not want to love Count Styvens. Then I ought not to want to be any more attractive to-night than usual. Am I a wicked girl? My cousin Maurice says, 'Coquetry is the cowardly woman's weapon, and I love you, little cousin, because you are not a coquette.'"

The mirror showed a lovely girl gowned in pale blue. The shoulders, slender and rounded, seemed to emerge from clear water made heaven blue by the reflection of the sky. The hair, so blonde it dazzled, made a radiant frame for the lovely face. The red mouth, half open, the white teeth, the wilful little chin, lightly cleft by an oblong dimple, made this delightful little maiden one of the most dangerous weapons that love ever fashioned.

When François and his family were announced in the salon of the Princess, the Minister hastened forward to convey Madame Darbois to a seat, after presenting her to the Dowager Duchess de Castel-Montjoie, Mlle. Jeanne Tordeine, of the Theatre-Française, and several other guests.

Esperance's entrance roused the curiosity of all. The Duke de Morlay-La-Branche, after conversing for a few minutes to François Darbois, whom he had met several weeks before, came up to the young girl as she was standing before the Countess Styvens, replying to the compliments the charming lady was paying her.

Sarah Bernhardt

"I am told that you are quite a clever musician." Esperance looked up to reproach the Count for his indiscretion in speaking about her playing, but her eyes met the ardent gaze of the Duke. She was agitated, thinking, "How handsome he is, and I had never noticed it."

"Yes indeed, Mademoiselle," he continued in his easy, agreeable manner, "we hear that you have captivated Count Styvens with your playing, and as perhaps you know he is recognized as being quite a dilettante authority."

Esperance strived to speak, but nervousness prevented her. She sat down quickly beside the Countess, and crept close to her. A completely new sensation seemed to invade her whole being. She had a strange feeling of uncertain joy tinged with pain and yet she loved this sensation that troubled her, this half-fright which gave her a slight shiver. The Duke brought up a chair and seemed to be exerting all his charm and animation for the Countess, but it was easy to see that all this charm, all this wit, were intended for the pretty creature who appeared powerless to resist his fascinating personality.

When dinner was announced the Duke offered his arm to the Countess, the Minister his to Madame Darbois, the Princess took the arm of the philosopher. While Esperance, naturally accepted the arm of Count Albert. She looked at him more attentively than she had ever done before, and involuntarily made a comparison between him and the Duke not altogether to his advantage.

"How easy and graceful the Duke is," she thought.

"How heavy this man, and dull and slow. The Duke's face is at once kindly and spirited, the Count's brooding and awkward. The Duke is a man, the Count but a shadow."

At the same instant the Count's arm pressed her delicate wrist. She had again to restrain the repugnance she had felt before, and her terrible nightmare came back to her. She let herself fall rather than sit in the chair to which Albert Styvens had conducted her. Here she found herself between the Count and the young Baron de Montrieux, who attempted, with the most charming courtesy to forestall her every want and monopolize all her attention. The Baron was over-flowing with wit and Esperance listened with delight.

After dinner the Baron de Montrieux went to the piano. He was a very fair musician, and all the company were glad to listen to him. Albert followed him. He was really gifted and, if fortune had not otherwise favoured him, he could have made his name as an artist.

There was enthusiastic applause. The Count bent before Esperance, who, in a burst of artistic appreciation, expressed her admiration.

"Then," he replied, uplifted with joy to feel that he had really touched her, "shall we play our duet from Orpheus, Liszt's symphonic poem, to these good friends who are, I think, quite appreciative."

"Oh! no, I should be afraid. I dare not. You forget I know so little. I am an actress and I will recite for you if you like, but -"

The Duke came forward, and hearing the conversation

Sarah Bernhardt

joined in with a request that was almost like pleading. Styvens held out his angular fist to the young girl; the Duke extended a long white hand; and so both led her to the piano. The Duke's fingers pressed her palm lightly but with a suggestion of encouragement, while the Count's held her like a vice that would never open. In spite of her protestations, Esperance was installed at the piano, and Esperance resolved to put all her best into her playing with the hope of being able to transport her audience into the highest realms of the art that can express great aspiration blended with the pathos of suffering. Charles de Morlay-La-Branche withdrew to the rear of the long room, and stood alone, leaning against a beautiful Italian window, to listen and to watch. A conflict of feelings were struggling within him. He was fighting against the attraction of this slender creature, whose white shoulders and delicate body were swaying with a phrase now violent, now subdued, her whole person actuated, controlled by the rhythm of the music. The heavy frame work of Count Styvens seemed an anchor for the fragile idol. The Duke gnawed his lip in suppressed emotional anger.

As the young couple left their seats the room shook with applause. Everybody was delighted. The Princess took Esperance by both hands, gazing at her, stroking the tapering fingers that were still vibrating with the fever of the music. Esperance was so pale that the Princess led her into another room and made her sit down, praising her marvellous execution and striving to quiet the little heart she could feel beating with so much agitation.

"The Doctor who attends me," Esperance explained in a far-away voice, "has told me, Madame, that I must avoid all excitement if I wish to live a long time, but that I shall not live naturally if I am over excited or depressed by emotion."

They brought her a refreshing and soothing drink. The Princess's attendant bathed her temples with Eau de Cologne. Esperance breathed more quietly and rose, thanking the Princess; then suddenly collapsed on her knees, sobbing, without strength, without consciousness, and Madame Darbois was summoned to her side at once.

"Oh! great Heaven!" she said. "I have never seen her like this before; usually she controls herself when over-excited by music. See, dear, a little strength, stand up, and we will go home at once...."

But Esperance's head slipped from the mother's support into her arms, while her whole body was shaken by sobs. The Countess Styvens came in to find the girl exhausted by a storm of moans and sobs. They succeeded in placing her on a large soft couch and she fell asleep holding the Countess's hand, under the impression that it was her mother's.

In about an hour she awoke, refreshed, unconscious of what had happened to her or where she was. Her father and mother were beside her. She got up, and one of the maids came to her. She then remembered, and asked how long she had been asleep.

"You see, mama," she said, "you must not take me out any more, I am not fit for it." Then kissing her mother who had never left her, she expressed her sorrow for what had happened.

She thanked the maid and asked her to make her

apologies to the Princess.

"Would you not like me to call her?"

"No, please do not disturb anyone; I could not bear it."

In the ante-chamber two men-servants were in attendance. One of them was helping Madame Darbois, and Esperance, still confused, slipped her arms in the sleeves of her cloak, and then stopped short. Her bare arm had been touched, she was sure of it.

She turned quickly. Her eyes met the Duke's enquiring but not altogether pleasant glance. With a quick gesture the girl clasped her mantle about her, and haughtily moved away without acknowledging the Duke's bow.

Neither M. nor Madame Darbois had seen anything of what had just passed.

The Duke de Morlay's bad humour vented itself against Count Styvens.

"I have just passed the Darbois in the cloak-room. The little flirt was in a pitiful state: I helped her on with her cloak and her skin was like ice."

Count Styvens turned almost in anger and his hands furtively opened and closed. A feeling of enmity was rising in his generous soul. He felt that the Duke had spoken slightingly of Esperance to wound him. Twice, during dinner, he had caught the covetous glance of the Duke fixed on Esperance, and he had suffered acutely in consequence. He looked at the Duke coldly; his shyness would have made him dumb had it not been for the sustaining power of his anger.

"I cannot reply to you now," he said. "My mother is here."

The Duke de Morlay-La-Branche, who was, after all, a gentleman, came up to him.

"Albert, I am a fool. I beg your pardon."

And he went to take his leave of the Princess, who had quietly witnessed and understood the pantomime that had passed between these two men.

"You did right, my friend," she said to the Duke. "Albert is a brave and loyal fellow."

"He is an idiot," he replied, "whose idiocy we must respect."

"All the same he has a quality which you and most of the other men of your age do not possess, and he is not afraid of being laughed at; and that gives him enormous moral strength."

"You find that a virtue, Princess?"

"Indeed I do. He does what he wants without bothering about what people will say."

"But does he really know what they do say of him?"

"You know that Albert and I have been friends since childhood," said the Princess. "He is twenty-eight, I am thirty, which gives me a little advantage perhaps, and I talk to him quite as a comrade. It is true that he has never had any love affairs with women, and they joke him about it. Albert does not disguise it. 'I shall always be as I am,' he says, 'until I really love.'"

"But he is in love now."

The Princess saw that the Duke enjoyed seeing her hesitation before answering. So she said nothing at all, but held out her hand; which he kissed respectfully and went his way.

CHAPTER XV

Esperance had returned home quite furious with the manner of the Duke de Morlay-La-Branche, which she considered insolent. She had passed a bad night, waking every few moments. She compared the dignified and honourable affection of the Count with the offensive attitude of the Duke. Her thoughts flew to Madame Styvens as to a refuge. She was possessed of great tenderness towards this charming woman, whose life of purity and goodness won the admiration of all who knew her. On her side there was no doubt that the Countess loved the young girl, but although she did not cherish the narrow and false ideas of many of her friends against the theatre, she would have preferred to have Esperance give up her career....

General Van Berger, who always spoke his mind to her, reprimanded her severely on this point.

"It is impossible," he affirmed, "to let things go any further. Albert cannot marry an actress. I realize that the Darbois family is very respectable; the young girl seems to me above reproach or criticism, but she must give up this career. The Countess Styvens is not for the public eye, and if she loves him...."

"But she does not love him."

Van Berger was silenced for a moment. "What do you say? She does not love him. And you approve of such a union?"

"My son loves her so deeply, and knowing him as you do, you can not doubt the fidelity of his affection. Esperance is touched, flattered even, but she does not want to give up her profession; she would rather, I believe, remain single, or at any rate only marry a man who would allow her to continue her artistic life. If I refuse my consent to the question my son will no doubt soon ask me, he will not insist; but will enter a Chartist monastery. He has a friend, a Chartist in France, whom he visits often. I shall lose my child forever, and my sad life will end in tears."

The gentle woman began to weep quietly. Much touched, the General rose, twisting his moustache, "Courage, be brave, the assaults have not yet been launched and you speak as if the battle were lost! We have not got so far ahead yet, fortunately. Above all, don't cry, that is worse than having one's arms and legs broken. I am yours to command, you know that, heart and soul at your service; and I do not retreat, not I, whatever comes.... Still, dear friend," he said, sitting down beside her and taking her hand, "we must face the facts. Many of your dearest friends would cease to visit you and your house if you...."

"What do I care about the superficial friendship of such people, if the happiness of my son is at stake! Thank you, dear friend, for your loyal insistence. I understand it, but I know that even if you do not succeed in convincing me you will not desert me in my trouble. Thank you."

The Baron kissed the noble lady's hand.

The time of the trial performance at the Conservatoire was drawing near. Esperance had resumed her usual life, alternately calm and feverish. She was studying for the Competition. She often wrote to Countess Styvens, who had returned to Brussels, on the subject. Before she left, the Countess had come to see the little invalid, who had touched her heart so much that special evening at the Princess's. She had also got to know the professor and his wife more intimately. The family attracted her, and she felt a large sympathy for them all. Of course she was fully aware of the love her son had for Esperance and resignedly left events in the hands of God. What did disturb Albert's mother a little was the vehemence Esperance showed in regard to her theatrical career, and the way she rejected the most guarded remonstrances against her following that calling.

"No, no," said Esperance to Countess Styvens, "no, no, no; the theatre is not a house of evil repute, nor are its followers evil doers: the theatre is a temple where the beautiful is always worshipped; it makes a continuous appeal to the higher senses and natural passions. In this temple vice is punished, and virtue rewarded; the great social problems are presented. In this temple instruction is less abstract, and, therefore, more profitable for the crowd. The apostles of this temple are full of faith and courage; they have the souls of missionaries marching always toward the ideal."

The trials at the Conservatoire were to take place on the fifteenth of July. Esperance was ambitious and strove for the first prize in both comedy and tragedy. The year before the jury had only awarded her two secondary prizes; not that she had not deserved the first, but that on account of her youth they had thought it wiser to keep her back for another year. The young artist was to compete for tragedy in the first act of *Phedre*, for comedy in Alfred de Musset's *Barberine*.

The dawn of the fifteenth was clear and quiet. Genevieve and Jean arrived at eight-thirty in the morning to rehearse their scenes for the last time. Jean had in his hand a tiny package. As he was about to give it to Esperance, the maid entered with a large box marked "Lachaume," Florist, which she gave to Mlle. Frahender. On observing this, Jean quickly hid his package in his pocket. Esperance had opened the box and taken out a posy of gardenias, which she slipped into her belt. Again the maid entered with a similar box containing orchids. Esperance blushed, and then tore the bouquet from her belt so quickly that she hurt her finger. She had not seen that a card attached to the flowers by a pin read - "Duke de Morlay-La-Branche." Scornfully, she at once threw the bouquet aside. Mlle. Frahender spoke to her in English to rebuke her for such conduct, whatever its motive. Esperance excused herself. "Be indulgent to me, little lady," she said, in her most winning way; "I am a little nervous just now."

She put the white orchids that Count Styvens had just sent to her in her belt. Jean Perliez picked up the discarded bouquet and the card. He was more disturbed by her anger against the Duke than by her passive acceptance of the young Count's gift. She had talked to him continually of the Duke, criticizing him it is true, but Jean felt in these reproaches that Esperance was more or less practising some deceit. Esperance had wished to have Jean defend the Duke, heap on him praise rather than the blame he did. The young artist felt instinctively that this man - the Duke - would not marry his little comrade.

The three went back to work. When the rehearsal was finished, M. and Mme. Darbois came in gaily to take their breakfast coffee with them. Esperance kissed them tenderly and departed for the struggle on which, perhaps, her career depended.

A day of competition at the Conservatoire offers the spectators a series of amusing studies, instructive, puzzling and deceptive also at times. Ambition, jealousy, vanity border on loyalty, sensibility, and pride. Most of these young people are preparing themselves to begin a sharp and bitter struggle for life itself. Others - and these are very few - are in search of, if not fame, at least notoriety. They have elected to enter upon this career, led by enthusiastic hope, their love of the beautiful, and unconscious consecration to art; nor will they cease throughout their lives to spread their propaganda in behalf of all there is that is good.

When Esperance appeared for the scene of *Phedre*, a fluttering murmur of approval greeted her, while several little outbursts of applause were heard. She was so pretty in her gown of white crepe de chine! Her youthfully cut bodice revealed the slender flexibility of her neck; she might have been a bust in rose wax modelled by Leonardo da Vinci. She carried all before her by her interesting interpretation of the role. The tragic grief of the daughter of "*Minos*" and "*Pasiphae*" was a revelation for many there from one so young. Tears coursed down Esperance's pretty cheeks. The abandon of her graceful arms, her renouncement of a struggle against the gods, her longing for death, her shame after the tale of "*Oenone*," her radiant vision of

Sarah Bernhardt

the son of "*Theseus*," all was fully appreciated by the public, and by a distinguished company of connoisseurs, often strongly critical, but never insensible to real talent as it developed.

In the competition for comedy the young girl achieved the same triumph. When the jury proclaimed her first in tragedy, all being unanimously agreed on the verdict, a storm of applause and admiration greeted the announcement. Mlle. Frahender wept with pleasure, Genevieve Hardouin, enfolding her little friend in her lovely bare arms, kissed her on the hair. Esperance felt more touched by the affectionate admiration of her comrades, than she had been even by the applause the day of the first presentation of Victorien Sardou's play at the Vaudeville. In the afternoon she received the same kind of ovation for her competition for the first prize in comedy. When she came out of the Conservatoire they would have unharnessed her carriage, but Mlle. Frahender and Jean Perliez absolutely opposed this manifestation. Genevieve Hardouin had obtained a second prize in tragedy and an honourable mention in comedy. Jean, who had only entered the competition for tragedy, had a first, shared with two other comrades. The three young people were radiant, each neglecting his own fortune to magnify the triumph of the others.

When Esperance returned to the Boulevard Raspail, she found her parents much elated at her success. Count Styvens, who had been present at the competition, had hurried to tell them the good news and give them all the details of their daughter's significant triumph.

"She surpassed herself in *Phedre*," he had said. "She is,

I think, the equal to some of the greatest tragedienes,"
and when they told Esperance she said, "Is he still
here?" looking towards the salon.

"No, he did not wish to weary you. He only left this
note:"

*"You were divine in Phedre, delightfully feminine in
Barberine. No one is happier at your phenomenal
success than your always devoted, Albert Styvens."*

Esperance felt a world of gratitude to the young Count
for not having waited to see her. She went into her
room to undress, and in doing so drew gently from her
belt the white orchid. She was about to put it in one of
the two vases on the mantel-piece, when her hand
paused of its own accord and remained inert; her gaze
had been caught by the Duke de Morlay-La-Branche's
gardenias in the other vase. Radiant with freshness it
caught the eye, it invited her to come and smell. The
girl bent towards its whiteness. The intoxicating
perfume held her. Her head drooped nearer and nearer
the delicate blossoms. Her lip touched the smooth flesh
of the petal. She trembled violently and threw her head
back. It seemed as if a kiss had been given her! She
quivered, closing her eyes, longing for the unpleasant
feeling to pass.

After a few moments she looked at the poor orchid
which had dropped on the cold marble mantel-piece.
She lifted it up carefully and placed it in some fresh
water.

Then she sat down before the vases where the two rival
flowers displayed their charms. She was bitterly
conscious of being impelled by a new inner force, an

Sarah Bernhardt

almost evil force. And she looked from the mantel to the ivory Virgin, whose open hands seemed to be showering blessings.

Esperance looked back to the white orchid.

"If I do not marry that man I am lost," she thought.

Almost terrified, she got up and walked about to calm herself, to conquer the instinct which her reason told her was wrong. Still under the strain of the emotions of the triumphal day, and to escape the disagreeable thought the sight of the radiant gardenias provoked in her, she began to write a long letter to the Countess Styvens. That soothed her nervousness a little. She poured out all her heart in the letter, for she knew that this woman loved her independently of the love of her son - loved her entirely for her own self.

Two days later Esperance received a letter from the Director of the Comedie-Française, asking her to call at four o'clock that same day at the theatre. At the right hour she went with her mother and Mlle. Frahender. Without delay she was at once engaged, for Madame Darbois had the spoken and written authority of her husband to make what arrangements her daughter should desire. The Director was most complimentary to the young actress and asked what rôle she would care to choose for her debut. Esperance proclaimed her preference for "*Dona Sol*" in *Hernani* or "*Camille*" in "*On ne badine pas avec l'amour.*"

Her heart was filled with emotion as she was leaving the great house of which in future she would be a part. The Place du Carrousel, the perspective of the Tuileries, and the Champs Elysées seemed more beautiful than ever before. The passers-by were charming. Everything, everywhere, spoke only of happiness and hope.

"Mama, dear mama, I am so happy."

PART III. THE COUNTRY

CHAPTER XVI

After the recent excitement at the Conservatoire, following the competition, Esperance was delighted to act upon the Doctor's advice to leave Paris. Doctor Potain had told the philosopher that it was absolutely imperative that his daughter should have two or three months of absolute quiet. He suggested the mountains; but Esperance would have none of them. She loved far horizons and vast plains, but her real choice was the sea. So it was decided that the family should go to their little farm at Belle-Isle-en-Mer.

"You must go immediately," the Doctor commanded, "and to begin with you must have two weeks' complete repose, in the sun, in a comfortable reclining chair."

Esperance was beside herself with joy. To see the pretty farm again nestling in its circle of tall tamarisks, to dream for hours by the seaside, to breathe the breath of furze and seaweed! The windows of her room overlooked the land on one side, and on the other she had wild ocean, studded with black rocks gleaming under the sea's caresses.

Maurice Renaud, Jean Perliez and Genevieve Hardouin were invited by the Darbois to spend their vacation at the farm of Penhouet. Their arrival at the Gare d'Orsay was a complete surprise to Esperance, who threw herself on her father's neck, sobbing with pleasure.

He chided her gently, "Daughter, are you going to break your word to the Doctor?"

So she at once began to laugh in the midst of her tears.

"No, papa dear, only I have not yet begun to keep it. The cure will only commence with my first day in the long chair on the seashore. So you see I can still cry a little in gratitude for all your thoughtfulness."

The trip was gay, thanks to Maurice's nonsense. Modern painter, cosmopolitan, elegant, and cultivated gentleman, he could still become frolicsome and frivolous with nonsense in happy company.

M. Darbois, ordinarily so quiet, laughed at his antics till the tears came, while Mme. Darbois smiled that pleasant smile that had first long ago appealed to François's heart. As to Mlle. Frahender, the artist's wit fairly made her dizzy. As at Brussels, she soon gave up trying to follow him, for at the moment when she thought she had caught the trend of his humour he had already branched off into another anecdote, this time serious, and her laugh would come too late. So she tried to read the names of the little stations flying past, but the speed of the train was so great that, like Maurice's anecdotes, she only got as far as the first syllable. She closed her eyes and slept.

They changed trains at Auray about six in the morning. The young people took charge of the luggage while Maurice went to make sure that the portmanteau with

Sarah Bernhardt

his canvas and paints was securely on the right train. With his mind at rest, he joined them at the little buffet, where they were having shrimps, pink as roses, fresh eggs, coffee and the little cakes of the countryside.

"This way for Quiberon," called out the guard. And the train carried the whole family away to its next stage.

When Esperance breathed the life-giving breath of the sea, when she could distinguish the green line of ocean beyond the trees, she clapped her hands with ecstasy. She became a guide for Genevieve, explaining to her the conformation of Carnac, and recounting with pretty fancy the legends of the country they were passing through.

At last the train stopped at Quiberon. They stopped at the Hotel de France to speak to the Proprietress, Mme. Le Dantec, and get a picnic dinner from her to take with them. The boat, the *Soulacroup*, was filling the air with its second whistle, so they had to hurry along. The tide was not yet full, so they had to climb down the slimy quay, slippery with trodden seaweed, shiny with fish scales. The boat was taking on board a dozen red hogs that snorted mightily. Several women with well-laden baskets settled themselves in the fore part of the vessel, using the baskets as a barricade between themselves and the pigs. Our travellers settled themselves as well as possible, which was not well at all, on the little bridge under an awning. However, Esperance found it all delightful.

The trip was rather rough and uncomfortable, but most of the company made the best of it. Mlle. Frahender grew pale and ill, and her hair flew about in the most comic disarray. Cosily ensconced in a corner, Maurice sketched the various attitudes his companions assumed with every antic of the lightly-laden, wave-tossed Soulacroup. Hunched up on the seat, Esperance clung to the rigging. Genevieve clutched at her when a wave pitched the boat too far over. The others, well muffled up, waited in silence. Jean Perliez sighted the shore continually with his glasses, wishing it ever nearer so that his impatient idol might soon be safe on shore again.

In due course the port of Palais came in view. The Soulacroup's whistle shrieked through the air and in a quarter of an hour more they landed. First the red pigs were taken off, tottering even on solid land, no doubt brooding over the evils they had just passed through.

Maurice was enthusiastic when he caught a good view of the little port of Palais, filled with a hundred little boats lined with blue nets. The tuna boats carried from their ropes and around their sides long, stiff silver tunas, so bright in the sun's rays that they hurt the eyes.

"Oh! Do look," cried Esperance.

A little boat had just approached, overladen with sardines, and soon a silver shower was falling on the hard stones of the quay. It was a beautiful sight, and the excitement of the Parisians amused the jolly fishermen mightily.

François Darbois led his party to the carriage that was waiting, a brake with six seats, drawn by two farm horses. The farmer on the box seat was beaming with pride at the return of his patrons.

It is more than an hour's journey from Palais to Penhouet, but the road seemed short, on account of its variety of view. Leaving Palais, there was first of all the ropemakers rolling long strands of hemp with their fingers almost bleeding over the task. They had chosen a charming spot; shaded by a little orchard they worked and sang the ropemaker's song, with a lingering, dragging melody. And then, after passing a little wood, the island itself came into view. It was covered with gorse, like a series of Oriental carpets dotted with the gold of the broom in bloom, woven with rose heather, and red heather, and purple heather. The bright green foliage of the wild roses "appeared" like arabesques. The sky, hanging low, bluish green, without a cloud, seemed as a silken film stretched to filter the heat of the sun. At a turn in the road the plain disappeared to give place to little hills, which rise from every side to defend from wind and rain the beautiful golden wheat, with its heads drooping under the weight of the heavy grain.

"Ah!" cried Esperance joyfully, standing up in the carriage, "I can see there is the farm just ahead."

The road dropped abruptly so they had to put on the brakes in spite of Esperance's impatience.

And the two young girls, clinging to each other, saw the little red-roofed farm house enlarge, as they grew nearer. At last the carriage stopped, and the farmer's wife came forward to meet them with her three children. At twenty-six she looked forty, like most peasant women exhausted by work and child-bearing. Madame Darbois caressed the children, who had just been having their ears washed and their hair combed vigorously to prepare them for the advent of their master's family.

The farm house was long, and close to the earth, being only one story high. The front door gave directly on the same level into the dining-room, a large room which also served as the salon or parlour, with a bright kitchen to one side, where shining casseroles spoke of the order of the proprietors; to the left, was a large bedroom, sacred to the Darbois themselves. Close to the kitchen was a very comfortable room for Marguerite and the other maid. A wooden staircase led to six rooms above, which were very airy, and all hung with bright chintzes. Mlle. Frahender was installed next to Esperance, with Genevieve on the other side. The two young men were sent to what was known as the "Five Divisions of the World," being composed of five cabins, Europe, Asia, Africa, America and Oceania. These five rooms were always reserved for guests, were built of pitchpine, and their windows gave directly on the sea.

Farther away, at the edge of the fields, were the farmer's quarters, with a long pond full of reeds and iris, hard by and adjoining the pond a pigeon house with sixteen white pigeons which were very dear to Esperance. She loved to see them fly across the water, like pretty messengers disporting between two skies.

After a frugal dinner the young people climbed the dills as far as Penhouet. The bay was surrounded on all sides by high rocks, behind which were hidden smaller rocks, covered with mosses, and mussels; and on the right the cliff hollowed out into a dark cave facing the land. This little beach, cheerful by day, grew mysterious with the fall of night. Esperance could point out Quiberon, outlined across the way between land and sky like a ribbon of light. The little lighthouse, high on the plateau above the farm, sent out its long lunar arms regularly to sweep the country and search the sea.

CHAPTER XVII

Esperance kept her word to Doctor Potain, and spent fifteen days stretched out in a cosy lounge chair. The particular part of the beach had been chosen by Maurice, for it was during this time of forced repose that he intended to do his cousin's portrait for the next Salon. In a little hollow of the hill, he settled the chair. A great tamarisk with feathery foliage of bright green formed a background. To the right was the sea, to the left a glowering mass of dark rocks. Jean and Genevieve took turns in reading aloud, and the picture was said to be progressing famously. During the first two weeks Esperance spent about five hours every day in the chair, but from the sixteenth day she only devoted one hour for posing, after lunch, and then she began to organize excursions to explore the country round about.

One morning as the four young people were returning from a bicycle ride, they saw ahead of them the little brake on its return journey from Palais to the farm which Mme. Darbois had used on a shopping expedition with Marguerite. In the brake were two other persons - two men. The excursionists were still too far from the carriage to recognize the strangers. But Esperance, who was watching, stopped suddenly. Genevieve, who was behind her, almost rode into her, and had to jump lightly from her wheel. Maurice and

Sarah Bernhardt

Jean were some distance behind. She called to them. They were much concerned to find Esperance, with a pale face, clenching her hands on the handle-bar.

"What is it, cousin, what ails you?"

At first she did not speak at all, then her eyes lost their far-away look and she gazed at Jean.

"I don't know," she said in a changed voice, "I think I had some hallucination come upon me."

Then she pointed towards the distant brake which was approaching Penhouet at a great pace.

"What did you see?" Maurice insisted. "You have had a dizzy feeling come over you? You must be careful."

"Yes, perhaps so," she went on, shaking her head as if to rid it of some vague thoughts that were disturbing her brain, "perhaps so. But let us be quick, for one of the gentlemen was Doctor Potain."

"Were there two men," asked Jean.

"Yes, two."

And she started off again at a great pace.

Jean was dolefully perplexed.

When they arrived at the farm they were quite breathless from their long ride. The philosopher was waiting for them at the door.

"Esperance, my dear," he said, "Doctor Potain is here

with the Duke de Morlay-La-Branche. Your mother met them at the Palais, just as they had landed from the boat and were looking for a carriage."

"Very well, father, I must change my things and I will be with you as quickly as possible."

Jean Perliez understood the emotion of his dear little comrade. She seemed to him at once terrified and fascinated. Maurice was presented to the Duke, who immediately began to make himself agreeable. He was quite anxious he said to see the portrait of which M. Darbois had spoken, so Maurice led him up the hill side. The portrait was on an easel, and from a distance the Duke almost thought that he was seeing the real Esperance, the little girl who was troubling his life. He was delighted with the freshness of the colouring, and the perfection of the likeness, so necessary when the model is so beautiful.

Maurice was pleased by the appreciation of such a skilled dilettante, the praise was evidently sincere. He was very much taken with the Duke, who predicted a glorious future for him.

Jean waited at the foot of the staircase leading to the girl's rooms, and watched them descend. Esperance was looking radiant. She had dressed herself with particular care. He understood the tremors of her heart and decided to keep watch in case she should need him.

When the girls came into the hall, the Duke was talking to Maurice, and the Doctor to François Darbois. The gentlemen had not heard the door open, but intuitively the Duke turned around.

Esperance met his burning eyes which were veiled by an expression that suggested repentant submission. She inclined her head slowly and went straight up to Doctor Potain, thanking him for coming, and apologizing for having kept him waiting. Potain led her into her parents' room. He was much disturbed by the uneven beating of her heart, stormier than he had ever heard it.

"That is because I just rushed foolishly on my bicycle to see you, Doctor. I recognized you a long way off. So...."

The Doctor looked closely at the young girl. Her eyes shone with abnormal brightness. He sounded her, but found nothing wrong except the irregularity of her heart. He sent Esperance back to the salon so that he could talk with her father alone. The Duke hastened to apologize for having come thus without notice. He was staying at the Château of Castel-Montjoie with Doctor Potain, and when he heard that the Doctor was leaving for Belle-Isle, he could not resist the opportunity to come and ask pardon. He talked a long time, with ardent, almost brotherly tenderness; asked when Esperance thought of making her appearance at the Comedie-Française, urging her to play *"Camille,"* and spoke with considerable praise of Musset's heroine.

"The character of the young girl seems to have been caught alive. I criticize her only for her hardness."

"But," Esperance replied quickly, "that hardness is simply a light veneer, the result of her education. *'Camille,'* who knew nothing of life except through the disillusioned account of her friend in the Convent, would soon become human if *'Perdican'* had a less complicated psychology."

She stopped, and was silent a minute.

The Duke looked at her.

"All the world has not the candour of a Count Styvens," he said.

This unfortunate sentence exactly answered a fleeting thought that was passing in Esperance's brain.

"So much the worse for 'all the world,'" she said quietly and left him.

Her father and Doctor Potain came in at this moment.

"What are you plotting against me?" she said, going up to them.

François caressed her velvet cheek. "You shall soon know."

The Duke had remained dumbfounded in his chair. The sudden mastery of this child, who had for the second time rebuked him, touched his pride. His instinct as an irresistible charmer told him she was not indifferent to him. Still he could not define in what way he appealed to her. Was it physical? Was it of a higher order? After a little cogitation, he concluded that that was the secret. However, he was wrong. Esperance was subjugated by the attraction of his masculinity and strength, which was subtly energetic and audacious. His taste and independence appealed to her artistic nature. His vibrant voice, the grace of his slender hands, the lightness of his spirits always alert, his superiority at every sport, made the Duke de Morlay-La-Branche quite like a real hero of romance. He had expected to subjugate the little Parisian idol, and found himself thwarted by her. This rather annoyed him, and he vowed to conquer her.

Doctor Potain, who was looking at his watch, now chimed in with, "My dear Duke, we must be thinking of leaving; the boat will not wait for us."

Charles de Morlay thanked his farm hosts, and after bowing elegantly over Mme. Darbois's hand, looked for Esperance.

"Jean," said Professor Darbois, "look and see if you can find Esperance, and tell her to come and say good-bye to our dear Doctor."

But Jean returned alone. Esperance was not to be found. She had flown.

"She had not forgotten about the boat," said the young actor.

"Perhaps she has gone on her bicycle to gather news of old mother Kabastron, who is very ill. That is about ten minutes' distance from here. I will ride ahead on my bicycle."

The Duke laughed gaily, and prepared a scathing witticism with which to wither the young girl. But he did not have the pleasure of delivering it to Esperance, who had hidden herself behind her portrait at the foot of the rook.

She reappeared much later, and was rebuked by her

father for having shown such discourtesy to his guests.

"You know very well, papa dear, that I am very grateful to Doctor Potain, and I should not have gone away if he had been alone."

M. and Mme. Darbois looked at each other and at Esperance.

"Yes, my dear little mother, the Duke makes himself too agreeable for your big daughter."

"But," said the philosopher, "I have never noticed it."

"You were absorbed in a philosophic discussion with the Doctor, and the Duke was not speaking very loud."

"Can you not be more definite?" asked François Darbois a little nervously.

Jean intervened, "May I say something?"

"Certainly, my boy."

"Well then. I heard the Duke de Morlay-La-Branche make fun of the honesty of Count Styvens, and at that Esperance abruptly broke off the conversation."

François turned towards Esperance.

"That is so," she said, kissing her father, "so tell me that you are not angry with your little daughter."

For answer he kissed her tenderly.

"Ah! if I could find a way to shelter you from so much

admiration, from being so much sought after. Yet I don't know very well how to defend you."

"Do not reproach yourself, dear father, you have been so good, so trusting. I will never betray that confidence, and my godfather will be obliged to consume all his own horrid prophecies."

CHAPTER XVIII

When Esperance's portrait was finished, the family could not admire it enough. Maurice who was for himself, as for others, a severe critic, said, "It is the first time that I have been satisfied with my own work. Little cousin, you have brought me luck, so if my uncle will permit me I am going to teach you to ride a horse."

"My goodness!" said Madame Darbois, "still more anxiety for us!"

But Esperance clasped her hands with delight.

The first riding lessons were a source of new joy for Esperance. Maurice was an excellent rider, and his passion for horses had made him expert in handling them. He had chosen a horse for his cousin from a stable in the Cotes-du-Nord, the private stable of the Count Marcus de Treilles, the horse had been secured at a bargain on account of some blemishes of his coat. He was very gentle, however, and the Darbois soon felt confidence in him. Doctor Potain had recommended a great deal of physical exercise for the patient, to counteract the excess of mental work which had weakened her heart.

"Riding, fishing, walking, tennis," the great specialist

Sarah Bernhardt

had said to François Darbois, "will be the best thing for your daughter, and," pressing his hand, "let her get married as soon as possible."

Long excursions about the little island became for Esperance the most delightful part of their country life. Very often M. and Madame Darbois, Mlle. Frahender and Genevieve Hardouin would follow in the brake. They carried their lunch with them and ate it sometimes in the little wood of Loret, sometimes on the cliffs amidst the broom, furze and asters with their golden flowers and silver foliage.

The philosopher's fishing fleet was composed, as he laughingly said, of a blue boat with blue sails, and a little Swedish whaler. François went every evening about six o'clock to set the nets with the farmer's eldest son, whose portrait Maurice intended doing for the following Salon. All the little colony gathered at nine in the morning on the beach, ready with baskets to bear away the catch.

Maurice, Jean and Esperance went out with the Professor to get the nets. Sometimes they had been put far out and then Esperance would row with the others, for which rough sport her delicate arms seemed out of place. The young people would cry out with delight every time they saw the fish under the transparent water held by the meshes. Sometimes they had quite a big draught; two or three rays, several magnificent soles, with mullets, and flounders. Sometimes a great lobster would give the net such tweaks that they guessed his presence before they saw him. And sometimes it happened that the catch was nothing but a few sea crabs, who would half devour the other unfortunate fish imprisoned with them. Another day a great octopus appeared, and Esperance grew pale with fright at sight of his long clinging tentacles.

Esperance often made a selection of the seaweeds in the net, and she and Genevieve commenced an album in which they pasted, in fanciful designs, these plants, fine as straws or solid and sharp of colour. This album was intended for Mme. Styvens, and the girls worked at it lovingly. Maurice would sometimes assist them with his advice or make them a sketch which they could copy as carefully as their beautiful materials would admit. Mlle. Frahender devoted infinite patience to gluing the tiniest fibres of the sea plants. Some were bright pink, suggesting in formation and colour the little red fishing boats. Others were gold with their slender little flowers rising in clusters. The long supple green algaes, swelling along their stems into little round beads, like beads of jade, looked as though they wore some Chinese costume. As the album grew it gave promise of wonderful surprises.

On the first of September François Darbois received a letter from Count Styvens, asking permission to come and submit to him a philosophical work that he had just finished. He begged to present his compliments to Mme. and Mlle. Darbois. The professor read the letter aloud after dinner.

"I hardly think," he queried, "that I can well refuse this pleasure to my favourite pupil?"

Maurice, Jean, the old Mademoiselle and Mme. Darbois seemed very happy at the prospect of a visit from the Count.

"He is a very good musician...." " He can row

splendidly...." "He has a heart of gold...." concluded the philosopher.

A dispatch was sent to Albert Styvens, telling him they would all be delighted to see him. Only Esperance showed some reserve, and Maurice cried out, "My cousin is in dread of musical evenings, I see!"

They all laughed at this quip, which had a very close resemblance to the truth.

"Yes, papa, but no music after dinner: our evenings would be lost! It is so pleasant to go for long walks on these wonderful moonlight nights! The piano is for the town, here we only want to enjoy the harmonious music of nature, the sea that croons or roars, the wind that whistles, whistles or scolds, the plaint of the sea-gulls in the storm, the cry of the frightened gulls and cormorants, the clicking of the pebbles rolled over by the waves; all these charm me strangely and I often sleep on the little beach, soothed by these melodies which you will find echoed in the themes of our great masters."

The philosopher drew his daughter on his knee.

"Very well. We will not mention music to your lover."

The word had slipped out but it stung the young girl, however, she would not let her resentment appear.

"So," she thought, "they all accept the courting of Albert Styvens. My father himself is part of the conspiracy against me."

She led Genevieve outside and confided to her her

apprehensions. Her young friend did not deny that the coming of Count Styvens had the appearance to all of an approaching proposal of marriage.

"My God," said Esperance, pressing her friend's arm, "it seems to me that I shall never be able to say 'Yes.' I am so happy as I am."

The two girls were sitting on a little mound. The moon was reflected in a sea as quiet as the sky.

"See," said Esperance, "that is the image of my life. At this moment I am calm, happy, and my art is like that bright star. It brightens everything for me without troubling me.... I do not love Count Styvens. Oh!" she went on in answer to a movement from Genevieve, "I like him as a friend, but I do not love him. I know he is a gallant gentleman, a fine musician, and a splendid athlete; I recognize that he is very generous and that he is entirely unselfish - for these I greatly respect him, but these qualities alone have nothing to do with love."

"He is a very good-looking man," said Genevieve.

"His arms are too long and he has not any decided colour. His face, his hair, his eyes are all of a neutral tint which you cannot define."

"But handsome men are very rare!"

Esperance did not answer.

"There is the Duke de Morlay-La-Branche, too. Do you like him any better?"

The moon shone full on Esperance's face.

Sarah Bernhardt

"Great Heavens, dearie," exclaimed Genevieve quickly, "you are not in love with that man, I hope."

"Don't speak so loud," said Esperance, frightened. "No, I am not in love with the Duke, but he bothers me, I confess. He is continually in my mind, and the thought of him makes the blood rush to my heart. When he is present I can struggle against him, but I have no strength against the picture of him I so often conjure up. That dominates me more than he can do himself. That seems innocent enough, but I know very well all the same, that I find every excuse for dwelling on the thought of him. No, I do not love him ... but still...." she murmured very low.

Genevieve took her friend in her arms.

"Esperance, darling, save yourself! Think of the downfall of your mother's happiness, think of the fearful remorse of your father. Think of your godfather's iniquitous triumph. Ah! I beg of you, accept the Count's love, become his wife, you will be constrained by your loyalty to save your father's honour. But the Duke...."

"My father's honour is precious to me, and you see, I am defending it badly," said Esperance. She wept quietly. Genevieve drew her head down on her shoulder. Esperance kissed her.

"Come, we must go back, it is getting late. I thank you, Genevieve, and I love you."

A letter arrived the next morning which announced that the Count would pay them his visit on Thursday.

There were just three days before his coming. Esperance had made up her mind, after her talk with Genevieve, to accede to her parents' wishes. She and Genevieve went to inspect the room that had been prepared for the Count. It was a little square apartment very nicely arranged. On the floor was a mat with red and white squares. The windows looked out on the rocky coast. The young people decided to hang some small variegated laurels from the ceiling to decorate it. On the mantel they put some flower vases on either side of a plaque representing the golden wedding of a Breton couple. Mme. Darbois opened for them what Esperance called her "reliquary," and they found there flowers and ribbons. They chose wisteria, and lavender and white ribbons, then went to work on their wreath. A large crown of pretty bunches was hung from satin ribbons. When it was ready the four young people went with ladder and tools to hang the wreaths, Maurice standing high up on the ladder drove in the peg intended to hold the crown.

"As reward for this service, you know," he said, "I must be allowed to put the wreath on your pretty head, the day that you are married."

Esperance blushed and sighed sadly.

The room was charming in its decoration, though when it was finished it seemed more fit for a young girl than for a big, broad-shouldered man.

M. and Mme. Darbois went to meet Count Styvens at Palais. François had taken his glasses and pointed out the boat to his wife.

"There is the Count," said Mme. Darbois. "I recognize

his tall figure."

In truth, Albert Styvens was stepping ashore, holding in his arms a child of two or three years. He put it down carefully, and held out his hand to a poor, bent old woman, who tried to straighten up to thank the kind gentleman.

François and Germaine came up to the young man, who pressed the philosopher's hand and presented his respects to Mme. Darbois: and seeing them look with some curiosity at the old woman, he said, "Here, Madame, are some good people deserving of your kindness. Mme. Borderie is this little chap's grandmother. Her widowed son died five months ago of tuberculosis, and as the child was coughing she gave everything she had to take him to a specialist in Nantes. The rough sea to-day made the poor little fellow ill, bringing on a horrible coughing attack. The poor woman was too weak to hold him during his convulsions, and he rolled away from her, and she was so frightened when he did not move, that she was going to throw herself overboard. I rushed with the other passengers to stop her, we calmed her finally, and after some little time I was able to resuscitate the child, who had gone off in a fit."

The poor woman wept as he talked, and showed a banknote he had slipped into her hand when he said good-bye.

"You must put that away. You will need it," said the young Count, smiling.

"Where do you live?" enquired Germaine.

"At Pont-Herlin."

"That is some distance away?"

The old woman shook her head and feebly shrugged her thin shoulders.

"I must go there."

"Well, Mme. Borderie, we will take you there."

Without further parley, Albert picked the old woman up lightly and set her down in the brake. The baby was deposited on her knees where he promptly fell asleep. The Count's little trunk found place beside the farmer on the front seat. A basket of osier, which the young man had handled very carefully, was also placed in the brake, and then they set off for Pont-Herlin.

They were growing anxious at the farm of Penhouet, at the non-appearance of M. and Mme. Darbois, Pont-Herlin lies some way from the Point des Poulains and the roads are not in very good condition, especially for a two horse brake. But soon the wind brought the sound of horse's hoofs and shortly after the brake drew up before the farm. Albert went white at sight of Esperance. She had come forward first, fearful on account of the delay. Mme. Darbois explained the cause, and spoke of the Count's great kindness, to the old woman and her boy.

Esperance raised her pretty eyes, damp with emotion; she looked at Albert, wishing she could admire his person as much as she did his mind. And, somehow, as she looked she was agreeably surprised.

"After all, he is not ugly, if he is not handsome," she thought, "and he is so genuinely good."

In this state of mind she left her hand an instant in his and he trembled.

The young people were anxious to lead Styvens to his room. François, however, was not allowed to accompany them. They marched two ahead, two behind, with the Count between, like a prisoner. Never before had Albert seen Esperance so naturally gay, never had he found her more fascinating. He was almost delirious with happiness. Life seemed to him only possible with this lovely creature for his wife! His wife! Such an accession of blood gushed into his heart at the thought that he stopped giddily.

Jean and Genevieve, who closed the order of march, bumped against him, for he stopped so suddenly that they thought something must be wrong.

"Good Heavens! are you ill?" asked Genevieve.

The Count smiled. "Excuse me, I am sorry. It was my mistake."

As they went on again Maurice whispered to his cousin, "You know, Esperance, you have it in your power to make that man happy for ever. I can see it. Why it seems to be almost a duty. It will be like offending Providence to refuse the wonderful future that lies open before you."

Esperance was very thoughtful, but her gay spirits returned when they arrived at the "Five Divisions of the World." The little cortege climbed the narrow staircase, crossed the little ante-chamber which opened on the opposite side on a court cut out of the rock. Each room had a door on this natural court. Stopping before the last door, on which was written "Oceania," the young people bowed before the Count.

"Behold the prison of your Highness!"

When he was left alone the Count examined his surroundings. His simple chamber seemed to him sumptuous. He smelt the flowers on the mantelpiece, half suspecting that they were an attention of the young girls. The wreath suspended from the ceiling made him smile. It had been hung there in his honour, there could be no doubt about that. There was a knock on the door. Marguerite entered, followed by the farmer bringing the trunk and the osier basket.

He stopped the old servant as she was going out. "Wait a moment and help me, please."

He cut the string which held the basket and took out four bouquets as fresh as if they had just been gathered.

"See, Marguerite, the name is pinned on each bouquet; be so good as to give them to the ladies."

At half-past one the Count appeared walking up and down before the door of the dining-room. He did not want to be the firs t one to enter. Maurice joined him.

"I would love to see the portrait of your cousin," said Albert.

"I will show it to you after lunch."

"Is it finished?"

"Yes; but I still have some retouching to do to the background, and I shall be glad to have your advice upon it. It is not perhaps exactly necessary, yet every time that I look at it, I feel the need of some slight change."

Genevieve and Esperance came in together. The contrast of this double entry was striking. Genevieve, dark, with regular features, framed by a mass of heavy black hair; Esperance, shell pink, aureoled by her wavy blonde hair. Genevieve was so beautiful that Maurice was moved. Esperance was so dazzling that the Count mentally praised God at the sight of her. He was warmly thanked for his pretty flowers, several blossoms of which each girl had pinned to her dress.

When the fish appeared, Maurice rose gravely.

"This magnificent fish, sir," he said to Albert Styvens, "was caught by me for you; it is for you to decide whether to share it with us or whether you prefer to eat it alone."

The young attaché arose and with more humour than they expected from him, took the platter and bowed with it towards Mme. Darbois. The conversation raced merrily along, and they were soon disputing about sports. The Count learned that Esperance rode on horseback. He was delighted, and inquired if he would be able to procure a mount. Jean offered his, but the Count, who knew of his love for Esperance and divined what a joy these excursions must be to him, refused this sacrifice. The farmer's wife, who helped to wait at table and was ignorant of social customs, forthwith entered the conversation.

"Ah! if Madame will permit me, I can bring you to the Commandant, who has a fine horse to sell."

"You may have no fish this evening," said the professor genially. "As I was away meeting you, I could not put out my net."

"But we did it, father," said Esperance, "and I hope that Count Styvens will have some magnificent luck. We go fishing this evening."

"So, you are a fisherwoman too, Mademoiselle?"

"We fish every morning, and we shall be very glad to have you join us," said the girl quietly.

After lunch the Count joined the four young people in a ramble along the cliffs. Esperance and Genevieve went arm in arm, the three young men followed; with Styvens in a dream of delight, happier than he had ever been in his life. Maurice was watching Genevieve every day seeing her more beautiful, and abandoning himself without much effort to this new passion. Jean Perliez contemplated Esperance and smiled sadly, if gladly too, at the thought that she was going to be delivered from the dangerous Duke de Morlay-La-Branche. They sat down on a high rock overlooking the little beach of Penhouet and remained silent for a while.

"How very beautiful it is," murmured Albert at last. "You love the sea, do you not, Mlle. Esperance?"

"More than anything else in nature. I love great plains

Sarah Bernhardt

too, but I like them best because they are like the sea when they billow under the breeze."

"You don't like the mountains at all?" asked Genevieve.

"Oh! no, I stifle there. I dream at night that they are pressing in to strangle me. I went to Cauterets with mama after she had bronchitis. I spent all my time climbing to get a view of a horizon and breathe better. As soon as mama was well the Doctor sent us away saying that it was not good for me."

"And the forest?" asked Albert.

"The forest hides the sky too much. Nothing makes me as sad as the deep woods."

"And the lakes, cousin, what do you say of them?"

"A lake makes me shiver. I feel constrained before a lake as before a person whom I know to be false and perfidious. Of course, the sea is dangerous, but no one is ignorant of its caprices, its violence, its tragic love bouts with the wind. The sea is open, whether in laughter or fury. See, look off there," she said, standing upon the rock. "This evening it is calm as a lake, and still the waves are all rippling, preparing for an assault on this rock! It is so immensely alive, even in its great reserve!"

The silhouette of the young girl, cut against the horizon, was blurred by the passing night mist. She seemed a flower blooming by moon-light. Maurice said in a low tone to Genevieve, "See if you can realize this picture. It is beyond the power of any painter."

"One of the aboriginals might have succeeded. He would not have been guided by any of the conventions that are introduced in all the arts and bar the way to the realism of the ideal, which is dear to all true artists."

"The realism of the ideal is very true, but how are you going to make amateurs or critics feel that?"

"Oh!" replied Genevieve, with much conviction, "There is always an amateur of the beautiful, there is always a critic who describes his emotion sincerely, it is for them that I give my tears when I am on the stage."

Esperance dropped on her knees, and taking her friend's head in her hands, "You are always right, Genevieve," she said. "It is a great gift to have you for a friend."

"My little cousin speaks truth," concluded Maurice.

Genevieve stretched out her hand with a smile to thank him. The young man kept the contact of that charming strong hand and kissed it with more warmth than convention required.

"Monsieur Maurice," murmured the girl with trembling lips. But she could not voice a reproach. She got up to hide her blushes.

"Is not this the time for us to go back? The air is getting sharp, and you have no wraps, Esperance."

Count Styvens stood up to his full height and stretched his hands to his little idol to help her up, but she had withdrawn before the two arms stretched towards her, and recoiled in a kind of fright.

"Did I startle you?"

"Oh! No," she said nervously, "But I was dreaming, I was far away...."

"Where were you, cousin?"

"I don't know. Thoughts are sometimes so scattered that it is hardly possible to give a clear impression."

Putting her hands in the Count's she jumped lightly to her feet. The young men led the girls back to the farm, and silence descended upon the Five Divisions of the Globe.

But love made every one of these young creatures somewhat unsettled, and it was long before either of them slept. Esperance and Genevieve talked low, and long silences broke their confidences. Count Styvens had brought cigarettes for Maurice and Jean. All three stayed and talked a long time in the painter's room. Alone with men, Styvens lost all the timidity that sometimes made him awkward. His broad and cultivated mind, his humanitarian philosophy unaffected by his religious beliefs, the sincere simplicity with which he expressed himself, made a great impression on Jean and Maurice.

"That man," said the latter to his friend, "is of another epoch, an epoch when he would have been a hero or a martyr!"

"Perhaps he may yet be both," murmured Jean.

CHAPTER XIX

Next morning Albert Styvens asked Maurice to show him the portrait of Esperance. He gazed at it a long time in silent admiration. He could gaze his fill at a portrait without outraging the conventions.

"What marvellous delicacy! Oh! the blue of the eyes! The mother of pearl of the temples!"

He sat down, quivering with emotion, and looked frankly at Maurice.

"I love your cousin; you know that, don't you?"

Maurice nodded.

"I have loved her for a year, and you see me here, still hesitating to speak to her father."

"Why?"

"Because I know that she does not love me.... Oh! I believe," he went on sadly, "I hope, at least that she does feel some friendship for me - but if she declines my proposal... what else would ever matter to me?"

Maurice came and sat down beside him.

"Your mother?" he queried.

"My mother loves Esperance devotedly, and she has a very real admiration for your uncle as well. She is very religious. M. Darbois's philosophical books, which deny nothingness and proclaim the ideal, have been a great comfort to her in her voluntary solitude. She would be very happy to know if I could be happy."

"But," objected Maurice. "I am afraid that my cousin does not wish to give up her art - the stage."

"Yes, I am aware of that, but my mother and I have not the stupid prejudices of the multitude. Undoubtedly, this union, under such conditions, would estrange us from many of our so called friends, and I should have to give up the diplomatic service, but that would not trouble me. No," he went on, resting his hand on Maurice's knee, "the hard part would be to see her every evening surrounded by the admiration of so many men. I suffered when she was playing at the Vaudeville, and then she was scarcely more than a child, but I heard them all commenting on her beauty and it was all I could do to control myself. What shall I be if she becomes my wife? Ah! my wife! my wife! I really believe, M. Renaud, that her refusal would drive me mad; so, I hesitate. Hope is the refuge of the sick; and I am very sick - sick at heart."

Maurice felt strangely drawn to this man, so simple, and so frank, and so innately refined in thought.

"From to-day I am your ally, and I hope soon to be able to call you 'dear cousin.' As to her artistic career, Esperance will have to sacrifice that for you. We will all try to lead her to this decision, but you must not make her unhappy about it."

"I am already disposed to all concessions except those which touch my honour, and I assure you that my mother and I are both ready to scorn all idle talk."

The girls came up with Jean Perliez. The Count said, "Your portrait is a perfect likeness and is, moreover, a beautiful picture. But," he exclaimed, "you are all ready for riding!"

"Yes, we are going to Port-Herlin. Won't you come with us? Mama, little Mademoiselle and Genevieve, are going in the carriage to carry some provisions to poor old Mother Borderie."

"Your invitation is very tempting, and I am going to surprise you perhaps by declining. The farmer arranged to have the Commandant's horse here for this morning, but he comes accompanied by many warnings and I want to try him out when you are not here; if M. Perliez will be my guide to Port-Herlin to-day I shall be glad. To-morrow I hope you will offer me the same chance again...?"

Esperance smiled delightfully.

"Suppose we have lunch there," said Maurice.

"Papa would be left alone too long, and I want to see if M. Styvens can fish as well as ride. We will come back to pull up the nets about five o'clock, and then we will have tea in the boat."

The carriage was ready, the horses saddled. The Count had the pleasure of assisting the young actress to mount, and then Esperance and Maurice set out together, followed by the brake. The Count and Jean Perliez took a more roundabout and a steeper way. Albert wanted to study the character of his horse. The first to arrive at Port-Herlin were to await the others, and together they were to go to visit old Mother Borderie.

The dwelling was one of the White Breton houses with thatched roof. There were three rooms, the kitchen, where one entered, and two little rooms. In the first, fitted in the wall one above the other were two narrow beds edged with carved wood; in the second room, four similar beds. Large bunches of box, which had been blessed, ornamented the beds where the woman's four children had died. The father of the little grandson was the last to go. The kitchen was unlighted except when the door was open. The bedrooms had each one narrow opening like a loophole.

The old woman was sitting beside the hearth, by the side of which was an armful of furze. The evening meal was slowly cooking in a marmite suspended from a hook. Between her knees she held the child, combing his hair. She stopped when she saw the visitors enter, and the child ran towards the Count who took him in his arms.

The presents they had brought were unwrapped by the girls. Blouses, trousers, clothes for the baby, a woollen dress, a muslin dress, with two beautiful fichus in true Breton style for the grandmother. One box contained sugar, coffee, and six jars of preserves; another, smoked bacon, salt pork, two bottles of candy and prunes, and six bottles of red wine. The old woman looked, caressingly felt everything with her old knotted fingers, while the tears ran down the furrows that sorrow had hollowed in each cheek.

"Ah! if my son had had such good things, perhaps he would not have died!"

And she stood before the food with her hands crossed, her eyes lost in the distance among old far off memories. Esperance undressed the little fellow, and Genevieve looked for water to wash him before putting on his new clothes, but despairing of finding any, she tried to draw the old woman back from her dream.

"Water?" she said. "I have been too weak these three days to go to the well. There is none here but what is in that pitcher there, on the board, but don't take it, Mam'selle, the baby is always thirsty."

Genevieve raised her beautiful arm in its loose sleeve and picked up the pitcher. She looked at the water and asked with surprise, "This is the water you drink?"

"Yes, the cistern is empty, on account of the drought we have had these two months, and the spring is a mile away. It is too far for me, and especially for the child who is not strong. I don't dare leave him alone in the house here; and I don't dare leave him with the neighbours. They are too rough and they knock the little fellow about and he doesn't understand it is only done in joke, and he cries and calls for me and gets such a fever that he almost died one day when I left him to go do washing still further away."

"But couldn't you get the neighbours to bring you some water?" asked Esperance.

"My young lady, there are thirteen in that family, and one of them is ill to death!" she added sighing.

Albert joined in, "Where is the spring?"

"Over there, near the church in the next village."

"Very good, we three will go there," he said, calling Maurice and Jean, "and we will bring you back lots of water?"

"Wait till I give you...." she opened the cupboard. "Here is the pail. Take care, it is very heavy."

Albert began to laugh. "Come along, my friends. I have got an idea."

Esperance watched him as he went out and for an instant she loved him.

While waiting for the young men to return she settled her mother on a chest. The only chair in the house was a straw arm-chair with a high back, on which the old Borderie was sitting and which she had not thought of offering.

"No doubt," said Mme. Darbois in a low tone, "little by little she has had to sell everything she had."

The girls opened a bottle of wine, the jar of prunes and the jar of candy, and arranged them on the board pointed out by the poor woman, who thanked them simply and said, "Ah! my little lad, how good it will be for him!"

"And for you too, you know. Now drink some wine

and take some coffee," said Esperance, caressing the grandmother's hands.

"I haven't got enough wood to boil the water."

Madame Darbois looked at the girls contritely. "Wood," she said. "And we never thought of it."

"If you aren't poor, you don't have to think," muttered the old woman.

A contraction of the heart, the sting of remorse, pierced Mme. Darbois and the two girls.

"To-morrow you shall have plenty of wood, Mme. Borderie."

"That will be very good, kind lady, for then we can have a little heat, and that is what the little one needs. The sun never comes into my room, ah! it can't, the hole is not big enough. And then in the evening when the fog begins, my little boy, he coughs so, and that makes me shiver; then I take him in my bed, but my blood is not warm enough so he can't get warm. Ah! but that will be good for him, to have wood! Thank you."

For the first time her face broke into a smile, for she had almost forgotten how to smile. Her life had been nearly all tears. Suddenly she raised her head in fright - "What may that noise be?"

At the door a cart stopped. On the cart a big barrel.

"Here is some water, Mme. Borderie, that we are going to pour into your cistern."

With the help of the carter and Maurice, Albert got to work and behold! the cistern half full. Albert tried the pump.

"Don't waste any, in Heaven's name," cried the old woman.

"No, no, never mind. Anyway there is another barrel on its way."

In fact another cart was stopping before the door. This barrel being smaller. Albert, impatient at the peasant's slowness, picked it up himself and rolling it along, emptied it like the first in the cistern.

"Look there, will you, Mother," cried out the second carter, "that isn't any cheap water. The fine gentleman has given a hundred francs to the town so you could have that water there."

The Count coloured to the roots of his hair. He thought that Esperance had not heard, but he met her contrite glance, full of gratitude. With Genevieve's help she washed the little fellow, who was very docile, sniffing with pleasure the "good smell" of these ladies. Bathed, combed, in his new clothes, he was a darling.

"I don't know you any longer, little boy. Who are you?" chuckled the old woman. And she kissed the child, saying, "On Sunday, we will go to Mass, you will be as fine as the other little boys."

She saw all her visitors to the door, and when Esperance jumped on her horse, "You aren't afraid up there? You know horses aren't exactly treacherous, but they are uncertain, and then these dreadful flies make them wild. *Au revoir*, Madame; my good gentlemen, thank you. Good luck, Mam'zelle."

The four riders returned together. Passing the little village of Debers, they had to stop; a big hay wagon barred the way. The peasant who was driving was abominably drunk. He swore and struck his horses and jerked them violently towards the ditch. Maurice ordered him to make way. He laughed foolishly and swore at them insultingly. Maurice and the Count started forward, and the peasant menaced them with the scythe resting on the seat beside him. In a flash Albert leapt from his horse, threw the reins to Maurice, and went straight to the drunkard. The fellow tried to brandish his scythe, but already Albert had wrenched it from him and threw it aside. Then seizing the man, he pulled him down on his knees and held him there until he begged for pardon. The rustic, suddenly sobered, and raging with impatience, paid in full the apologies exacted by the Count, before he was allowed to get up.

Jean, during this contest, had led the horses out of their way. The driver, pale with fury, swung his whip at large and it struck Esperance's horse. The poor beast, mad with fright, took the bit between his teeth and started out on a dizzy run. Albert saw at a glance the only possible way to stop his course.

"Go to the left and cut across the road," he cried, "I'll take the right."

And he put his horse across the fields.

Esperance's horse did not follow the bend of the road as Styvens had expected. Blinded by fright, it made straight ahead towards the cliffs.

Sarah Bernhardt

Once on the rocks, there was the precipice and certain death.

The Count's horse leapt as if it understood what it had to do.

The Count came up just as Esperance lost her seat and fell with one foot caught in the stirrup. Her lovely blonde hair swept the earth. Twenty yards more and that exquisite little head would be crashed upon the rocks.

With a desperate effort, Albert by spurring his horse furiously was able to reach her horse's head, seize him by the bridle and swing himself to the ground.

Braced against the rocks, he succeeded in halting the trembling beast, and bent in anguish over the fainting girl. But just as he freed Esperance's feet, the horse, still trampling and plunging, kicked him full in the head. He went down like a stone.

Maurice and Jean had now come up. One calmed the horse, the other went to the aid of the wounded man. Albert, his face streaming with blood, was murmuring feebly, "No, she is not dead; no, she is not dead...."

He fell back unconscious.

Jean was kneeling beside Esperance. He raised his eyes to Maurice, moist with tears, but bright with hope.

"She is alive," he said, "she has just moaned feebly. It is only a little way to the farm. Hurry Maurice, go for help. God grant the Count's wound may not be fatal...."

The peasants who were haymaking nearby had left their work and come upon the scene. One man offered his cart and Albert was lifted, unconscious and bloodstained, and laid on the hay.

Esperance had come to her senses. She could see, but could not understand. A peasant woman, kneeling beside her, washed her face in water from a pool in the rocks.

Suddenly she recollected her comrade.

"Jean," she cried with fright, "Jean, Count Styvens?"

Jean sorrowfully showed her the wagon where he lay. Esperance, leaning on the young actor, stood up to be able to see, and a great sob shook her from head to feet.

"My God! my God!" she moaned, "is he killed?"

"No, I don't think so, not yet at least...."

"And his mother, his poor mother.... But what happened? I don't remember.... It is terrible...."

Jean described what had happened, and how the Count had snatched her from certain death.

Esperance began to cry bitterly.

Meantime Maurice was returning with the victoria in which were M. and Madame Darbois. The wagon was sent on its way very slowly. François stepped down quickly and took his daughter in his arms, intending to carry her to the carriage.

"My father, I am able to walk...." she stifled with sobs. "But he...."

The philosopher put her in the victoria beside her mother, and begged Jean to stay with them. Then he rejoined the cart, and climbed up beside Maurice who was supporting the limp head on the hay.

The professor had studied a little medicine. He could see that the wound was grave, but the young man was robust and he allowed himself to hope.

Maurice recounted the accident with all its details.

"Brave fellow," said François, taking the cold hand. And tears, he could scarcely restrain, began to fill his eyes.

Soon they all arrived at the farm. Marguerite, as she had been instructed, had prepared the Darbois's room to receive the wounded man. Esperance, exhausted, was put to bed, and was soon asleep, watched over by Mlle. Frahender, who prayed silently, counting over her rosary.

They had difficulty in moving Albert Styvens. His great body was heavy and difficult to raise. Finally, after they had washed and bound up his head, they succeeded in undressing him and making him as comfortable as possible in the great bed.

A quarter of an hour later he opened his eyes, and, in response to the anxious faces leaning over him, smiled sweetly.

"And she?" he asked in a feeble voice.

"Thanks to your courage, she is all right," said Mme. Darbois. "You have the blessings of a grateful mother."

She put the young man's hand to her lips. Two warm tears fell down on it. The young man trembled, then his face grew radiant. They followed his glance. On the threshold stood Esperance, leaning upon Genevieve. A half-hour of profound sleep had completely restored her. She had waked suddenly, and seeing Genevieve and Mlle. Frahender beside her, had asked, "How is Count Albert?"

And in spite of the protests of both women, she had got up. She wanted to be sure, she wanted to see!

The wounded man looked at her fixedly.

"Tell me that I am not dreaming," he implored.

"Albert," she murmured, going up to him, "I owe you my life."

She knelt beside the bed and her delicate hand rested on his strong hand.

"God is very good," he sighed, closing his eyes.

He went so pale that François came forward quickly to feel his pulse. He was silent a moment, then covering the patient's arm with the sheet again, looked at his watch.

"If only this doctor would come...." he said.

Almost immediately the head doctor from the barracks at Palais was announced. He was a man of forty,

Sarah Bernhardt

handsome, a little over-important, but he understood his business well enough. He diagnosed the wound as a fracture of the head and dressed and bandaged it, promising to return that evening with a soothing potion.

For Esperance he prescribed a healing lotion for the many little scratches, which were of no gravity. The girl was so insistent that she was allowed to watch beside her deliverer. Genevieve and Mlle. Frahender also stayed in the room, ready in case she needed help. A dispatch was sent to the Countess.

Quiet redescended on the farm. A heavy atmosphere of sadness seemed to envelop it. Lunch was served disjointedly, nobody cared to eat. Genevieve and Mlle. Frahender had been relieved by the maid, but they were anxious to return to their posts, and when François began to fold his napkin, they pushed back their chairs and quickly returned to the sick-chamber. The patient was becoming delirious. The name of Esperance was continually recurrent in his confused talk. Once the young girl trembled; the Count's expression had become so ferocious that she was terrified. Genevieve and the old Mademoiselle had just come in. She clung to them, clenching her hands and hiding her face. She pointed to the Count, who, with his brows contracted and his lips sternly set, was talking volubly. All three trembled. He ground out the name of the Duke of Morlay-La-Branche in a kind of roar. Mlle. Frahender, more composed than the girls, took the potion left by the doctor to calm the fever when it should become too raging. Esperance hardened herself against the weakness which had made her leave the bedside, and while Genevieve held the bandaged head she poured the liquid between the sick man's lips.

At the same time she spoke to him very gently.

The well-known, much-loved voice had more effect than the potion. The wounded man grew gradually calmer, and still unconscious, slept quietly once more. Then Esperance sank back in an easy chair, begging Mlle. Frahender to see that no one should make any noise. When the doctor returned at nine, he found the patient had been sleeping for an hour. He was well satisfied, and waited a half-hour more before disturbing him to dress the wound. He could say nothing definitely as yet, except that the patient had lost no ground.

He took his leave until next day, and when François asked him to insist upon his daughter's rest, he refused, saying, "I shall do nothing of the kind. She risks nothing except a slight fatigue, and she is performing a good work. It may be that she is the real doctor."

A telegram from Madame Styvens announced that she would arrive next day with the doctor who had attended Albert from childhood, and a friend. She asked that rooms be reserved at the hotel at Palais. But François would reserve only the "Five Divisions of the World" for the three travellers. They prepared one of the rooms as a dressing-room for the Countess, and Maurice and Jean went to lodge at the farmer's.

It was with infinite discretion that Esperance broke the news of his mother's coming to Albert.

"Poor mother," he said, "she must be living through hours of anguish in her anxiety. But the doctor said that I am out of danger."

"What! you were not asleep!"

He smiled with the almost childish smile of the very ill returning to life.

"Then I shall be on my guard, henceforth," she threatened him gently with a slender finger.

He stretched his hand out towards her. She pressed it tenderly.

"Be careful, Albert, don't move too much."

They had completely dropped the "Monsieur" and "Mademoiselle," and this intimacy filled the young man's heart with joy.

CHAPTER XX

François had made a special arrangement with the captain of the *Soulacroup*, so that the charming Countess need not risk travelling with geese and pigs. At Quiberon he had reserved a special room that she might have at least an hour of rest. She went pale as death when she saw the philosopher and his wife waiting for her at the train, although they had sent her reassuring telegrams every few hours. But feared that something serious might have happened while she was on the way.

François said with emotion as he kissed her trembling hand, "Everything is going well, Madame, be assured."

She breathed deeply and the colour returned to her face, which was still so youthful in appearance. She presented Doctor Chartier, who had been present at Albert's birth, and had cared for him ever since, and General van Berger. Several peasant women, who had heard the news of her coming, pressed around offering flowers.

"Your son is saved, Madame," they said.

Her mother's soul was overcome with sorrow and joy, for she felt that they spoke the truth.

Sarah Bernhardt

Esperance, who had been watching for her coming, threw herself into her arms sobbing, but quickly realizing her impatience - "Come, come, he is expecting you."

In spite of her efforts to keep calm the poor woman cast herself upon the bed and embraced her son, interrupting her sobs with words of endearment, crying, laughing, delirious with happiness, for he was indeed alive, and she had feared.... But she cast away the terrible thought.

The doctor from the barracks entered for a consultation with Doctor Chartier, who issued the smiling command, "Leave him to the doctors now, good ladies."

The Countess pressed a last kiss on her son's hand and went away with Genevieve and Esperance.

After Doctor Chartier had examined the wound, he congratulated his *confrere*. "You have cared for our patient admirably, and you will find that his mother is eternally grateful to you."

And indeed the Countess did press his hands and expressed with noble simplicity her gratitude to everyone for all that had been done for her son.

The doctors were to return in the evening. Albert begged his mother to take a little rest.

"If I have your word, dear mama, I declare to you I will go to sleep, I am so relieved to know your anxiety is over."

"I will take care of your mother, Albert," said Esperance. "You take your medicine and go to sleep. Genevieve has promised to come and fetch me if you do not."

The Countess smiled as she went out with the young girl. She looked at the pretty face, which was still scarred by the marks of her fall. She listened, trembling with terror, but admiring the coolness and courage of her adored son, while the little artist gave her an account of the accident. Then she sent for Maurice and Jean Perliez that she might thank them repeatedly. She loved them all for their goodness and simplicity.

"The maid is at your disposal, Madame, I will send her to you." said Esperance. She bent to kiss the Countess's hand, but found her face caressed by it.

"My daughter, my dear daughter," said the Countess, kissing her tenderly.

Esperance went away mystified, and in a daze.

In eight days, Doctor Chartier left them. The invalid was now convalescent, but still confined - to his room for several days. The head wound was closing little by little. Happily the cut had been a clean one and there had been no complications; but fatigue was to be avoided, and the young Count was not allowed to exert himself in any way. He usually settled himself in a big arm-chair near the window, and while his mother did some embroidering, Esperance read aloud. Every two hours they were relieved by Madame Darbois and Genevieve. As to Maurice, he had made a plot in concert with Esperance and Albert, of offering a portrait of her son to the charming Countess. Baron van Berger played endless games of cards with François. The days passed quickly and everyone seemed happy. Esperance's face was as lovely as ever, for every scar had disappeared.

The accident to Count Styvens had made a great stir in the fashionable world, where the young Belgian diplomat was much esteemed and even loved, and the artistic world was interested on account of Esperance. Telegrams and letters came in every day. The Duke de Morlay-La-Branche had shown such an interest that the object of it (the Count) grew exasperated. The Duke had even expressed a desire to come and see the sufferer, but the philosopher, warned by Jean Perliez, replied coldly, pleading the doctor's orders.

At last the day came when the Count was permitted to leave the sick room. He was allowed to take a walk, and felt so strong that when Maurice offered his assistance he refused it quite gaily. Esperance and the Countess walked on either side of him; but suddenly he grew dizzy, and stretched out his arms. Maurice started forward to catch him as he tottered, and the Count saved himself by catching hold of the shoulder of Esperance. Under this heavy burden Esperance shuddered and nearly fell, and grew so pale that Genevieve came to her.

"Give me your arm, darling, and walk a little behind with me, you seem so shaken.... Oh! I guess why...."

Maurice and General van Berger supported Albert, who had lost his self-reliance and was a little crestfallen.

"Yes; I have been tortured again by some sort of repugnance," said Esperance. "I know that I should devote myself to loving that man. But...."

"That will make for the happiness of all who love you."

"Yes, but it will be like condemning myself to death."

Genevieve shivered and grew silent, while pressing Esperance close to her side to give her courage. Her friend's confidences troubled her sadly. She also saw the shade of sorrow hovering over this pure face. She was on the point of encouraging Esperance to refuse the union which would no doubt be proposed for her, but the recollection of the Duke haunted her. Was not this man more to be feared than death itself?

"These are silly notions that crowd your brain with presentiments and nightmares. You must rouse your energy, my darling, and chase everything that threatens to hurt your life."

"I swear to you, Genevieve, that I make superhuman efforts; but no one is master of his thoughts. They are so impulsive and rapid that they seem to escape the control of the will."

"Nevertheless we can deprive them of power!"

"Alas!... But I do not want to sadden you. Look! Maurice is getting anxious. Ah! you are going to be really happy, you are. I feel it. True happiness is always found where love is equal."

Maurice could not resist crying out, at sight of the two

girls, "How grave you both look! What were you talking about that you should spoil your beauty with furrows?"

The Count looked straight at Esperance and she could not prevent herself from blushing.

"My God, have pity on me," she thought. "Help me to love this man."

After fifteen days of long walks, which grew longer every day, and constant care, Albert became completely cured. They had a party at the farm house to celebrate his recovery, with the garrison doctor for the only outside guest.

The portrait of the Count that Maurice had done proved to be quite a remarkable picture - life-like and natural. It was placed on the mantel-piece in Mme. Styvens's room, where she found it when she returned after lunch. It was accompanied by a very simple letter, but a very sincere one, recalling the courage of the young Count and nobly expressing the gratitude of all. It was written and signed by the philosopher, Mme. Darbois and Maurice. The beautiful portrait, so delicately presented, was a source of happy comfort to this lonely woman.

The next day the Countess had a long talk with her son. He was sitting at her feet.

"Reflect very carefully," she said to him, "reflect very carefully. I believe that that child, whom I love, whom I find absolutely charming, will not willingly renounce her art. However, I am ready to do all I can to persuade her to accede to our desire and leave a career which would be an endless source of worry and suffering for you, my dear son."

"Mama, do not trouble her too much. She is honest and loyal, and I have nothing to fear for the honour of my name."

And before his mother could speak he went on: "I am jealous, it is true, but what happiness is not willing to pay for itself with a little pain? Then, perhaps, she will understand. I love her so much, dear, dear mother."

She took the head of the dearly loved son in her hands, and looking deep in his eyes, said fervently - "Dear God! May happiness reward so great a love!"

The young Count returned with his mother to the farm where François Darbois and his wife waited for them by agreement. After a quarter of an hour's conversation, Esperance was asked to come to her parents. She was in her room. Her heart beat as if it would break. She had been warned by Maurice of her family's interview with the Countess. Genevieve was with her, extolling the advantages of such a union, at the same time exalting the real goodness of the Count.

"Think also of your father, who at last will be able to realize his dream of becoming a member of the Academy. You know as well as I do that he has every chance of being elected, but he will never present himself as long as you are on the stage. You know the straightlaced, old-fashioned ways of that assembly...."

"But most of them are poets and dramatic writers," replied Esperance. "Why should my father care to belong to the Academy at all?"

Sarah Bernhardt

As Genevieve rebuked her, her eyes filled with tears. "You see, Genevieve, I am becoming ungrateful. My nature, that I believed so frank and straightforward, seems to get tangled in unexpected twists trying to go the right way. Yes, yes, you are right; I must save myself from myself."

Just then the maid came into the room.

"Monsieur wants to see Mademoiselle. Madame and Countess Styvens are with him."

"Very well; say I will come immediately."

Esperance threw her arms around her friend's neck.

"If you could only know how I thank you."

She went to obey the summons of her parents, resolved and comforted by her friend's words. Her father gave her in a few words the Countess's message. She went forward, very much agitated, her lips trembling, her voice uncertain - "Madame, I thank God for giving me another mother who is so good, so lovable."

The Countess drew her to her, and held her in a long embrace. The saintly woman was praying that happiness should descend on this little creature who was to be her daughter.

Maurice, the Baron, Jean, Mlle. Frahender and Genevieve were all, during this interview, walking nervously in different directions about the farm Albert was in his mother's room, sitting down, his head in his hands, awaiting the decision which was to settle the joy or sorrow of his life. Maurice entered suddenly.

"Come on, cousin," he said, "they are waiting for you."

The young man sprang to his full height with complete command of his over-excited nerves.

"Ah! Maurice, Maurice...."

He threw his arms about the young man and was off on a run for the farm. He entered like one distraught, bent over his mother's hands, and covering them with kisses, murmuring half-finished phrases. Esperance was beside the Countess. He stood an instant in silence before her, looking at her questioningly. Blushing and embarrassed the young girl held out her hands to him and replied low to the question in his eyes, "Yes."

Then he bent over her hand, and his lips murmured, "I thank you, Esperance, oh! I thank you."

They all pressed the hands of the two fiancés. Mlle. Frahender and Genevieve kissed Esperance tenderly. The Baron thundered in his military voice, "There has been no battle, and yet here is the breath of victory. That is very good, but a little stifling. Let us have some air!"

The good man had expressed the general sentiment.

The Darbois, Mlle. Frahender and Jean were sitting in the shade of a little thicket of low, dark-needled pines and other trees with foliage green like water. Climbing flowers interlaced in the branches, making flecks of pink and white and violet. It was an ideal refuge from the heat and the wind. Maurice and Genevieve walked on ahead. Esperance and Albert sat down on the high point of rock that dominated the little landscape. For an instant they looked quietly without speaking.

Albert broke this restless silence, and said, as he took Esperance's hand, "I love you, Esperance, and I will do all that is in my power or beyond it to make you happy."

"I believe you, Albert, and I hope to be worthy of so devoted a love."

He looked at her very penetratingly. "I know that you are not yet in love with me."

"I do not know just how I love you, my dear, but I should always have turned to you if I had been in trouble."

"Have you never been in love?"

"No, I have been and am deeply touched by Jean Perliez's devotion, but I have never thought of the possibility of being happy with him."

"And the other?" asked Albert, looking straight at her with his clear eyes.

She did not answer at once.

"The Duke?"

"Yes, the Duke."

"I do not love him," she answered frightened. "At moments I even hate him, and...."

"And?" insisted the young man, pressing the hand he

was still holding.

"... I am happy to be your fiancée!!!"

Her voice vibrated, her eyes were tender with gratitude.

During the dinner Countess Styvens announced that she must go next day.

"I will take my mother to Brussels," said Albert, "and if you will permit me, I will return immediately."

The dinner was very gay, for they were all happy. Esperance herself, so restless, so disturbed only that morning, talked animatedly, keeping them all delighted with her grace and indefinable charm. Genevieve was astonished, doubting for a little while whether she was simply purposely creating a false excitement. But no, she was really happy.

Baron van Berger rose for a little toast.

"Dear friend," he said, bowing to the Countess, "I am delighted to see that you are reinforcing the ranks and enlisting the younger class. This reinforcement will bring you light, the joy of its twenty years. I drink to your sun of Austerlitz."

Then, turning towards Albert, "I drink to the line of little soldiers that you will give to Belgium, my boy."

The Count became scarlet. Esperance dropped her eyes. Maurice could hardly restrain his desire to laugh.

"Do not forget that life is a battle," continued the

General. "Do not shut yourself up in your happiness, but be always on your guard...!"

"I drink to you, Lady Esperance, who bear a name of hope for the future, for you will certainly understand that the most beautiful role to play is that of wife and mother, which has nothing to do with your theatrical fictions...."

Esperance rose, but Albert restrained her, looking at his mother. The charming woman said tactfully, "My good friend, I think that you have spoken according to your own convictions. Esperance will conduct herself always as seems best to her."

"How kind you are, Madame!" And the young girl went and kissed her hand.

This little incident had interfered with the quiet of the evening. But Esperance resumed her serenity, as she understood that her future mother-in-law had quite recognized the possibility that she might remain faithful to her art.

As to Maurice, the Baron had put him in such spirits that he was sparkling with wit, and the dinner ended in the most delightful camaraderie and good feeling. Esperance, before they had time to ask her, went gaily to the piano; Albert sat down beside her and begged that she would sing.

She agreed sweetly, on condition that her fiancée should accompany her. Her voice was very pure and clear, and she sang a simple ballad with exquisite taste.

"You have no middle voice," objected the Baron.

"Quite true," agreed Esperance with a silvery laugh; "you are terribly frank."

When the girls were alone together finally, Genevieve complimented her friend upon all that had happened.

"You were adorably gracious, dear little Countess, and I believe in your happiness!"

"No, Genevieve," said Esperance, "I shall not be happy, I know it, except in so far as I can give happiness. I love Countess Styvens very deeply. I am touched by Albert's love, I see that I shall be forced by loyalty to renounce the theatre; I shall be torn by regret, for I fear my life will be spoiled, and I am not yet twenty!"

She was sitting on her bed, looking so forlorn that Genevieve slipped down beside her and drew the little blonde head to her shoulder.

"You, dear," asked Esperance, "will you renounce the theatre if Maurice tells you that he wishes it?"

"I shall not even wait for him to tell me.... If Maurice wishes me to be his companion through life, I will sacrifice everything for him, with only one regret, that I have not enough to give up for him!"

"Oh!" said Esperance, miserably, "you are in love, but I am not."

And the unhappy child, stifling her sobs, hid her head in the pillow.

Two days later, the Countess, her son and the Baron

Sarah Bernhardt

left for Brussels.

Madame Styvens had questioned Esperance very adroitly, and she left Penhouet with a pretty good idea of her tastes and preferences.

It was then the end of August, and the banns were to be published for November. The Baron was to arrange for the marriage in Brussels, but it was agreed that the young couple should live in Paris, and the Countess proposed to pick out a pretty house to shelter the happiness of her son. She herself would live in Paris; but she refused to share their home.

"I shall look for a house or an apartment near by."

The adieux were tender on both sides. Esperance was so sensitive to the charm of her mother-in-law that it made her seem devoted to her fiancée....

CHAPTER XXI

The news of the engagement of Esperance and the Count Styvens was known all over Paris. Letters came to the farm of Penhouet, done up in packets. Many expressed to the philosopher and his wife their joy at hearing that their daughter had decided to leave a career so ... so very ... in which ... in fact that...! Every absurd prejudice, so puritanly ingrained in the minds of most middle class divisions and sections and even amongst the more cultivated, was endlessly repeated upon with the usual banalities in the large correspondence of their friends and others. Poor actors, so misunderstood! so misrepresented! The philosopher showed all the letters to Esperance, who shrugged her shoulders, astonished to find there was so much prejudice in the world against her beloved calling. One letter, however, she took quite seriously. It was written by the most eminent of all the Academicians. One sentence in the epistle wounded the poor child very deeply. "Now I shall be able to go about your election with more confidence and security. Dare I admit to you, my dear Professor, that the only obstacle I encountered, and which seemed to me insurmountable, was the career chosen by that lovely child, your daughter, whose talent we all admire so much! Now I can start my campaign, and I am very sure, my dear Darbois, of achieving our ambition without much difficulty. Therefore, perhaps, I shall not altogether deserve your thanks."

What Genevieve had said was patently true; her father had sacrificed his dearest hope for her, and he had done it so all unostentatiously.... Ah! how she loved her father, who was unlike other men! He was standing there before her, smiling, a little scornful of all these little souls. And as he handed her another letter - "No, father dear, no, I beg you. Pardon me the wrong that I have been doing you; I admire you and I love you, dear papa, but leave me with the noble feeling of your supreme kindness; I would rather not know any more of the little meannesses of the world."

She climbed on her father's knees and covered his forehead with kisses.

"Look," said Mme. Darbois, holding up a letter "eight pages from your godfather."

Esperance jumped up laughing, "That I certainly shall not read."

"I am going to write to the Countess that I give up my art...." And swift as a shadow she was gone.

The philosopher sat hesitating, his expression troubled. Had he the right to compel this sacrifice, knowing, realizing, as he did, that his child had based all the happiness of her life on the career she was now voluntarily giving up for his sake? Germaine looked at him questioningly.

"Do you believe, my dear, that I ought to let Esperance write to the Countess, as she proposes? I fear that she is making this sacrifice to gratify my vanity."

"François!" exclaimed Mme. Darbois indignantly.

"My pride, if you prefer it," he said. "But what is such a satisfaction in comparison with the happiness of a life? To me it seems very unjust!"

Germaine adored her husband and her daughter, but she believed more, than in anything in the world, in the noble genius of the philosopher.

"Esperance's sacrifice," she said, "is very slight. She is making a superb marriage into one of the noblest, richest families in Belgium. Albert worships the ground she walks on. The Countess will be more than indulgent to her. She is realizing the most perfect future a young girl can hope for. I see nothing to regret, because she is making a slight concession to her father."

François looked a little sadly at this mother who had never comprehended her daughter's psychology. He knew that for this sweet woman the happiness of life began with her husband and ended with him.

He did not want to argue and rose, saying, "I must do some work."

Ho kissed the unlined forehead of his beloved wife, and then as he was leaving the room added, "Tell Esperance I should like to see her letter before she sends it."

Esperance sat at her desk in her own room, but she sat with her head in her hands, unable to begin her letter. Presently Genevieve came in.

"Is anything the matter, dear?"

Esperance told her what had just happened downstairs.

"I have learned once more that all your reasonings and counsels are always wise, dear sister.... I am sitting trying how to write to the Countess to tell her that I am not going back to the stage!"

Genevieve kissed her. Esperance let her head fall on her friend's bosom, and raising her eyes to her face, said slowly, "But oh! I have not the courage."

Genevieve knelt beside the desk, and dipping the pen in the ink, put a fresh sheet of paper before Esperance, saying with a laugh, "Mlle., get on with your task. I am the school mistress to see that you write properly!"

The smile she brought to Esperance's lips chased away the nebulous uncertainties, and so she wrote her letter to her dear little "Countess-mama," as she had called her since her engagement. When her mother came with the philosopher's message and saw the letter, she was delighted with the phrasing and thanked her daughter warmly for the joy it would give her father.

"Ah! mama, I believe that I am the happiest of the three Darbois, dear ridiculous mama!" And she gave her a quick embrace.

Life was again travelling the simple, daily country round. It was after lunch, three days after Esperance had written her letter.

"Why so pensive, little daughter? Where were your thoughts?"

Esperance jumped up at this question from her father.

"I was dreaming. I am so sorry. I was in Belgium, near the Countess Styvens when my letter would be brought in to her, for, as nearly as I can make out, it ought to arrive to-day."

"No," said M. Darbois, "that letter has not been delivered; it is still in my desk."

Their faces expressed the great astonishment that they felt.

"You did not like it, papa?"

"Very much, very much. It is quite good - and - and pathetic."

"Then, darling papa?"

"I want to talk with you a little more before you send it."

Everyone drank their coffee a little quicker, and five minutes later François found himself alone with his daughter. Even Mme. Darbois had withdrawn, afraid that she might show her own anxiety too much.

"I am listening to you, papa."

"You are going to answer my questions with perfect frankness, Esperance?"

"Yes, father."

"Had you thought of writing to Countess Styvens

Sarah Bernhardt

before you read that letter?"

He drew the Academician's letter from his portfolio and placed it before her.

"No, father, dear."

"Then it was on my account, and to facilitate my admittance to the Academy, that you wrote?"

"Oh! no," replied Esperance quickly, "I would not do you that injustice, knowing how much you love me, and knowing the purity of your heart, the nobility of your ambition. I am sacrificing what I believe, perhaps wrongly, to be my happiness, to the demands of a misunderstanding world. I knew, when I read that letter, that I had no right to drag a man of your merit, my dear mother, and all the family, into the troubles of a life in which they have no real interest. I did not want you to have the sympathy of the world. Sympathy is too often akin to scorn!"

François would have spoken, but Esperance interrupted him.

"Oh! father darling. You are so good. Don't torment me further, send the letter. I am still so new to this role. I need your sincere, your constant help."

Just then Marguerite came in and handed the philosopher a letter, bearing an armorial seal, which had just come from Palais. He quickly opened it, seemed surprised and passed it to his daughter.

"What! The Duchess de Castel-Montjoie is at Palais," she said. Then she read: "My dear Philosopher, the

Princess and I will come, if agreeable to you, after five. I name this hour because the Princess's yacht has to leave to take up friends who are waiting for us at Brehat."

"What time is it?" said Esperance, turning round.

The professor consulted his watch.

"Twenty minutes past three. Quick, Marguerite, tell the men to harness the victoria with the two horses at once."

A quarter of an hour later the carriage was ready to leave. When it had disappeared round the corner from the farm, Genevieve and her friend prepared to go for a walk. Esperance told her mother and Mlle. Frahender that they would be back again in half an hour. They climbed down the cliff, and were soon out of earshot of everyone - they were quite alone. "Genevieve, Genevieve," said Esperance, "I feel that a new danger is threatening me, ready to destroy all my new illusions. Do not leave me, darling."

"What is it that you fear?"

"I can only be sure of one thing, I am in such horrible distress, and that is that the Duke de Morlay-La-Branche is at the bottom of this visit. Ah! if I could be sure that I should never see him again, never, never!..."

And she cried in her great distress like a little child.

Genevieve stayed at her side, without saying a word, only stroking her hands from time to time. Presently Esperance grew calmer.

"Come," she said, rising from the boulder on which they had seated themselves. "We must dress to receive the enemy's emissaries." Her voice was light, but her heart was heavy.

Maurice, who had been strolling not far off with Jean, came up and noticing Esperance's tearful eyes, said: "What is the matter?"

"I dread this visit," exclaimed Esperance.

"What is the reason of this sudden call?" ejaculated Maurice.

"I think I can guess," said the actor.

"Well, tell me!"

"But if I should be wrong?" said Jean.

"What a frightful lot of circumlocution," cried Maurice impatiently, pretending to tear out his hair.

But Esperance replied, "No, Jean, you are not mistaken. I can guess your thoughts. I am afraid, as I just now said to Genevieve, that the Duke de Morlay-La-Branche is connected in some way with this visit of the Princess and her friend!"

"If the Duke comes here, but I do not believe he will, Jean and I will not leave him alone a minute. I assure you that he will get more of our company than he will appreciate. But, knowing that the Count is not here, I do not think he will come. He is too correct for that! Come, let us dance in honour of Albert!"

Taking his cousin's hands and Genevieve's, he nodded his head to Jean to do the same thing, and led them into a whirlwind dance upon the sands of the beach, until the girls laughed as though no heavy thoughts were weighing in their hearts.

Two hours later the victoria arrived from Palais. The young people could see that it contained only two ladies and the philosopher, and Genevieve breathed again.

The Princess descended lightly before the front door. She kissed Esperance, and after speaking to Mme. Darbois, had Maurice, Jean and Genevieve presented to her.

"You did the portrait of which the Duke de Morlay has spoken so highly?"

Maurice bowed.

"Would it be impertinence if I asked you to let me see it?" she said with a smile.

"I thank you, Madame; you flatter me by your request."

The Dowager Duchess, with whom the Princess had been spending three weeks at her Château of Castel-Montjoie, was now presented to Mme. Darbois. She was a lovable and delightful old lady, with a great appreciation of art and science. Both ladies had been present with the Duke at the last Conservatoire competition, and they expressed to Esperance, Genevieve and Jean the enjoyment their performances had given them. The Duchess was much struck by Genevieve's proud beauty, and said to Maurice, "Ah! Monsieur, what another beautiful portrait you could make! This young lady is much more beautiful close to than even on the stage!" And she added a kind and appreciative word for the classic talent of Jean Perliez.

Tea was to be served in the little beautiful convolvulus garden. When they entered this shelter, which a poet might have designed, the Duchess exclaimed enviously, "What a heavenly spot. Who is the inspired person who has arranged this mysterious flowery retreat for you?"

The philosopher pointed to Maurice and the girls.

The Princess admired it, and the conversation rippled on. "We are come to trouble your bower with a plea for charity! Every year, the Duchess gives a garden party in her beautiful park at Montjoie for the benefit of the 'Orphans of the Fishermen.' There is a little open-air theatre, where some of the greatest actors have appeared. Little rustic booths, shops where you pay a great deal for nothing at all, and a thousand other distractions. We are come, the Duchess and I, drawn by a very pretty star, Esperance. She will not deny us her light, our lovely little star?" she concluded, bending towards Esperance.

"But, Madame," murmured Esperance, "my decision - my promises do not depend on myself alone, now."

The Duchess extracted a letter from her gold mesh bag and held it towards her.

"You are perfectly right, my dear child," she said easily. "I also foresaw that objection, so I wrote to your fiancé, even before speaking to you, for which I must apologize, and here is his answer."

Esperance read the little missive bearing the Styvens's arms and handed it back to the Duchess.

"I will not be," she said smiling sadly, "more royalist than the king. Madame, I am at the service of your work."

This was a great delight to the two kindly disposed women, but the young girl's heart was torn because her fiancé would not see! It is true that his letter ended with the words, "I agree with both hands to whatever Esperance shall decide," so that little choice was left.

The garden party was to be the twentieth of September. It was then the end of August.

"And of what nature is to be the modest contribution I can make to your fête?" asked Esperance, half humorously.

"Modest! Of course you will be the principal attraction. My guests, knowing that they will see you for the last time before Count Styvens carries his little idol away from the public...."

Esperance was saying to herself, "so this cultivated, broad-minded lady thinks just as the others do."

The Princess continued, "We want you to play with your fiancé the Liszt symphonic poem that you played one evening at the Legation; and to take part in some tableaux vivants that we are all to appear in. The Duke de Morlay-La-Branche is directing and staging this part of the programme. The performance will be given only by people we know - no professionals."

The Princess had spoken quite quickly, without reflection. She blushed slightly when she remembered Esperance and Jean Perliez, but she had made the mistake and there was no way of calling it back. She thought that Esperance belonged to that circle where a compliment effaces what might seem like an impertinence.

At first the name of the Duke de Morlay had fallen like a pebble in the stream and began to ripple the waters; a spreading circle of thoughts, fears, resentments began to move in every heart. The philosopher himself was troubled, for he had been prompted by Maurice to observe the assiduous attractions of the Duke, and the agitation he caused Esperance whenever they had been together. Esperance and Genevieve both grew pale. The young painter raised his head, ready for some sort of a return reply. Without hesitation he had decided on the plan to follow. He must not only be invited to the fête, which would be easy enough; he must take part in it, so as to be able to shadow and watch the manoeuvres of the over agreeable Duke.

"If you will allow me, Madame," he said boldly, "I should like to contribute my mite to your fête by painting the scenery?"

The Princess clapped her hands with delight at the suggestion and this new support.

"How pleased my cousin de Morlay will be," she exclaimed. "He has just been saying to me, 'For the scenery we shall require a painter, a real artist.'"

"A professional," said Maurice, bowing ironically.

The Princess was somewhat provoked, but she appeared not to notice the rather pointed remark.

"You might also design the costumes for the tableaux vivants," she continued.

"My cousin," exclaimed Esperance, "has a great gift for arrangement and composition. You will be able to judge for yourself soon; I will show you how beautifully he has painted my portrait."

"True. May we see it now?"

This made a welcome change for the four young people. They all went towards the "Five Divisions of the World." The Duchess stopped every now and then on the way to admire the sea and the luminous quality of the air. She was really amazed when she was shown the picture. It had been installed in the little court, under a kind of alcove that Maurice had made for it. He had found in his aunt's "reliquary" some pretty hangings which hid the alcove, and the picture lost nothing by the arrangement of drapery.

"You have indeed a beautiful portrait there," said the Princess sincerely. "Every year for his birthday I give my husband some work of art. If you do not find me too unworthy a subject it shall be signed this year, 'Maurice Renaud.'"

The young man bowed. "I shall be very happy indeed, Madame, and very highly honoured."

"Then, as our friend and collaborator," said the

Duchess, "you must, I think, come with us at once so as to be able to get to work with the Duke without delay."

"Give me time to pack by bag, Madame," returned the triumphant Maurice, "and I will join you at the carriage."

"I will come and help with your packing, cousin. You will excuse me?" she added turning to the Princess.

And Esperance, followed by Genevieve and Jean Perliez disappeared together.

As soon as she was sure she was out of ear-shot Esperance threw her arms about her cousin's neck. "You were simply wonderful."

"Yes," joined in Maurice, "the enemy has fallen into the ambush, as Baron van Berger would say. I will be back as soon as possible, but I must take time to rout our amiable Duke. He is the real enemy, and the most difficult opponent, but I am confident. With my most diabolical scheming, little cousin, I am going to have great fun. All the same, I foresee that I sha'n't be able to stay away long." And he kissed Genevieve's hand tenderly.

They soon finished the packing, and Jean closed the suitcase, and the young people arrived at the carriage just as it drew up.

"How very good it is of you to accept this sudden demand upon your services with such good grace!"

"I must remind you, Madame, that I suggested the

work myself and I am glad to do it. I am also quite happy to be carried off by you, as it is such an unlooked-for pleasure."

Two days later the professor had a letter from Maurice, which he read aloud to the family as they drank their coffee.

"My dear Uncle, - This letter is to be shared by the whole community. I have found a world gone mad in this magnificent château. We are twenty-two at table. I have been cordially welcomed by all the strangers, to whom this cursed Duke, delightful fellow, has graciously presented me. I set to work at once to unravel and discover the plans of Charles de Morlay. But more anon. This is the programme: an orchestra composed of excellent artists are to play while the guests arrive, inspect each other, and take their places. We begin with a little ballet, entitled, *The Moon in Search of Pierrot*, acted and danced by some very good amateurs. I am to paint the drop for this ballet, and the authors (it has taken three of them to elaborate the stupidest scenario you ever yawned through) have called for a Scandinavian design and I have promised it, and shall paint it at Penhouet. Then, the great attraction, the tableaux vivants. That is where I lay in wait for our astute Duke. I will spare you details of nine of the tableaux. There are to be twelve, but Esperance appears only in three, which are the best. In one she represents Andromeda fastened to the rock, and Perseus (the Duke) delivers her after overcoming the dragon. In the second, the 'Judgment of Paris,' she appears as Aphrodite, to whom Paris (the Duke) gives the apple. The third is 'Europa and the Bull,' Europa being personified by Esperance. The Duke does not wish to look ridiculous in a bull's hide, so takes liberties with the legend and transforms the bull into a centaur. I have said 'Amen' to everything. Finally to complete the fête, which will no doubt be well attended and very profitable, there will be little shops of all kinds. Esperance is to sell flowers from the Duchess's gardens. I have my own idea on this point, which I shall later confide to you. I can easily get her fiancé to agree. Your nephew, dear uncle, should live in the land of honey for the future. I have already had orders for three portraits, and of three pretty women, which assures me that the portraits will be successful. Ahem! I am taking all my notes to-day and will be with you the day after to-morrow. It is up to you, dear uncle, to distribute in unequal or suitable doses my respects and love and affection amongst all those anxious to receive such privileges. Your affectionately devoted, Maurice."

"It seems to me," said Genevieve, as she left the dining-room with Esperance, "that your cousin has arranged everything very well, and that you ought to be quite happy and content."

"Oh! I know very well that I shall be taken care of, but how can I struggle against the tumultuous ideas that assail me? The vision of the Duke has haunted me ever since Maurice left. I have never seen the château, but I am sure that I shall recognize it. I would like to fall ill with some complaint that would send me to sleep and sleep. Oh! if I could get a little ugly for a little while, just long enough to make the Duke lose interest in me, I should be so glad. Dear Genevieve, can't you give me a little dose of the elixir of your happiness. I need it sorely just now."

The girls had been walking as they talked down to the

little beach at Penhouet. The sea was at low tide, and the golden sand, dried by the sun, offered them a restful couch. They stretched themselves out upon it, and Esperance soon fell asleep. Jean Perliez appeared on the crest of the little hill that hides the bay from the sightseeker. Genevieve signed to him to come down quietly. He had a telegram, a dispatch from Belgium. He pinned it to Esperance's hat lying on the sand at her side, and dropping down close to Genevieve, began to talk in low tones. For both he and Genevieve were uneasy concerning their little friend.

A farm dog at the moment began to bark furiously. Esperance woke quickly, looking pale and worried, with her hands pressed on her frightened heart. She saw the telegram and opened it quickly.

"Albert will be here this evening by the second boat. What time is it?" She showed a little emotion, but only a little, though she felt deeply.

She looked towards the sun.

"It can't be four yet."

Jean took out his watch.

"Twenty to four," he said.

"The boat can't get here before five-thirty. Quick, quick, run, Jean, and ask to have some conveyance got ready. I must go and tell my father and get his permission to go with you and Genevieve to meet my fiancée. Ah! what good luck!" she said with a long breath, "What good luck!"

François Darbois was delighted for his daughter to go
and meet Albert, and departed so radiantly that he said
to his wife, "I believe she is getting to love this brave
Albert?"

Genevieve, who had heard, as had also Jean, said to the
young man in a low voice, "But, my God! suppose she
is beginning to love the Duke?"

CHAPTER XXII

The boat approached the little quay of Palais slowly with Count Styvens standing well forward, his tall figure silhouetted against the grey of the sea. He caught sight of Esperance immediately, as she stood up in the brake, waving her handkerchief. Great happiness was in his heart, and in his haste to be ashore, he went to assist them to lay down the gangplank, and was at the carriage in a second, kissing most tenderly the hand Esperance held out to him. A great basket was placed on the seat. The girls blushed with pleasure, for a sweet odour was wafted to them from it.

All the way home Esperance heard from Albert in detail all that had happened to him since she had last seen him. She talked incessantly, as if to drown her thoughts under a sea of nonsense. At the farm the young man could see the pleasure they all showed at his return. Of course he was somewhat astonished to learn that Maurice was absent with the Duchess, for he had not yet heard of the events that had happened during his absence.

They all gathered together in the dining-room. The Count took out of his pocket a little case, and asking Esperance to give him her hand, slipped on to her middle finger a magnificent engagement ring. Somehow her hand went cold as death as Albert held it, and

Sarah Bernhardt

her face contracted strangely.

"Do you regret your word already, Esperance?" he asked in a nervous, low voice.

"No, no, Albert," she said quickly, nervously twisting the ring on her finger, "but this is a very serious moment, and you know that I incline to taking things seriously here," and she put her hand across her heart. Then she smiled, pressed his hand, and showed the ring to Genevieve. They all examined and admired the beautiful jewel. When the philosopher turned to praise it Albert had disappeared.

The basket was opened revealing a bouquet of magnificent white orchids, marvellously fresh, held in a white scarf with embroidered ends.

When they assembled for dinner an hour later Esperance was not present, and Albert began to look uneasy. But they had not long to wait, and when she did appear she was dressed all in white, an embroidered scarf fastened about her waist, and several orchids arranged like a coronet in her hair. At that moment she seemed almost supernaturally beautiful.

"What a pity that Maurice is not here! You are so lovely this evening," said Genevieve.

"Oh," said Esperance smiling, "that is not the only reason you regret his absence?"

Next day they were surprised to get no word from the painter to tell them which boat he would take. It was warm and they had coffee served in the convolvulus bower. The breeze came through an opening from the sea.

"Look! isn't that a pretty boat?" cried out Genevieve.

A white yacht was sailing slowly towards Penhouet. The philosopher got his glasses.

"It is the Princess's flag," he exclaimed.

"Yes, yes," agreed Albert, "it is the Belgian flag. Listen, there is the salute."

Jean ran to the farm, calling back, "I will answer it. All right, M. Darbois?"

The flag sank and rose three times, then the yacht headed straight for the little bay. Genevieve climbed on a high rock and clapped her hands. "It is he, oh! it is he."

She turned radiantly back to the party in the grove. Her "It is he" made Albert smile. It was so charming, so sincere that they all shared the quality of her joy.

It was indeed Maurice returning on the Princess's yacht. The tide was so high that the boat could get quite close.

Everyone went down to the beach where the waves were washing the little rocks. Albert jumped on the largest rock which seemed to recede to sea with him. Genevieve would have followed him but he cried out, "Look out, it is very deep here."

She stayed where she was, but so woebegone did her face become that Albert leapt ashore again, and before she knew what he was doing, picked her up, and was back on the slippery rock with her.

"Oh! the bold lad!" said the Professor.

The little sloop had been launched and Maurice could easily land on the big rock. He kissed Genevieve, and told the Count of his delight in seeing him again. Then he looked around him. The water surrounded them on all sides. He looked at Genevieve questioningly, but by way of response Albert simply picked her up again and went ashore with her. Maurice was quick and agile, he was even strong in a nervous way, but Albert's strength and agility filled him with wonder.

Esperance congratulated the Count on his prowess and his kind thought in enabling Genevieve to see Maurice a little sooner.

"It is because I know what that joy is myself," he answered simply.

Esperance's eyes grew moist as she turned to Albert.

"You are so good, you always do the right thing. I am prouder every day to be loved by you."

During dinner Maurice gave them an account of all that had happened to him, with many new incidents.

"I am not telling you anything new," he added to Albert when they were alone. "You know as well as I do that the Duke is in love with Esperance. We all know it here."

Albert agreed with a rather sad smile that he did

know it.

"Now that my cousin is your fiancée, he is too much of a gentleman to seek her, but he certainly wants to be near her, to talk to her, in short to flirt with her."

"You believe that he would dare?"

"My dear cousin," said Maurice, half jestingly, half serious. "I believe him capable of anything, but he knows that you are here ... and perhaps is afraid to take liberties."

"To put an end to his manoeuvrings we must somehow make him look ridiculous, and expose his folly. The fête, I think, will give us our chance."

Albert said, "I will follow your advice, Maurice."

"Very good. I will give you particulars of my plans. By the way, I have brought all your invitations. I will go and deliver them." So they went to seek the others, and Maurice gave each one a card with a personal invitation for the twentieth of September. Genevieve blushed.

"I am invited as well," she said.

"Of course; and I believe the amiable Duchess intends to ask you to recite the poem she has written. It is very touching. I will find it for you to-morrow. Ah! yes, you have made a great impression on that delightful lady. She talked about you to me all the time. You would have supposed she was doing it to please me."

Genevieve became purple. It was the first time

Sarah Bernhardt

Maurice had expressed himself so frankly. When they left the table she led Esperance aside and kissed her until she almost stifled her.

"Oh! how happy I am, and how I love him!"

Maurice and Jean passed by talking so busily that they did not see the girls.

"You are sure?"

"Absolutely. Since I have been away for four whole days I am convinced more than ever that I adore that girl and shall not be happy without her."

"You have written to your father?"

"Not yet. I must first of all talk to Genevieve."

"You are not afraid of what she will say? Of her answer?"

Maurice smiled.

"I want first to tell her of my future plans, and to have a confidential chat with her about everything."

"You will be my best man, old fellow," he went on, clapping Jean on the shoulder. "You have chosen the role of actor, with the temperament of a spectator; strange lover!"

"Like any other man I follow my Destiny. You were born for happiness, Maurice, one has only to look at you to be convinced of it. You breathe forth life, you love, you conquer. Youth radiates from you. I have asked myself a hundred times why I have chosen this career, and I am persuaded that I must live, if at all, the life of others."

"Are you very upset - unhappy?" asked Maurice.

"No, oh no; I don't suffer much, but of course I am a little disturbed. I am like a reflection. Esperance's happiness elates, her sorrow depresses me. I love her purely as an idealist. I would like Count Albert to look like the Duke de Morlay-La-Branche, and still keep the noble soul that we know he possesses. If your cousin should die, I truly believe that I would die. My life would be without aim, without soul; bereft of light, the reflection would vanish."

They walked slowly down to the beach to join Albert and the girls. The night had broken soft and limpid, full of stars, full of dreams. They sat down on the sand, silently admiring the prospect. The waves broke regularly as if scanning the poem of silence. A fresh scent rose from the rocks which were clothed with sea moss. Far away a dog was barking. The young people were silent, united in a mood of wonder before the depths and lights of the night.

Sarah Bernhardt

PART IV. THE CHÂTEAU

CHAPTER XXIII

On the fifteenth of September the girls had to tear themselves away from their quiet retreat at Belle-Isle, and leave Penhouet and all else to travel with Mlle. Frahender, Jean and Maurice to the Château de Montjoie. When they arrived there, at ten in the evening, Esperance recognised the Duke in the distance as soon as the carriage stopped. He was looking out of one of the great windows above the terrace. He was, in fact, awaiting the coming of Esperance. But he pretended not to have seen the carriage and continued to gaze up at the stars. Esperance trembled and her lips were icy cold. Albert had also seen the Duke, and was not deceived by his attitude. He had resolved to be calm, but a sullen, unbidden anger arose within him.

When the housekeeper had installed the two girls in a tower of the Château, she left with them a little Breton peasant girl.

"She will be devoted to your service," she said. "Her name is Jeanette. Her room is above yours and, when you ring this bell, she will wait upon you at once."

Esperance threw herself on her bed, still dressed, for

her heart was overflowing.

"Ah! why, why is Albert so trusting? Why did he let me come here? Would it not have been better to have run the risk of offending the Duchess?"

And when Genevieve tried to reason with her, "I am suffering, little sister," she replied, "I am so unhappy; for the sight of the Duke at the window distressed me. I tremble at the idea of seeing him again, and yet I long for the time when I can give him my hand."

"But this is serious," said Genevieve. "I thought you had recovered from all that nonsense, or rather, I thought you would be less affected."

She helped Esperance to undress. The poor child let her do so without a word.

She slept badly, haunted by dreams and troubled with nightmare. At six o'clock in the morning she woke up feverishly, and rang for the maid.

The little Breton appeared five minutes later, her eyes still full of sleep, her cap crooked.

"Will you get me a little warm water?" asked Esperance. "It is cold from the tap."

"It is too early, I am afraid. Mademoiselle must please to wait a little."

"Well, be as quick as you can, please. I want to go for a walk in the park while there is no one about."

The little Breton laughed. "You won't run any danger

of finding anyone at this hour. What will the ladies take for breakfast?"

"Two cups of chocolate, please," said Genevieve, beginning to get up.

"Be so good as to make haste, Jeanette, get us our hot water and our chocolate, like a good girl and say nothing to anyone."

Jeanette looked in the mirror, adjusted her cap, put back a stray lock of hair, and opened the door. But she stopped, looking at the girls craftily.

"Which way were you going, Mademoiselle?"

"That all depends. Which way is the prettiest?"

"When you leave the Château you must turn to your right and walk to the first thicket. About ten minutes through the thicket and you will come out on the big terrace. That is where they always take the guests and say how beautiful it is!"

"Thank you," said Genevieve, "to the right, then the thicket and the terrace. We aren't likely to meet anyone?"

"Nobody is abroad but the cats at this hour, and...."

Outside the door she made a face like a mischievous child who had just played a trick. Running rapidly across the long corridors, she mounted to the second storey, opened an ante-chamber which led to another room and knocked lightly. The Duke opened the door.

"You here, Jeanette! What is it?"

"My godfather," she said very low, "the young ladies are getting up now, and I think they are going to walk in the grove to the right of the Château."

"They are going ... alone?"

"Certainly. No one else is awake, but they may be going to meet their lovers."

"Why did you come to tell me yourself, instead of sending my man?"

"Because he is a lazy fellow who would have taken an hour to dress and then would have told a lie and said I told him too late."

"Very well, run along now, and don't get caught."

So Jeanette sped quickly towards the kitchen to get the hot water in a great copper can, which she half emptied on the way to ease the weight.

As soon as they were dressed, Esperance and Genevieve made quick work of their chocolate, and started out. It was very still.

"It is the Sleeping Beauty's wood," said Esperance.

They went towards the grove they saw on their right. At the entrance to it Esperance closed her parasol and stopped suddenly, pressing Genevieve's hand.

"Some one has been here already."

Sarah Bernhardt

They both stopped motionless, listening. Not a sound. They slowly continued on their way, but the thicket did not lead to the terrace, and ended in a little enclosed dell. On a pedestal a figure of *Love in Chains* overlooked a stone bench.

"We have lost our way," said Genevieve. "Let us go back."

"No it is charming here. Let us go on to the bench. I am a little tired and my heart is beating so.... What was that?"

She put her companion's hand above her heart.

"Why what is the matter with you. Why are you so nervous?"

"Ah!" replied Esperance, with great apprehension of she knew not what, "I feel as if I could not struggle.... The presence in this house of the Duke de Morlay overcomes me. I don't know whether that is love; but at least it tells me that I do not love Albert. Come dear, let us rest a moment."

Just then a man stepped out from the thicket and barred their way.

The Duke stood before them.

Esperance uttered one cry and fell in a faint.

The Duke started forward to catch her, but Genevieve repulsed him.

"It is a cowardly trick you have played on us, sir. I

understand now that we did not lose our way but were duped by your orders."

As she spoke, she was trying to support Esperance, but almost falling herself under the weight of the inert body. She cried at her own impotence, but she was obliged to accept the Duke's help to get Esperance as far as the marble bench.

"Try," she said holding out Esperance's tiny handkerchief, "to get me a little water."

"Instantly, Mademoiselle ... there is a fountain near at hand."

When he came back Genevieve moistened the poor child's temples. The Duke was very pale.

"Mademoiselle, believe me that I am greatly upset at what has happened. I had no idea...!"

"I shall be very glad to excuse you. Esperance looks a little better, had you not better go away?"

"But I cannot leave you all alone like this."

He took Esperance's hand, and it seemed to him that warmth came back into it.

Esperance opened her eyes. Still half unconscious, she looked at him curiously, then she cried sharply out, "Have mercy, go away, go away!"

And she gave way to hysterical sobs.

The Duke said humbly, "I will leave you."

Sarah Bernhardt

And then kneeling before her, "Forgive me, I am going; I am leaving you ... but I entreat you to forgive me."

He was sincere in what he said. Both girls felt it.

Esperance had risen gently.

"I am betrothed to Count Styvens," she said. "You know that. I know that my emotion just now was foolish, but I am sick at heart and I am not always able to control myself. You are good, I see that. Please help me to cure myself. I will be grateful to you all my life."

"I give you my word...." his voice trembled. "I will make myself...." and he went away.

As soon as they were left alone the two girls took counsel as to what course they should pursue. Esperance, in despair, threw herself on Genevieve's judgment, and Genevieve asked permission to consult Maurice.

"Could we not keep it as a secret?"

"I am afraid, darling, that that would not be right. We are sure of Maurice's discretion, and we need advice as well as help."

Esperance looked at her companion.

"How could the Duke have known? Oh! I suppose the little Breton girl who waits on us was the culprit. We must get rid of her. We have only three days to spend here, and then, too, I am sure that the Duke will keep his word. I was struck by his pallor, and his eyes when he looked at you were full of tears, but I believe he was sincere; there is less to fear from staying than fleeing perhaps, since we know that. Let us go back."

She helped her dear little friend to get up and they returned to the house as they had come. Mademoiselle Frahender was just coming out to look for them.

"Here we are, little lady, don't scold," said Esperance playfully.

The little old lady shook her head chidingly.

"You do not look well, my child. You are up too early. Six o'clock, that pert little Breton told me, when I found her fumbling in our trunks. When I told her that I was going to complain of her she said, 'Oh! don't do that, Madame, my godfather, the Duke de Morlay, would never forgive me!'"

The girls looked at each other.

"I promise to say nothing, but you must watch her carefully."

They were just going in when Maurice joined them, out of breath.

"Hello! cousin. Where do you spring from?"

"I have been looking for you for half an hour to give you the programme, edited by Jean and enlivened by your humble servant. Here you are, and here you are, naughty lady, who gives no word of warning to her lover of early morning escapades."

"Oh! Maurice, it was I who led Genevieve astray, and I am doubly repentant. She will tell you why."

Maurice grew serious.

"What means that haggard face, cousin, and the collar of your dress is all wet? Come, come, Genevieve herself seems ill at ease. I would like to know what you two have been up to."

"Well! take her into that grove, you will find a bench there, and she will tell you all about it. I am going to rest," replied Esperance.

Genevieve and Maurice sat down in the grove. After she had told him what had happened, she added, "What seems to me to make it really serious is that I believe the Duke to be in earnest."

"Love and flirtation often look alike," said the young man shrugging his shoulders.

"I don't think so," said the girl with conviction, and continued sadly, "Esperance is fighting against this infatuation with all her strength, but I am very uneasy. And if the Duke should love her enough to offer to marry her!"

"You think that likely?"

"What can resist love? Tell me that."

And her beautiful eyes, swimming with tears, looked anxiously, trustingly into the young man's face.

"I tell you what I truly believe. And that is, that

Esperance loves the Duke."

The young painter meditated for a long time.

"Come on, we must go back," he said finally. "We must get ready for the rehearsal." He left the girl with exhortations to reason with his cousin.

"What the deuce is our will for if we can't exercise it?"

"Maurice, I am brave and determined, you know that. My sister and I have struggled unaided, she since she was thirteen! I since I was eight. I thought that she was enough to fill all my life, and now...."

"And now," he asked tenderly, taking her hand.

"All my life is yours! I should not tell you this, but you can judge by my doing so the impotence of will against...."

She drew away her hand hastily, ran to the staircase and disappeared. He heard the door open and his cousin's voice saying, "How pale you are, Genevieve!"

"What are you dreaming about, Cousin Maurice?" said Albert, putting his hand gently on his shoulder.

That hand felt to Maurice as heavy as remorse.

"Let us go and see what is going on," said the young painter. "There is Jean coming to look for us now."

CHAPTER XXIV

In the great hall of the Château a charming theatre had been built. Everything was ready for the rehearsal. An enormous revolving platform held three wooden squares which would serve as frames for the tableaux vivants. The mechanism had been arranged by an eminent Parisian engineer. A curtain decorated by Maurice served as background. There were eleven little dressing rooms, seven for the women, four for the men.

Maurice saw the Duke seated straddlewise on a chair, and smoking a cigarette. The three men went up to him before he was aware of their presence. At sound of Albert's voice he sprang to his feet, almost as if expecting an attack. His nostrils were dilated, his face set. In an instant he resumed his usual manner, and shook hands with the young men.

"You were asleep?" suggested the Count.

"No, I was dreaming, and I think you must have figured in my dream."

"Let us hear of the dream."

"Oh! no, dreams ought not to be told!"

And he pretended to busy himself with some orders.

The guests who were to take part in the tableaux vivants began slowly to stream in. Maurice took Jean aside and told him what had happened that morning.

"You must keep watch too. I am not going to leave the Duke."

When Esperance and Genevieve came in, Maurice caught the Duke's expression in a mirror. He saw him move away and join a distant group where he lingered chatting. Jean thought Esperance looked uneasy. Albert came up to her and kissed her hand. She smiled sadly. She was looking for some one. The Duke had disappeared before she had seen him.

After a long discussion it was decided to have a dress rehearsal. Esperance was not in the first picture so she would have had ample time to have dressed at leisure, but nevertheless she put her things on quite feverishly. Her costume consisted only, it is true, of a light peplum over a flesh-coloured foundation. Genevieve helped her to dress. In each dressing-room was one of Maurice's designs illustrating just how the dress, hair, etc., were to be arranged. For Andromeda, Esperance was to have bare feet, and wear on her hair a garland of flowers.

The three first tableaux revolved before the Duke and his staff, composed of Albert, Jean, Maurice and some of the distinguished guests; and the order was given to summon the artists for the second set, which was composed of the next three pictures.

The first tableaux of the second group represented

Circe with the companions of Ulysses changed into swine. The marvellous Lady Rupper was to represent Circe. She entered dramatically, half nude, her tunic open to her waist, caught at intervals by diamond clasps, her peplum held in place by a garland of bay leaves. She was very beautiful. Her husband, a wealthy American, laughed at sight of her, a coarse laugh, the laugh of all Germans, even when Americanized.

The second picture represented Judith and Holofernes. The beautiful brunette, the Marquise de Chaussey, in a daring costume designed by Maurice, held in her hand a magnificent scimitar, the property of Morlay-La-Branche. She was to pose, raising the curtain, as in the picture of Regnault.

The third picture was the deliverance of Andromeda. When Esperance appeared, so slender, so fragile, her long hair waving in floods of pale gold almost to the floor, a murmur of almost sacred admiration rang through the hall. Lady Rupper approached her, and taking the child's hair in her hands, cried out, "Oh! my dear, it is more beautiful than the American gold."

The Duke came up to Esperance.

"I should have preferred enchaining you to delivering you, Mademoiselle."

"I can speak now in the person of Andromeda and thank you for that deliverance ... which you promised," she answered with a little smile.

She had spoken so low that only the Duke could hear the ending which he alone understood. He had promised to deliver her from his love, but at that instant he revolted against the thought and the admonition.

"Why not?" he muttered to himself. "She must be happier with me than with that insufferable bore! I will keep my word until she herself absolves me from it."

They had to arrange her pose against the rock. Maurice and Albert helped her, while the Duke watched from a distance, and criticized the effect. All at once he cried out, "That is perfect. Don't move. Now the mechanician must mark the place to set the fetters for the hands and feet."

Maurice stepped back by the Duke to judge of the effect.

"It is excellent," he said, looking only, thinking only as an artist. "That child has a beauty of proportion, a dazzling grace, and the most lovely face imaginable."

As the Duke did not speak, Maurice looked at him. He was standing upright, leaning against a table, pale as death.

"Are you ill?" asked Maurice.

"No ... no...."

He passed his hand across his forehead and said in an unnatural voice, "Will you see to it please, that they do not leave her suspended that way too long? Tell Albert to raise her head, it seems to me that she is going to faint."

He started forward.

"I will go," said Maurice, stopping him.

When the machinist finished screwing the rings in the rock Maurice asked whether it would not be better to repeat this tableaux at once. The Duke approved. The terrifying dragon was properly arranged on the ground - the wonderful dragon which was the design of a renowned sculptor and perfectly executed by Gerard in papier maché. Perseus (the Duke) with one foot on the head of the vanquished monster, bent towards Andromeda. The breath of her half-opened mouth was hot on his lips, and he could hear the wild beating of her little heart. He felt an infinite tenderness steal over him, and when a tear trembled on the young girl's eyelashes he forgot everything, wiped the tear away tenderly with the end of his finger and kissed it lovingly. Happily the turning stage was almost out of sight and nobody except Genevieve had caught sight of the incident.

Esperance breathed, "God, my God!"

The Duke raised the poor child, and said to her very low, "I love you, Esperance."

She murmured, "You must not ... you must not."

While he was loosing her chains he continued, "I love you and I will do anything to win your love."

She strengthened herself desperately.

"You do not need to do anything for it, alas!"

And she fled.

When the Count came to find her, there was only the Duke talking to the stage hands.

"Where is Esperance?"

"I have no idea," replied Charles de Morlay dryly.

Albert turned on his heel, delighted to see the Duke out of humour.

Genevieve caught up with Andromeda who was running away out of breath, seeing nothing, hearing nothing. Genevieve saw her enter the grove leading to the clearing and there she joined her.

"Esperance, my darling, my little sister, stop, I beg you."

Her voice calmed the girl. She caught hold of one of the branches and clung to it, gasping.

"Genevieve, Genevieve, why am I here?"

Her eyes shone with a wild light. She seemed to be absolutely exalted.

"He loves me, he loves me...."

"And I love him." And she threw herself in her friend's arms. "I am as happy as you now, for I love.... The thick cloud that hung over everything is gone. Everything is bright and beautiful. This dark grove is sparkling with sunlight and...?"

Genevieve stopped her.

Sarah Bernhardt

"Little sister, you are raving. Your pulse is racing with fever. We must go back. Think of poor Albert."

Esperance drew herself up proudly, replying, "I will never betray him, I will tell the truth, and I will become the wife of the Duke."

"You are talking wildly, dearest, the Duke will not marry you."

"He will marry me, I swear it!"

"Albert will enter the Chartist Monastery and the Countess Styvens will die of sorrow."

"The Countess Styvens," said Esperance slowly.

As the sweet face of the mother came before her mind's eye she began to tremble all over.

Maurice had followed the girls into the grove, and he found them now in each other's arms.

"Genevieve," said Esperance, "not a word of what I have said!"

"Have you both gone crazy? They are looking everywhere for Esperance for the 'Judgment of Paris,' and here you are congratulating and kissing each other!"

"Cousin, I needed the air, don't scold. Genevieve looked for me and found me before anybody else, and I kissed her because I love her most."

She spoke fast and laughed nervously.

"Who freed you from your chains?"

"Perseus, it was his duty!"

"And now he is going to give you an apple."

"Then," she said very prettily, "I must try to deserve it. Come help me to make myself beautiful."

She led Genevieve away by the hand.

Maurice remained rooted to the spot. Somehow he guessed what sudden change had operated upon his cousin's spirit. Something must have taken place in the corridor between these two! He murmured sadly, "Poor Albert, poor little cousin!"

The young Count appeared before him in his most radiant humour.

"I have just met Esperance," he said. "She was joyous, brilliant, I have never before seen her so happy!"

Maurice gnawed his moustache, and moved rather angrily.

"We should never have come here," he said, "success has turned her head."

"She was born for success," said the Count. "I often ask myself whether I have a right to accept the sacrifice she is making for me."

"My dear friend, when things are well you should leave them alone."

"When you love as I love, you desire above everything the happiness of the one you love."

"Unless the one you love should prefer someone else to you?"

"You are wrong, Maurice. I would sacrifice myself for Esperance's happiness if I knew she wanted to marry another man."

Maurice shrugged his shoulders.

"We are not of the same race. Your blood runs colder in your veins than mine, for mine boils. But, perhaps you have a better understanding of these things?"

And he left the Count to go and help the Duke prepare the "Judgment of Paris."

Three young girls had been chosen for this tableau. Mlle. de Berneuve, a beautiful brunette (Hera); Mlle. Lebrun, with flaming hair (Athene); and Esperance, delicately blonde, was to represent Aphrodite, to whom the shepherd Paris would award the prize for beauty.

To personify Aphrodite the girl wore a long pink tunic, with a peplum of the same colour heavily embroidered. Her hair was piled high on her head, leaving the lovely nape of her neck half covered by her draperies, her exquisitely delicate arms emerging from a sleeveless tunic. To represent the shepherd Paris, the Duke was wearing a short tunic embroidered with agate beads to hold the stuff down, and a sheep skin. A red cap was on his head. He was magnificent to look upon.

The stage began to revolve. Paris held out his apple to

Aphrodite, who went crimson at his glance. The girl's blushes did not escape the audience, where the comments varied according to the person who made them.

Maurice, Genevieve, and Jean understood what Esperance read in Paris's eyes. A sad smile gave a melancholy grace to the lovely Aphrodite. Both the actors had forgotten that they were not alone. Hypnotized under the gaze of Paris, the young girl made a gesture towards him. A sharp, "Don't move" from the prompter brought her back to herself. She turned her head, saw the audience, with the eyes and glasses of everyone focussed upon her. It seemed to her that they must all know her secret. She tottered; and supported herself upon Athene. She must have fallen from the frame and been badly hurt, if the Duke had not caught her just in time. A cry escaped from the audience. The Marquis de Montagnac gave a sign to the stage hands to stop revolving the stage.

Albert climbed up on the stage at once. He thrust Paris quickly aside, picked up the girl and carried her out on to the terrace. Maurice and Jean followed him. She was not unconscious, but she could not speak and she recognized no one. Genevieve knelt beside her. At first delicacy - discretion - held the spectators back, but curiosity soon drove them forward. But the Duke did not appear. He had seemingly vanished.

The Doctor of the Château was called from playing croquet. He began by ordering the crowd away. Esperance was stretched out on an easy chair on the terrace. The Doctor looked at her for a moment, amazed at her beauty, then sat beside her, feeling her pulse. Genevieve described what had happened. He

Sarah Bernhardt

listened attentively.

"There is nothing serious," he said, "only a little exhaustion and collapse. I will go and mix a soothing drink for her."

Esperance, still unconscious, was carried by her fiancé to her room, where Genevieve and Mlle. Frahender put her to bed. Albert went back to wait for the Doctor. Maurice went in search of Charles de Morlay. He met a forester, who told him that the Duke had gone for a ride in the forest, and had sent word to the Duchess that he might not be back to lunch.

Maurice returned disturbed and thoughtful. Genevieve was waiting for him with the news that the Doctor had himself administered a sleeping draught to Esperance which he said should make her sleep at least five hours.

"So much the better! That will give us a little time to consider and to decide what is to be done. The truth is that we ought to clear out this very day! Love is a miscreant!"

"Not always, fortunately," murmured Genevieve.

"You, Genevieve, have a balanced mind, calm, just. If only my cousin had your equilibrium!"

"Oh! Maurice, Maurice...."

A tear ran down Genevieve's eyelashes. She closed her eyes. He took the lovely head in his hands and his lips rested on her pure forehead. They remained so for one marvellous, never-to-be-forgotten second.

When he left her Maurice met Albert Styvens. They walked side by side towards the woods.

"I am very much alarmed," said the Count, "not about Esperance's health, but about her state of mind. I am a poor psychologist, but my love for your cousin has sharpened my wits. It seems to me that the Duke is trying to make Esperance love him."

"Possibly; I had not noticed."

"Yes, Maurice, you have noticed and you have no right to deny it. I want to ask your advice. The Duke and I both love your cousin. One of us must lose. Just now I repulsed the Duke so rudely that he could have demanded satisfaction, but I foresee that he will let it pass. That attitude, so unusual to his temperament, proves that he wants to avoid scandal. Why? What is his object?"

"I don't know," said Maurice. "He has gone riding in the forest, probably to calm his nerves with solitude. He loves your fiancée, but his honour forces him to respect her."

"Perhaps," said Albert.

"I think," said Maurice, "that we should all leave this evening or to-morrow morning at the latest. Esperance is not ill, only worn out. She is easily exhausted."

"And if she loves the Duke?" pursued the Count.

"Then it is my place to ask you what you are going to do about it?"

Albert was silent a minute, then raising his pale face, answered slowly: "If she loves the Duke, I shall have to ask him what are his intentions; and if, as I believe, he wishes to marry her, I shall die a Chartist!"

The third gong vibrated, announcing lunch.

After lunch, Albert, Maurice, Jean, and Genevieve settled themselves under a great oak, which was said to have been planted by a delightful little Duchess of Castel-Montjoie, who had been celebrated at Court during the Regency. A marble table and a heavy circular bench made this wild corner quite cosy, and sheltered from the sun and from the curious. The tree was just opposite the tower where Esperance was sleeping so deeply, and Mlle. Frahender was to give a signal from the window when she awoke. Neither of them felt much inclined for conversation, for their eyes were fixed on the window opposite. About half-past four Mlle. Frahender appeared, and Genevieve hastened to the room.

Esperance was sitting up in bed, remembering nothing.

"Albert, Maurice, and Jean are over there. Do you wish to see them?"

Esperance rose up quickly, wrapping a robe of blue Japanese crêpe embroidered in pink wisterias about her, and gracefully fastened up her hair.

"Let them come, if you please, now."

The young men entered and stopped in amazement at the change that had already taken place in her. Instead of finding her a wreck they discovered her pink, gay and laughing.

"What happened to me?" she asked. "My little Mademoiselle does not know, she was not well herself. There is my Aphrodite costume. What happened to me?"

"It was very simple," explained Maurice. "You stayed too long with your head hanging down during the rehearsal, and as you were tired it made you ill. Albert brought you here and you have been asleep for five hours. Now you are your charming self again. We will leave you so that you can dress, and then if you feel like it we will take you for a drive."

"I will be very quick; in ten minutes I will be with you."

The young people did not know what to think. It would now be very difficult to suggest that Esperance should withdraw from the fête, as apparently every trace of her indisposition had disappeared.

Then Albert spoke:

"I am going to ask Esperance to give up appearing at this performance as a favour to me," he said. "I shall contribute largely to the charitable fund, and we can go back to Penhouet."

He had hardly finished speaking when Esperance came into the little salon.

"Here I am you see and the ten minutes is not yet up!"

A discreet tap at the door made them all turn round.

Sarah Bernhardt

The Dowager Duchess appeared.

"Ah! my dear child, what a joy to see you so restored."

"I must apologize, Madame, for the trouble I gave you. It is all over, all over," she said, shaking her pretty head; "and I am as well as possible."

"I am more than delighted," said the Duchess, sitting down. "You have no idea, my dear Albert, of the perfect disaster Esperance's absence would have caused. She is the star of our bill, as they say, and on whom we all rely. You know that my son wants to be elected Deputy, and this fête will secure him the votes of the whole community. More than fifteen hundred people have taken tickets. The local livery stable men count on making a fortune. All the villagers are getting their rooms ready to let. If that adorable child had failed us nothing could have made it up to them, and my son would have been ruined."

She rose up.

"But," she added, with the sweet smile that won all hearts, "you see me so happy, so reassured, that you must all be joyful with me."

The young people led her to the foot of the stair. The carriage was waiting to take them for their drive.

The visit from the amiable Duchess rather disconcerted Albert, and Jean, and Maurice and Genevicve. Everything seemed like the warring of an implacable destiny. All four felt absolutely impotent.

The drive was stimulating. Esperance drew life at

every breath. They could watch the colour coming back into her cheeks.

As the carriage came out into a clearing, the Duke de Morlay rode wildly by. His horse was covered with sweat and trembling so that he had some difficulty in mastering it. The Duke inquired for Esperance's health and decided that it must be excellent from her looks.

"But my dear Albert," he said, laughing, "you almost knocked me over this morning, however, I do not blame you, I would have done as much myself in your place. However, I must be off, my horse is fagged. I shall see you later."

And he was gone.

"How pale the Duke looked," exclaimed Esperance.

"He is fatigued, he has been riding since this morning."

"Did he not lunch with you, cousin?"

"No."

"Why did he go away in such haste?"

"You are too curious."

Then, looking hard at her, "Perhaps he thought, like the good Duchess, that your weakness was serious, and that all his little arrangements were going to fall through."

"I understand that the Duchess cared, since the election of her son is at stake, but the Duke, how would it affect him?"

Albert sitting opposite her in the carriage, looked her full in the face.

"Perhaps he will never find another opportunity to pay his court to you."

"Whew, that is straightforward bluntness for you!" thought Maurice.

Esperance grew red. The recollection of what had happened began to come back little by little. She closed her eyes to be able to think more clearly. Albert left her in her silence a minute, then he said, "We had planned to carry you away to-day, but you heard what the Duchess said just now. I feel bound by the confidence of that old friend to remain. My fate is in your pretty hands. Be circumspect with the Duke. Frank, and loyal with your fiancé."

And he took her hands, in a long kiss.

The coachman was told to turn around, for it was getting late. The horses set off at a trot.

Nothing more was said between them, about the Duke.

After dinner, the Duke arose, and announced, "The fête will be the day after to-morrow. We have only rehearsed once, and then, not in full. I feel somewhat responsible for the exhaustion of our little star. Her head, hanging down, was so beautiful, that I thought only of the pose, without realizing how painful it must have become to the artist. I ask Mile. Darbois' pardon. Also, I should like another stage director. I propose M.

Maurice Renaud, our ingenious collaborator, to whom we owe our magnificent costumes, and originality of our decorations."

Everyone applauded, and Maurice was proclaimed director of the fête.

"I thank you, and accept", he said simply.

He thought, "That is his way of getting rid of me."

"I hope, my dear Director," continued the Duke, "that you will make us rehearse hard to-morrow. If anything goes wrong we shall still have the morning of the following day, for the fête does not begin until half-past two."

Maurice rose, and in a comical tone announced, "Ladies, gentlemen, and artists, I beg you to be prompt for a rehearsal of the tableaux vivants to-morrow at ten o'clock. Any artist who is late, will pay a fine of a hundred francs, to the poor of the Duchess." And as they laughingly protested, "There is a quarter of an hour's grace accorded as in the theatres, but not one instant more. My stage-manager is empowered to collect the fines."

They followed the action of the Duchess and rose from their seats. The Duke went over to Maurice.

"I would like to talk over some of the details with you. They must interest us, but they mean nothing to the others. A cigarette?"

They strolled to the end of the terrace. A pretty Chinese umbrella sheltered a delightful nook. The

Duke and Maurice dropped into easy chairs.

"Will you give me your word that what I am going to say to you will be for you alone; that you will not repeat it?"

The young man refused, "How can I give my word without even knowing the subject of your confidences?"

"It concerns your cousin."

"Then it concerns Count Styvens."

"Indirectly, yes."

Maurice got up.

"I would rather not listen to you, for my duty as a man of honour would compel me to speak, should it be necessary."

The Duke sat still and reflected for a minute.

"Very well, you shall judge when you have heard me, what you think you had better do. I leave you free. I love your cousin Esperance: she is the fiancée of Count Albert, but she is not in love with him."

Maurice had thrown away his cigarette and leaning forward, his hands clasped, his eyes on the ground, listened intently.

"I have paid her in a way attentions for a year; I admit it was wrong for I had no definite intentions. A visit to Penhouet, however, completely changed my opinion of this little maiden. The atmosphere of beauty, of calm in which she lived, the liking and respect I felt for M. and Madame Darbois, and the free play of intelligence and taste I there discovered, made a deep impression on me and I could not forget. The ordinary life of society, so artificial, so devoid of real interest, this life that eats up hours and weeks and months in futilities, in nothings that come to nothing, all this became suddenly quite burdensome to me. I continuously thought of the adorable child I had seen at Penhouet, brighter than all else in that radiant place. I was travelling, and did not learn of the accident to your cousin and Count Styvens until I returned to Paris. Then I wrote for news."

"I came back here to my old aunt's, my nearest relative. I wanted to ask her to invite the whole of the Darbois family to spend a month here at Montjoie. A letter from Count Albert, announcing his engagement to Esperance, was a terrible blow to me. I conceived the detestable idea of revenging myself on Albert, but every scheme went against me. I have been beaten without ever having fought." Then he paused.

"Since you have done me the honour to make me your confidant, permit me to say that the little ambush you laid for Esperance this morning...."

The Duke interrupted, "That ambush was a vulgar trick, theatrical and cheap. I spare you the trouble of having to tell me so. I was about to disclose myself to the young ladies when I heard your cousin speak my name. Then I kept still, hoping to learn something. What man could have resisted? I heard these words spoken to Mlle. Hardouin, 'Yes, the presence of the Duke of Morlay disturbs me; I do not know if that is love, but I do know that I do not love Albert.' They

Sarah Bernhardt

went on towards the clearing; I was compelled to leave my hiding place. You know the rest. The cry the child gave, and her look of reproach unmanned me. I understood at that moment that I loved in deadly earnest; that my intention of avenging myself on Albert was nothing but a vain manifestation of pride, that the ambush was a cowardly concession to my reputation as a - well, deceiver of women. You know what I mean."

He shrugged his shoulders scornfully.

"The man I was trying to be has left the man I am, and now, Renaud, here is what I want you to know. Esperance Darbois loves me, I was convinced of that at the rehearsal. I love her ardently in return. She will not be happy with Albert, and I want to marry her. I will employ no 'illicit means,' as the lawyers say. On other scores I shall feel no remorse to have broken your cousin's engagement. My fortune is twice Albert's; he is a Count, I a Duke, and what is more, a Frenchman."

Maurice stood up nervously.

"You are a very gallant man, Duke, and my sympathy was yours from your first visit to Penhouet, but I am greatly distressed that you should have made me your confidant, for I must in honour bound support Albert."

"I do not see why! It seems to me that the happiness of your cousin might count before any friendship for Albert Styvens."

"But where is her real happiness, I might say her lasting happiness?"

The moon had risen radiantly pure. From their

elevation on the terrace, they could overlook all the garden and park sloping gently to the lake. In a boat two young girls were rowing. They were alone.

"You leave me free to act?"

"Absolutely."

"Till to-morrow," said Maurice pressing his hands.

The Duke remained alone on the terrace. He saw the young man go rapidly towards the lake. He heard him hail the girls and saw him climb into the boat with them, then disappear after he had waved with Genevieve's handkerchief a signal of adieu.

CHAPTER XXV

When Maurice and Esperance and Genevieve landed, the Duke was still pacing up and down on the terrace. Maurice had jumped lightly on to the shore, and had helped the young girls out, and having taken them to the Château, rejoined the Duke who was waiting for him.

"You are right. Esperance loves you. My uncle comes to-morrow evening. He is a man of such uprightness that he will find, no doubt, the best solution of this most complicated situation. Only I beg you to spare Albert."

The Duke replied instantly, "I will make every effort to be generous; but this morning he thrust me away from your cousin in a deliberate attempt to insult me. I pretended to blame it on his anxiety, but I may not be able to control myself again, if he drives me so far."

"Alas! I am afraid that you are both of you at the mercy of the first thing that happens. For the love of God, keep cool. And don't forget to come to-morrow at ten for the rehearsal."

And they parted.

Maurice did not sleep a wink. Esperance and

Genevieve went to bed very late, after talking for a long time of the future.

"Poor Albert," murmured the little star still as she closed her eyes in the very moment of gliding into the unreal life of dreams.

Mlle. Frahender had some difficulty next morning in waking the two young girls. Another maid waited on them, for the Duke had sent his goddaughter back to her family.

"Let us all three take our chocolate together on this little table. The sun is so gentle this morning, to-day ought to have a beautiful life ahead of it. My parents come at six and we must go to meet them."

She chattered on all through the breakfast, and kissed Genevieve in overflowing happiness.

"I love to see you so, Esperance," said the old Mademoiselle. "You have scarcely seemed yourself lately, even at Penhouet. Now you are truly yourself, you are radiant with your seventeen years. It is a pleasure to look at you and to listen to you."

When the two girls came into the hall the Director, Maurice Renaud, the Marquis Assistant, and the stage-manager, Louis de Marset, were the only others who had arrived. The manufacturer of the paper models was arranging the rock, the dragon, and the headless horse in the middle of the room. He held a brush red with dragon's blood, gave it a touch, and recoiled to admire the effect; then taking the sea weed he had gathered from real rocks, began placing it in little bunches on his pasteboard rock.

"In regard to the half white horse, a magnificent cardboard mount," said Maurice, flatteringly, "we shall not use it. Another tableau has been substituted for that one."

The Assistant came up to Maurice. "Can you tell me, sir, why they will not give the 'Europa and the Bull'?"

"Because Mlle. Darbois has been far from well, and the Duchess has requested that she shall not appear in more than two tableaux. She is to play a very difficult duet, as well, you know, and afterwards she will have to talk to all the people who crowd around her to buy flowers."

Jean was charged with excluding all those who were not in the tableaux. Albert was included in those not admitted, and he certainly would have held it against the Duke, had he still been Director; but Jean explained to him that Maurice had taken this means of making the rehearsal go more quickly. Genevieve, who was also excluded, kept the Count company, and tried to distract him; but he was in a very despondent humour. When he saw the Duke arrive so late, he said, somewhat crossly, "He is delaying the rehearsal."

"Oh! no," said Genevieve, "he does not come on until the second group, and there is no need for him to appear in costume."

When Andromeda was extended upon her rock the Duke took his position. They were alone in their wooden frame.

"Won't you trust yourself to me?" he breathed.

"I love you with all my soul."

"My life is yours," she replied.

The scene had turned very quickly, the curtain, had fallen. Maurice came up and helped the Duke to unfasten the girl. She was radiant. He was transformed. Maurice guessed that they had spoken together, but he asked nothing.

The second tableau was given immediately. Paris was not in costume. He held the apple to the glorious Aphrodite, the picture turned, the rehearsal was over for Esperance. The Duke still had to take part in two other scenes.

When Esperance was dressed she followed Maurice's advice to go join Genevieve and Albert.

"What a relief," he exclaimed at sight of her, "I began to think it would never be over."

"Yet we did not lose any time."

"Oh, no! but now it will go more slowly. The Countess de Morgueil will have to make several repetitions of her tableau of the enchantress Melusina."

It was the little de Marset who had spoken. Esperance started. For a long time it had been rumoured that the very pretty Countess de Morgueil, widowed two years ago, was violently infatuated with the Duke de Morlay, who was said not to be indifferent to her affection.

Afraid apparently that his meaning had not been plain, Marset insisted, "she is always circling about

Sarah Bernhardt

the Duke."

"But does he care for her?" asked a young woman with a hard face, who was just going to give herself a dose of morphine, and who was never seen without a cigarette between her lips.

"Who knows?" queried Marset, with a knowing air.

Esperance had grown very pale. Albert was controlling himself with difficulty. He observed Genevieve's constraint, and the trouble of his fiancée.

"Shall we walk a little?"

They walked towards the woods and Maurice, in some excitement, soon joined them. He was greatly troubled, and longed to be able to tell Albert how things were going. He was very fond of this fine fellow, and at the same time felt great sympathy for the Duke. He understood perfectly well why Esperance should prefer him to the Count, but at the same time he blamed her a little for causing so many complications. When he saw her so fresh and charming beside Albert, he grew more disturbed. Genevieve quietly drew him aside.

"You are getting excited, Maurice, and I see clearly that you are blaming Esperance, but let me tell you, dear love, that you are unjust. At this moment Esperance is walking in a dream. Nothing real exists for her. For three months she has suffered very much, struggled very much, and felt so much. Events have come very quickly. She finds herself all of a sudden at the fount of the realization of all her fondest hopes; to be loved by the one she loves!... Be patient, Maurice, she is so young and so sensitive...."

"Your heart, dearest Genevieve, is an admirable accountant. It adds the reasons, multiplies the excuses, subtracts the errors, and divides the responsibility. You are adorable and I love you with all my heart. Come with me, it is time for the concert. You go on immediately after Delaunay. The Duchess is unable to contain herself at the idea of hearing you recite her poem."

The Duke passed by, accompanied by the pretty Countess de Morgueil, at whose conversation he was smiling politely and replying vaguely. He seemed not to have seen the others. Like Esperance, he was living in a world of dreams, happy in a realm where there was neither impatience nor jealousy. He knew that he was loved.

After lunch Esperance said that she was going to rest, so as to be fresh for next day. Her father and mother were to come on the Princess's little yacht. She and Mlle. Frahender were to go alone to meet them. That gave her several hours of solitude to think of him, only of him.

Maurice repeated his last orders for the engrossing fête, against which he railed ceaselessly, in spite of Genevieve's constant efforts to calm him.

"Oh! of course, it is perfectly evident that I am unreasonable, I know it; but if I break my leg slipping on an orange peel, you would not prevent me from swearing at the person who had peeled the fruit there, would you?"

Genevieve laughed in spite of herself. "Be a good boy, tell your uncle everything as soon as he comes; but say nothing against Esperance, for that would not be right."

Her lovely face was very sad. Maurice looked at her with a world of tenderness, "My darling, forgive me; the truth is that I am so worried. Albert's face is hard and set. He knows nothing, cannot know anything, but he is gifted with the intuition that simple souls often possess. I am very uneasy, I can tell you. Say nothing to Esperance. Come now, let us stroll into this thicket and talk just by ourselves for awhile."

They entered the thicket, holding each other close, in silence. When they came to the clearing they stopped short. The Duke was there, stretched out upon the bench, smoking, dreaming.

He got up, surprised, and apologized.

"I had just come back here to live over an unforgettable moment."

"This corner must be the rendezvous for the slaves of the little god," said Maurice, bowing to the statuette of *Love Enchained*. "We will leave you."

"No," said the Duke quickly, "Please stay. Your happiness shows me the vision of which I dreamed. Art is the inspiration of the beautiful, and I believe, that artists have a more delicate sense of love than other people.

"I believe, in truth," said Maurice, "that artists, move in a much larger world than that which is inhabited by either the bourgeoisie or the aristocracy."

They talked for a long time, and returned to the

Château together.

Albert was beneath the green oak, talking to the Dowager Duchess, who was telling him how much she admired Genevieve. She had repeated her poem so wonderfully to her alone that morning! They did not see the trio emerge from the thicket, and Maurice was glad of it. He felt more and more constrained. The complicity against the poor fellow's happiness seemed to him a form of treason. He looked at his watch. It was only five o'clock.

"That is impossible. This watch must have stopped."

The Duke went to his room. His man gave him an elegant little note, and as his master threw it down on the table, "They await an answer."

"Very well, I will send one."

The servant withdrew. On the stair he met an English maid waiting the answer.

"Monsieur will send an answer."

"The Countess will be displeased. These French gentlemen are more gallant but less polite than our English lords. She is as much in love as Love itself."

"He also is in love."

"Then it ought to be easy enough, for Madame is a widow."

"But it is not your mistress that he loves."

"Ah! who then?"

"Ah! nothing for nothing." And he held out his hands.

"Ah! shocking!"

"Very well," and he started, as if to return to his master.

She stopped him.

"Monsieur, Gustave you know very well that I am promised."

"Nothing for nothing."

Again he held out his hands. She hesitated a moment, looking up and down, and then let him have her finger tips. With a brutal gesture he caught her to him and kissed her furiously. The little English maid, blushing and rumpled, drew back and announced coldly, "You French are brutes. Now, the information I paid for in advance."

"Very well. He is in love with little Esperance Darbois."

"The actress? But she is engaged to Count Styvens."

"It is the truth I have told you," replied the valet, proud of his own importance, "and if you will meet me in the grove, during dinner, I will tell you some more."

"Thanks, I know enough now," said the maid dryly, leaving him.

She disappeared, but Gustave preened himself, certain of success. As he went downstairs he saw Count Albert, helping the old Mademoiselle and her charge into the carriage. Instinctively, he looked up to see his master's silhouette at the window. Albert was asking to be allowed to go with them, but Esperance had promised herself a quiet and restful drive.

"No, Albert, we shall be four with my father and mother, and this is a small carriage."

"But I will sit with the coachman."

"Look," said the young girl, laughing, "at the size of the seat, and remember that there will be two large bags and a hat box, a very big hat box, to hold a hat for mama, one for Genevieve, and one for me."

Albert sighed sadly and closed the carriage door, after he had kissed his fiancée's hand. As the carriage drove away he went up to the room his mother was to occupy when she arrived next day, and looked to see if all was ready.

He took a book and tried to read, but after a couple of minutes he threw it aside and went out of doors again. He stopped a moment on the terrace, considering where to go. A young lady stopped him as he was preparing to go down the steps.

"All alone, Count, and dreaming! Ah! you are thinking of her. Come, let us stroll along together."

And the young Countess de Morgueil took his arm before he had time to answer.

Sarah Bernhardt

"You were not at the rehearsal this morning. You know that they have given up the tableaux of 'Europa.' Did you insist upon it?"

"No, why should I have made myself so ridiculous?"

"But the Duke pretended...."

"Dear Madame, the Duke could not have pretended anything except that he did not wish to appear without any clothes on, a decision that I heartily approved of."

"They say that he tries to fascinate every woman he meets. What do you think?"

"And what do you?" said the Count, looking her straight in the eye.

"Oh! he would never cause me great palpitation," she returned meaningly.

"Are you making any allusion to Mlle. Darbois?" he asked, stopping abruptly.

"I am engaged to Mlle. Darbois, I believe you know, Madame. You are piqued because you love the Duke de Morlay and he seems to be deserting you to hover near my fiancée. Do as I do; have a little patience; to-morrow by this time the fête will be over and I shall have left with Mlle. Darbois. Don't be either too nervous or too malicious, it does not agree with your type of beauty. I kiss your hands."

He went towards the Château, and took up his vigil in the little salon adjoining Esperance's room.

The Countess of Morgueil was confused and mortified. "He is not so stupid as he looks," she thought.

Albert was reading, but listening all the time. Finally a carriage stopped before the Château. He went down quickly and caught Esperance in his arms so tightly that the young girl gave a little scream.

"Oh! pardon, pardon. It is so long since I have seen you."

He kissed Mme. Darbois's hand and almost crushed the professor's fingers in his nervous grasp. He asked anxiously concerning Penhouet, and expressed his desire to return there immediately. Maurice and Genevieve came running up.

"How happy every one looks here," said Mme. Darbois.

"Don't believe it, my dear aunt; we are standing on a volcano."

"Ah! the cares of the fête weigh upon you. It always seems as if everything were going wrong at the last moment."

She laughed, proud of her penetrations. Genevieve tugged at Maurice's vest as he was about to set the dear lady right.

"Ah! well, I leave you to dress. This evening, uncle, I want to have a chat with you as I have something serious to say to you."

The philosopher and his wife looked at each

other understandingly.

"Very well, my boy, I shall be entirely at your disposal for as long as you like, for I can guess...."

And he looked at Genevieve. Maurice despaired of ever making him understand.

CHAPTER XXVI

Everyone greeted the philosopher with delight when he appeared in the ante-chamber where the guests were assembled before dinner. The Duke came to present his greetings to Mme. Darbois and stayed talking to her for some time. He saw that she liked him, but foresaw at the same time that it would be very painful for the good woman to have to accept another son-in-law. During dinner the Duchess steered the conversation towards philosophy, wishing to please François, who was placed on her right - art and science being to her the highest titles of nobility.

"Ah! I am no philosopher," protested the Marquis de Montagnac. "I accept old age only as a chastisement, and not having committed any criminal act, I revolt against the injustice of it."

And Louis de Marset, bending towards his neighbour, who had had a great reputation for beauty before age and illness had pulled her down, remarked, "One cannot be and have been, is not that true, Madame?"

"You are mistaken, my dear sir. There are some poor people who are born fools and never change."

A smile of delight appeared on every face.

The Duke found himself in an argument with Lord Glerey, a phlegmatic Englishman, whose marital misfortunes had made both London and Paris laugh.

"You seem," said the Duke, "to confuse indifference with philosophy."

"I do not confuse them, my dear sir. My apparent indifference is simply scorn for the sarcasms, the cruelty of the people of society who are always ready to rejoice when anyone attacks the honour or love of another."

The Duke murmured slowly, "Certainly what they call 'the world' deserves scorn. And all the same, taken separately, every individual of this collectivity is a man or woman like any other, a suffering being, who laughs just the same, like an eternal Figaro, for fear of being compelled to weep."

Count Albert was talking to an old sceptic.

"But," the Countess de Morgueil addressed him suddenly, "What would you do, if on the eve of attaining the longed-for happiness, you found yourself suddenly confronted by an insurmountable obstacle."

"Everything would depend on the quality of the happiness in prospect, Madame. Some happiness easily abandoned, and some happiness is to be struggled for until death itself."

Maurice had guessed the point of this sudden attack. He was none the less surprised by Albert's answer.

"Decidedly, it is going to be even more difficult than I

feared," he thought.

Indeed, Count Albert had evidently assumed a change of attitude. Love and jealousy had transformed this simple and generous heart into a being of metal; he had not lost any of his goodness, but he had put his soul in a state of defence and prepared himself for the struggle. He did not know anything, but his presentiments filled him with anguish. He was not unaware that his austerity provoked irony, but now it seemed to him that the irony was taking a form of pity which enraged him.

Dinner was over, the great hall filled with groups gathered together as their tastes dictated. Bridge and poker tables were produced, and some of the young people gathered about a table where liqueurs were being served. Maurice took his uncle by the arm and led him away.

"Let us go to your room, for no one must hear what I have to say to you."

"Not even your aunt?"

"No, uncle, not even aunt."

François was astonished, for he had supposed that it was of his own future that Maurice wished to speak. They went towards the Tower of Saint Genevieve.

"Uncle, what I have to say to you is very grave."

"What a lot of preamble! Well, I am listening."

"The Duke de Morlay-La-Branche loves Esperance passionately."

"Well, that is a pity for the Duke, but he will console himself easily enough."

Maurice was silent before he continued, "Esperance is madly in love with the Duke!"

François started violently.

"You are raving, Maurice; she is engaged to Count Styvens and has no right to forget him."

"She has never been in love with the Count, and can hardly endure him since she has foreseen another future."

"What future?"

"The Duke wants to marry Esperance."

"But it is impossible, impossible," said the philosopher violently. "A word that has been given cannot be taken back so lightly."

"Calm yourself, uncle, if you please. For three days I have been wandering about in this untenable situation. We must make a decision. Every instant I fear an outbreak either from Albert or from the Duke."

"How have Esperance and the Duke contrived to see each other?"

"I will tell you all that uncle, later, but the how and the why are not very important at this moment. I want you to send for Albert. Esperance does not wish to marry him. She has loved the Duke a long time, but did not know that he loved her, and did not suppose an alliance possible between our families, even though you have made the name illustrious. For that matter I should never have supposed myself that the Duke would consent to make what would generally be considered a mésalliance."

"It all seems unbelievable," murmured François.

And with his head in his hands he groaned despairingly, "How can we sacrifice that noble and unfortunate Albert?"

"One of the three must suffer, uncle. It would be a crime to sacrifice Esperance who has the right to love whom she pleases and to choose her own life. The Duke Morlay is loved, Count Albert is not and never has been. He knows it as you know it now. Esperance consented to marry him through gratitude to you."

"Ah! I feared as much," said the professor prostrated.

François Darbois remained a long time in thought, then he got up, his face lined with sadness.

"Tell your cousin to come to me, I will wait for her here."

"I will send her to you at once. Forgive me for having so distressed you, dear uncle."

"It was your duty!"

François pressed his hand affectionately. Left alone he

felt despairing. The futility of the precautions he had taken, the inanity of all reasoning, of all logic, plunged him into the scepticism he had been combatting for so many years.

Maurice found his cousin talking to Albert, the Marquis of Montagnac, and Genevieve.

"Your father is feeling a little indisposed and is going to bed. Would not you like to say good-night to him?"

Esperance rose immediately. Albert wanted to go with her, but Maurice held him back, and began asking under what conditions he proposed to play the duet with Esperance next day.

"It is all one to me," replied the Count wearily. "I am in a hurry to get away from here. I find myself too much disturbed by my nerves, and you know, cousin, how unusual it is for me to be nervous."

At this term of family familiarity, Maurice shivered. He thought of the interview now taking place in his uncle's room. Genevieve joined them and they strolled up and down, but Albert made them return continually near the tower.

When Esperance opened the door of the little salon where her father was waiting, she saw him in such an attitude of distress that she threw herself at his knees.

"Father, darling father, I ask your pardon. I am ruining your life just as you begin to reap the harvest of so many noble efforts. You have been so good to me," she sobbed, "and I must seem to you so ungrateful. Do not suffer so, I beg you. Take me away with you, let us go and I will do my best to forget; let us go!"

"But," said the Professor, hesitatingly, "Albert would follow."

The girl rose.

"Oh! no, not that. I wish I could marry Albert without loving him; I have tried, but I cannot go on to the end, I cannot!"

"You really love the Duke?"

"Father, for a whole year I have struggled against that love."

"Why have you never told me?"

"Because I saw nothing in the Duke's attentions except the agitation they caused me; and I was too ashamed to speak of it to you. I thought, considering the position of the Duke, that I was an aspiring fool. He overheard me talking to Genevieve. When he appeared before us, I so little expected to see him there at such an hour - six o'clock in the morning, in the grove - that my heart could not bear the shock, and I fainted. From that instant I understood how much I loved him. I had no idea before of the power of love, but now I feel it the master of my life. I will sacrifice that to your will, father; but I will not sacrifice the immense happiness of loving. Even if the Duke did not love me, I should still be uplifted by my own love."

She sat down beside her father.

"Who knows what unhappiness may not be lurking for

Sarah Bernhardt

me, ready to spring at any moment?"

She drew near him shivering.

François took her charming head in his hands. He looked at her tenderly, but with an expression almost of terror in his face.

"Alas! all happiness built upon the unhappiness of others always risks disillusionment - and collapse."

"Dear father, my life has been bathed in such sunlight for the last three days, that I shall keep that glow of warmth for the rest of my life."

"I only ask, you little daughter, to do nothing, to say nothing, before the end of this fête. We have no right, however grave our personal troubles and responsibilities are, to betray the hospitality of the Duchess. To-morrow, after the fête, I will talk to Albert. Go, my darling, go back to that poor boy. I hate to send you to practice a dissimulation that I abhor, but we are in a situation of such delicacy and difficulty.... God keep you!"

He kissed her tenderly. She went back to her fiancé, to find to her surprise that the Countess de Morgueil had just passed by with him. Maurice pointed them out where they were walking slowly in the distance.

"Oh! so much the better," said Esperance. "That gives me an excuse to go to my room."

Maurice urged her to wait. "I am convinced that that woman is meddling in our affairs. It is plain enough that we have upset her."

"How? What do you mean, cousin?"

"Did you not know that the Countess is madly in love with the Duke, and that she had hoped to marry him this winter?"

"Poor woman," sighed Esperance, sincerely.

The Duke came by, and seeing them alone, he joined them.

"The three of you alone?" he cried. "Then you will allow me to join you for a moment?"

"Look," said Maurice, indicating Albert and the Countess de Morgueil.

"There is a dangerous woman who is making mischief at this moment!... And, nevertheless, I owe her the happiness this moment brings me."

"My father," said Esperance, "has been as indulgent to me as always."

"Thanks for these tidings," said the Duke. "Do you think he will receive me to-morrow, if I go to him?"

"Oh! certainly, after the fête; a little while after, for first he wished to speak to Count Styvens," she said timidly.

"Will you," the Duke asked Maurice, "make an appointment for me, and tell me as soon as you have an answer?"

"With pleasure."

The Duke bowed to the girls and withdrew. He took Maurice's hand, "I am happy, my friend, everything is going as I wish. I seem to hear laughter coming out of the shadows."

And he disappeared.

The young people waited for Albert a little while longer, but as he did not appear, Maurice advised the girls to retire, and he returned to sit down anxiously under the oak.

He had been there hardly a quarter of an hour when he saw the Countess de Morgueil go by. She was alone and walked nervously. On the doorstep she stopped and looked back into the distance. He saw her tremble, then go in quickly. He stood up on his bench to see what she had been looking at, but he almost fell, and had to steady himself by holding on to a branch. Albert and the Duke were together. Albert had put his hand on the Duke's shoulder, and the Duke had removed that great hand. They were walking side by side towards the extensive terrace that commanded the countryside.

"Oh! the wretched woman! What can she have said? And to be able to do nothing, nothing," he thought.

He lighted a cigarette, waiting, he did not know for what. But he could not go back to his room.

As he put his hand on the Duke's shoulder Albert had said, "I wish to talk to you."

"Very well. I am listening."

"I want you to answer me with perfect truth."

"Your request would be offensive, Albert, if it were not for your emotion."

"Is it true that you love Esperance Darbois?"

"It is true."

"Is it true that you want to marry her?"

"It is true."

"My God! My God!" muttered Albert, and he stopped for a minute. He was choking. The Duke felt a profound pity for this man who was suffering at this moment the most terrible pain.

"Do you believe that she loves you?" Albert still went on.

"I have answered you with perfect frankness concerning myself, but do not ask me to answer for Mlle. Darbois."

"Yes; you are right, you cannot answer for her. I know that she does not love me, but I hoped to make her love me. I wanted to make her so happy!... That love has made a different man of me. What I regarded yesterday as a crime seems to me now the will of destiny. One of us two must disappear. If you kill me, I know her soul, she will not marry you; she would die rather. If I kill you, the tender compassion she feels for me will be changed into hatred. What I am doing now is a brutal act, an animal act, but I cannot do otherwise! My religious education had restrained my passions! At least I thought so," he said, passing his great hand across his stubborn forehead. "But no! My youth denied of love takes a terrible revenge upon me now, and I have to exert a horrible effort now not to strangle you."

The Duke had not stirred.

"I am at your orders, Albert; only I think you will have to arm yourself with patience for several hours longer. This fête, given by the Duchess, cannot be prevented by our quarrel. I suggest that you postpone our meeting until to-morrow evening. Our witnesses can meet if you like at one o'clock at the little Inn of the 'Three Roads.' It is only ten minutes distance from here. The innkeeper is loyal to me, I am his daughter's godfather. The garden is cut by a long alley which can serve as the field of honour. I will go at once to warn De Montagnac and his brother; then I will go to the 'Three Roads.'"

"Good," said Albert.

"Naturally, we leave Maurice Renaud out of our quarrel."

"Certainly," said Charles de Morlay bowing.

They parted. From a distance the young painter saw the Duke enter the great hall. Several minutes later Albert's tall form barred the horizon for a moment. He looked at the Tower of Saint Genevieve, then he also entered the hall. Then Maurice decided to go in himself. He sat down by a little table littered with magazines and periodicals, and picked up one, without ceasing for an instant to watch the two men. The Duke de Morlay was standing behind the Marquis, who was still at the whist table. Albert Styvens had sat down beside a diplomat from Italy, Cesar Gabrielli, a serious young man, a clever diplomat, and a renowned fencer. When Montagnac finished his hand, the Duke offered him a cigar.

"Will you help me with some arrangements for the performance to-morrow?"

He was about to refuse, but the Duke said briefly, "It is important, come!"

The two of them went out, only lingering a little on the way for a joke with the men and a compliment to the ladies. Then Maurice watched the diplomat, who rose at the same time, and invited Albert to admire the moon from the terrace. Maurice saw them disappearing towards the corner by the Chinese umbrella. That was the end of the terrace, and was out of sight from all the windows.

"It is all plain enough," thought the young man, "but when, where?"

He understood that neither of the two adversaries could take him either for confidant or for second.

"However," he said, as he went to his room. "I want to know. I must know. I will know."

CHAPTER XXVII

The next day, the day of the fête, all the Château, from early in the morning, was in a violent tumult. Maurice, the Marquis Assistant, and Jean Perliez were busy to the point of distraction; fortunately for Maurice, who had been unable to sleep and had called Jean at six to share the secret which had not been confided to him. He could not think of telling Genevieve, and Jean should be able to help keep watch.

"You try," he directed, "to watch Montagnac; I shall not leave the diplomat."

The Duke came in search of Maurice to ask for Esperance. He looked a little pale but showed much interest in the fête.

"Our dear Duchess must be rewarded for all the excitement we have caused her house."

"There is no reason to suppose," said Maurice, "that all the excitement will cease after the fête!"

The Duke would not show that he had understood. Maurice went to smoke a cigarette in the garden and was hardly surprised to see the doctor, who had been attached to the service of the Duchess for twenty years, and attended all the guests in the Château, talking animatedly with the diplomat. The doctor raised his arms in a horrified gesture, letting them fall again tragically. He gave every evidence of a violent struggle with himself. The diplomat remained calm, determined, and even authoritative. The poor doctor finally yielded. The diplomat shook his hand and left him.

The doctor with an expression of great distress, walking feebly, passed by Maurice, who would have stopped him.

"No, no. What? It is impossible.... You are not ill.... Leave me, dear sir.... I ... I must..."

He stammered unintelligible phrases, hastening his steps. Maurice re-entered the hall. He met the musician Xavier Flamand, who said, "I just saw the Count Styvens go out."

"At this hour?" exclaimed Montagnac, looking at the Duke.

"He has gone to meet his mother at the station. She arrives at eight o'clock. It is only seven, he will arrive half an hour too soon."

"He is a dutiful son," said Montagnac. "I am surprised that he has not taken his fiancée."

Maurice raised his head. "Then the Marquis knows nothing!" he said to himself.

He reflected, "How dense I am growing. Evidently neither the Duke nor Albert has told anyone the motive of their quarrel."

Jean came up and cut short his monologue.

"I think that the two other seconds are Count Alfred Montagnac, the Marquis's brother, and Captain Frederic Chevalier. Here they come now."

Indeed the three seconds had just come up to the Marquis, who asked Maurice to excuse him. "I will be back in a few moments, dear M. Renaud."

The Duke dropped down by Maurice.

"I believe the fête will be a great success, but I wonder if you long to have it over as heartily as I do."

"I regret," replied Maurice, "that our hostess ever thought of it, and that we ever had anything to do with it."

"Would you also regret having me for your cousin?"

"No, you know very well that I would not, but...."

"But?"

"I know...."

"You know?"

"Yes, I know."

"Who has told you?"

The Duke's face grew stern.

"No one, I give you my word, but I have guessed; it

was not very difficult...."

"Then, my dear Maurice, I must ask you to remain absolutely silent. None of our seconds know the real reason of our meeting. None of them will ever know. This duel will be to the death, by the wish of Count Styvens, who has found himself justifiably offended."

"Where will you meet?"

"At the Inn of the 'Three Roads.'"

"When?"

"To-morrow, immediately after the fête. The Inn has been closed since this morning so as to receive no one except ourselves and our witnesses. Now, my dear Maurice, since you know, I want to ask you a favour. Here are some papers that I wrote last night. I am afraid my servant is on intimate terms with Mme. de Morgueil's English maid, and I dare not leave them in my room. I put them in your care. If luck is against me you will give these to the proper persons. If Count Albert is unfortunate, you will give me back the envelope. I'll see you later!"

He pressed the young man's hand in a close grasp.

The Duke de Castel-Montjoie, the Dowager's only son, had been chosen by the seconds as umpire. De Morlay and Styvens approved the choice.

The great hall had been invaded by a score of servants who arranged the chairs, placed the palms, and hung silver chains to separate the musicians from the audience. The curtain of the little stage was lowered,

Sarah Bernhardt

but a murmur could be heard through the pretty drop painted by Maurice. Among the servants set to finish the costumes was the Duke's sly goddaughter. Every time the Duke passed she gazed at him and her lips trembled. She who was usually so pert and smiling worked with set lips.

"Ha, ha!" said one of the maids, "you must be in love, eh, Jeanette?"

"Let me alone, stupid, to do my work," said the young girl with tears in her eyes.

She had been waked the night before by the noise of opening doors, she had got up and seen her godfather talking to her father. The Duke said, "You must close your Inn early as possible, you must refuse everybody, except the Doctor from the Château, Count Styvens and four gentlemen with the Duke of Castel-Montjoie. I shall probably get here first."

"Ah! my God," the Innkeeper had murmured, "the Duke is going to fight, I know that.... If only nothing happens to you, sir."

"I need not say that I count on your discretion as on your devotion. Have your best bedroom ready to receive one or the other of the adversaries and put yourself at the absolute command of the Duke de Castel-Montjoie. *Au revoir*. Try not to let your daughter know anything about this, and say nothing to hcr; but I know that even if she discovered she would not give us away. *Au revoir*!"

As soon as the door closed Jeanette ran to her father, bare-footed, her hair flying, just as she had jumped out of bed.

"Great Heavens!" said the Innkeeper, "you were listening."

"Yes, I was listening, I heard; I will prepare the room, but it shall be for the other!"

"Do you know who the other is?"

"No," she said quickly.

"Do you know why they are fighting?"

"How should I know?" she demanded.

She did know, however. However she sat mute under the gibes of the other servants.

Albert had returned with his mother, who seemed gayer, happier than usual. Esperance went at once to speak to her and was enthusiastically congratulated on her superb bearing.

The Countess kissed Esperance whose eyes were filling with tears, and she kissed the Countess's hands with so much emotion that the lady raised the blonde head, saying tenderly, "No, no, you must not cry! We must love each other joyfully. I have never seen my son so happy, I should be jealous if I loved him less. See, dear, I want to give you these jewels myself; I believe that they are going to suit you very well."

She clasped a magnificent collar of pearls around the young girl's neck. Esperance could not refuse them. She thanked the lovely lady affectionately.

"My father will tell me what to do," she thought.

Lunch was an hour earlier as the fête was to begin at half-past two. "Heavens," said Mme. Styvens with perturbation, "I shall never be ready."

Esperance left her, happy to escape from her torturing thoughts. "Deceit, deceit to this good woman!" Albert was waiting to lead her back. He admired his mother's gift, and spoke to her gently.

"It is just the tint of your skin," he said, "that gives these pearls their beautiful lustre. They ought not to flatter themselves that it is they who embellish you!"

All this was added anguish for the girl, his mother's kindness, Albert's gay confidence, and this fête which was, soon to begin, this fête where she must show herself publicly with him whom she loved so that she would die for him, with him who loved her more than life! She repulsed with horror the ideas that came crowding into her brain. If the Château should burn. If she should fall down the staircase and break a leg; if Albert should be taken ill and die within the hour.... If ... if ... and a million visions raced through her brain as she went back to the Tower of Saint Genevieve. But never once did the Duke appear as a victim of any of these misfortunes which her brain was conjecturing up so busily.

Lunch was a bit disorganized. The Duke avoided looking at Esperance. The sight of that child who loved him filled him with such emotion that he was afraid of betraying himself. The Countess de Morgueil, annoyed at seeing the two men she had sought to embroil talking together in the most courteous fashion, started to sharpen her claws once more.

"What a beautiful collar, Mlle. Darbois; this is the first time that you have worn it, isn't it? Count, I compliment you!"

"Mme. Styvens has just given it to me." The Duke understood the embarrassment the child felt - not yet eighteen, and forced to extricate herself from nets set by such expert hands as best she could.

At half-past two the great hall was crowded by women vying with each other in their beauty. It was a magnificent sight! Xavier Flamand went to his stand to conduct the orchestra.

He was heartily applauded and the spectacle commenced. More than two thousand people had come together for the fête. The hall could only accommodate eight hundred. Other chairs had been placed on the terrace. The tableaux began. The society assembled, appreciated a form of art which is pleasing and not fatiguing, which charms without disturbing.

The tableau of Andromeda was frantically applauded. The men could not admire enough the suppleness of Esperance's lovely body, the whiteness of her bare feet with their pink arches, the gold of her hair floating like a nimbus around the head of Andromeda, waved by the breeze as the stage turned. The women admired the Duke, so very beautiful in his gold and silver armour.

"How splendid the Duke is," remarked the Countess to Albert. "No one could have a prouder bearing. If I were in your place, my son, I should be jealous."

"Perhaps I am," said the Count, smiling.

The "Judgment of Paris" had the same success. Everyone waited for "Europa," and many were really disappointed. A hundred reasons were given for its withdrawal, and none of them the true one.

The philosopher and his wife were sitting with Genevieve behind the Styvens. Sometimes the Countess would turn around to compliment François, and the unfortunate man, so frank, whose whole life had never known deceit, suffered cruelly. There was an intermission to set the stage for the concert. The guests pressed around the Styvens's to express their admiration for Esperance, in the most dithyrambic, the most superlative terms. The concert began. Albert had to go upon the stage to play the Liszt duet with Esperance. He begged François Darbois to take his place beside his mother.

When the curtain went up after the quartette of "Rigoletto," Esperance and Albert were seated on the long piano stool. Loud applause greeted them. The Duke was talking to Maurice in the wings and seemed a little nervous. He envied Albert at that moment for his superiority as a musician. When they finished, a great tumult demanded an encore, but Esperance had come to the end of her strength.

As the public continued to applaud, Maurice and the Duke came forward to see why they did not raise the curtain. Esperance looked at the Duke.

"Oh! no, please do not raise the curtain; my heart is beating so fast."

Albert and the Duke supported her gently and she leaned upon them, her pretty head bending towards the Duke.

"I feel confused."

And she closed her eyes, afraid of giving herself away. Once more in the air and she began to feel better. She breathed the little flask of ether that the Doctor held under her nose.

"This poor heart is always making scenes. Ah! dear Count, you will have to set that in order."

The Duke had moved away. Annoyed by the insistence of the public, he told Jean Perliez to announce that Mlle. Darbois needed a little rest, and presented her compliments to the audience and excused herself from replying to the encoring. This was a real disappointment. There had been such enthusiasm for the two fiancés, an enthusiasm well-earned by the inspired execution of "Orpheus," that the attitude of this elite audience was a little indifferent to the artists who concluded the concert. The hall was half empty and several artists were too offended to appear.

Esperance went to her room with her mother and Genevieve, begging the Count to return to his mother.

"Your mother will be anxious, and my father can not reassure her, because he does not himself know the symptoms of this slight illness. Tell them that I will rest for a quarter of an hour and then join you at my flower booth."

When she was left alone with Genevieve she drew her

friend to her.

"My dear little sister, I cannot tell you the joy that pervades every part of my being. In an hour it will be over! My father will talk with Albert and I shall be free! free!"

"Poor boy," sighed Genevieve.

"Oh! yes, I am ungrateful to his great devotion, but I should be false to myself and to you, Genevieve, if I told you that the idea of his despair greatly troubles me. I know that every one about me regrets the breaking off of this marriage, and still I don't care. You all admire the Duke, but you blame him a little. I know that, but that is all submerged and forgotten in my great love. When I reason as I do now, I recognize at once the horrible storm I am causing, and yet I cannot feel sad. I find all sorts of excuses for myself, and cast back all the responsibility on Fate."

She was silent an instant.

"Do you think it will take vengeance?"

Mlle. Frahender came in.

"What will take vengeance?"

"Fate."

"My dear child, what is called Fate is simply the law of God."

"Then if God is just he will not avenge himself, for what has happened is not my fault."

The old lady looked at the young girl very tenderly.

"My dear child, do not get into the habit of throwing the responsibility of your actions upon others. Certainly we are not responsible for events, but we can almost always choose the way to meet them. Only, some flatter their passions and refuse to assert themselves against them! This weakness opens the door to all other concessions, and then it becomes difficult to make a loyal examination of our conscience."

"Is that my case?" asked the young girl with some anxiety.

"Perhaps," replied Mlle. Frahender, frankly.

"Oh! little lady, be kinder to me, I am so happy that I cannot believe such happiness comes from troubled waters.... And I swear to you that my heart is loyal."

The old lady kissed her charge, but her smile was sad. Esperance was now ready to go to her flower stall. A pretty dress, toned like a pigeon's breast, a round neck with a tulle collar, a wide girdle fastened with a bunch of primroses, a flapping hat of Italian straw tied with two narrow ribbons under her chin, created a delightful effect and a ravishing frame for her lovely face. When she passed lightly on her way to her booth, she caused quite a sensation. The Duke, Count Albert, Maurice and Jean Perliez were waiting for her. A crowd followed in her wake.

The Duke and Count had the same longing to see her, to be with her up to the last moment! They understood each other at that instant, and each outdid the other in courtesy. Albert was the first customer, passing a thousand francs for a primrose from her belt. The Duke made the same bargain. The girl's fingers trembled as she handed him the flower. Albert felt a choking feeling in his throat. The crowd pressed round. A German offered ten thousand francs for a flower which the young girl had put to her lips. At last Albert could work off some of his emotion. He repulsed the German.

"There is nothing more for sale, sir. I have just bought everything for fifty thousand francs."

The German would have protested, but he was pushed back by the crowd and landed at a distance.

"That was well done!"

"I did not know that he could be so impulsive."

"He was quite right."

"The poor people of the Duchess will become landholders!"

And the crowd scattered, making many comments on the way. Albert was soon surrounded, as everybody wanted to shake hands with him. The Duke had stepped back behind the booth. Esperance came out with Genevieve and Mlle. Frahender. He stopped beside her a moment.

"I love you."

"Oh, thank you."

"Forever, I hope!"

Then, as he saw that the Count was still surrounded and that Esperance would not be able to make her way to him, he offered her his arm.

"Let me take you to Count Styvens, who cannot extricate himself!"

With the help of Jean and Maurice, he dispersed the guests and led Esperance to her fiancée. At that moment anyone who had suspected the Duke of intentions to flirt with the plighted girl, must have abandoned their idea; and the motive of the duel, which was to bring one of these two perfect gentlemen to his death, became more and more obscure.

Count Styvens saw the girl coming to him on the Duke's arm, and he did not suffer from the sight; his suffering for the last two days had been too extreme to feel upset by any increase. He took Esperance to the door of the Tower.

"You were lovelier than ever before."

He kissed her fingers devotedly. The young girl felt a tiny tear fall like a terrible weight on her hand. He lifted his head quickly, looked fixedly at Esperance with a look of such goodness and faith, that she felt suddenly guilty and bent her head. The Count shook hands cordially with the philosopher.

"Do not forget," the elder man said to him, "that I want to have a little talk with you; it is more than a wish, it is a duty."

"I also have a serious duty to attend to," replied the young Count. "Excuse me if I have to keep you waiting."

CHAPTER XXVIII

Albert went immediately to his mother, who was taking tea with the Princess. He embraced her with such tenderness that she was astonished at his ardour. The Princess held out her hand.

"Do not wait too long to realize your happiness, Albert. You know how all your friends will rejoice with you."

He kissed her hand again, and went to join his two seconds at the gate of the kitchen garden.

The crowd had all dispersed to catch the last train.

The meeting at the "Three Roads" was for seven. They saw the Duke de Castel-Montjoie from a distance. He had had some difficulty in making his escape, having had to help his mother, the Duchess, with the last farewells. He bowed to the Count and led the way by a little door to the inn stable. He was carrying two sets of swords, done up in two cases of green cloth.

The Duke and his seconds were already there. Only the Doctor had not arrived. Morlay-La-Branche and Albert bowed to each other and got ready.

The little bowers, where the *habitues* of the inn often

284   Sarah Bernhardt

ate their midday meals, served them as dressing-rooms. The Doctor arrived out of breath, with the information that he had not been able to get a *confrere* and would have to serve both sides. The umpire, in company with the seconds, chose an alley of proper dimensions.

The adversaries were placed opposite, sword in hand. The Duke de Castel-Montjoie touched the points of their swords and said, "Go!"

The conditions of the duel were very strict. The first round should last three minutes, should neither of the adversaries be touched.

"Halt!" cried the Duke de Castel-Montjoie.

One minute was allowed them to breathe.

"Go," said the umpire, again joining the sword tips.

This time Albert made a furious drive against the Duke. There was a moment of suspense. The Duke did not give way. His arm shot out and the unfortunate Count turned completely round and fell. Charles de Morlay's sword had pierced beneath the right arm pit, entering the lung. The blood streamed from the wounded man's mouth. The Doctor and the seconds carried him into the room which Jeanette had prepared. The Duke, sorely moved, followed them. Albert saw him and held out a hand which the Duke pressed gently, bending his head. The Count signed to the seconds to withdraw.

"I was wrong, Duke," he murmured. "My love had blinded my wisdom with the heavy mask of egoism. On the threshold of eternity the truth seems clearer.

Forgive me, De Morlay, as I forgive you."

He choked. The Doctor came forward. The Duke, as pale as the dying man, pressed that loyal hand for the last time, and withdrew.

In her own room Esperance had just waked with an anguished cry.

"What is the matter with you?"

"I ... I ... I do not know ... a catastrophe ... where is my father?"

"In his room, and...."

At that very moment Maurice knocked at the door, and before they had time to answer him, he entered. His face was distorted with grief.

"A catastrophe, a catastrophe!" repeated Esperance, at sight of him.

"Get up, put on a wrap, put something on your head, and come, come quickly! A carriage is waiting for us!"

"A catastrophe, a catastrophe! Albert? the Duke?..."

"Albert!" he answered brusquely. "Come quickly! He wants to see you before...."

The words died in his throat.

He helped his cousin and led her rapidly to the carriage. Esperance was gasping with anguish.

"Tell me, Maurice, tell me."

But the young man could not answer. He knew only that Albert was mortally wounded. He had been waiting a few paces from the Inn to see the duellers come out. The Duke de Morlay-La-Branche and Castel-Montjoie appeared first, and as they were talking to the young man, the Marquis de Montagnac came out precipitately.

"I beg you," he said to Maurice, "to fetch the Count's fiancée. He wants to see her before his mother knows."

And Maurice had departed in hot haste.

As soon as they reached the Inn, Esperance jumped to the ground. Jeanette, who had kept a constant watch, ran along ahead of her and without a word showed her the door of the room where Count Albert lay dying. The Doctor stopped her.

"Very gently," he said.

But Albert had felt the presence of his dearly loved. He raised himself a little, holding out his great arms to the young girl.

"Come to me, my love, do not be afraid. I will never hold you again in these arms that frighten you. Listen carefully. I have only a few minutes to live! No one knows the real reason of my quarrel with the Duke.... You may have thought that it was about you. I swear to you," he laid stress on the word, "I swear to you that it was nothing to do with you!"

His glazing eyes cleared for an instant, illuminated by

the beauty of his falsehood.

"Marry the Duke, he is charming ... he ... he is loyal ... but do not abandon my mother; she will have only you!"

Two red streams trickled from the corners of his mouth. Esperance on her knees with her hands crossed on the bed, watched the blood run down on the face that had grown paler than the pillow. Her tears blinded her, and she shook as with an ague. Albert ceased breathing for an instant. The Doctor, who was watching closely from the end of the room, came near and gave him a dose of chlorate of calcium to stop the hemorrhage; then at a sign from Albert, withdrew again.

"Promise me," said the young man, "that you will always keep this necklace!"

"Albert, don't die! I will love you! I do love you! Have pity! I will always wear the necklace. You shall unfasten it every evening and clasp it every morning! Do not die! Do not die! I am your fiancée, to-morrow I will be your wife! You must life for your mother, for me!"

The door opened and the Countess, suddenly awakened, entered with the
Baron van Berger and the Duke de Castel-Montjoie.

"Mother, dear mother, forgive me.... I leave you Esperance, who will take my place with you. Forgive the Duke de Morlay the pain he has caused you. Our quarrel was so deep, we could only settle it by arms. It was I, I, who precipitated matters. The Duke acted like an honourable gentleman. Oh! do not weep, mother, do not weep!"

He raised his hand painfully to wipe with trembling fingers the tears burning the beautiful eyes that had already wept so much.

The Chaplain from the Château entered the room, bearing the Holy Sacrament. He was accompanied by the Dowager Duchess, the Prince and Princess of Bernecourt. A solemn hush quieted the sobs of the two women. The priest bent over the couch of the dying man. The Count summoned all his strength to receive the extreme unction, then, transfigured by his faith, he sat up, extending his arms. The two women threw themselves trembling into the open arms, which closed upon them in the last struggle of life. They remained there, imprisoned, not knowing that the soul had fled.

A terrible cry shook these souls sunk down in grief. Esperance shrieked, "These arms, these arms, loosen these arms which are strangling me ... Deliver me, deliver me from these arms ... I am choking...."

They had some difficulty in freeing her. Her pupils dilated by terror, she was hardly able to breathe. The Doctor did not disguise his anxiety.

"Save her, Doctor," said the Countess Styvens, "save my daughter. My son is now with God; he sees me, he waits for me, but I must obey his last wish."

They carried Esperance away unconscious, without tears, without movement, almost without life. François, who had just arrived with his wife, learned of the frightful tragedy and received in his arms the poor unconscious cause of the drama. Mme. Darbois did not wish to leave her daughter, but the philosopher insisted, until she could not refuse, that she should go back to the Countess Styvens.

When the professor arrived at the Château he found the Duke de Morlay at the gate waiting for tidings. At sight of Esperance unconscious, her head fallen back on her father's breast, he jumped on the step of the victoria.

"What more has happened?" he asked panting.

"The Doctor will be here in a few minutes. He will tell you...."

The carriage drove on to the Tower of Saint Genevieve. The Duke took the poor figure in his arms and carried her up to her room, followed by François Darbois, broken by sorrow. Genevieve was waiting feverishly for the return of Maurice and Esperance. She showed the Duke where to lay Esperance. He stretched the slender creature on her bed. Her eyes were open, but she recognized no one. The rigidity of her expression frightened the Duke, and he bent in terror to listen to her breathing. A faint burning breath touched his face.

The Doctor declared that he could give no decision at that moment, and ordered them to leave her to sleep.

"She must not be left for a second," he said. "Two people must watch so that she need never be left alone."

The Duke kissed the limp little hand, and recoiled - his

lips touched her engagement ring. As he went out he met the Countess Styvens and hardly recognized her, so terribly was she changed. She stopped him.

"Do not leave. I know from my son that it was he who provoked you. The cause of your duel is a secret that I shall never seek to know. May God pardon my son and free you from all remorse. I go to my daughter, all I have left to love and protect."

It was evident that the noble woman was making a great effort; the last words of her son were still ringing in her brain.

De Morlay knelt and watched the Countess disappear into the room.

CHAPTER XXIX

The Doctor declared that evening that Esperance had congestion of the brain, and that specialists who were sent for from Paris confirmed the diagnosis. The Dowager would not hear of having her taken away. The Tower of Saint Genevieve was put entirely at the Darbois's disposal. Twos sister were sent for, and Jeanette volunteered to do the heavy work. All the other servants were forbidden to approach the Tower.

The Countess Styvens, accompanied by the Duke de Castel-Montjoie, the Prince and Princess de Bernecourt, and the Baron van Berger, had taken the body of her son to be buried in the great family mausoleum which she had raised to the memory of her husband at her country place of Lacken.

Maurice and Genevieve were greatly relieved when they learned that the Countess had not remained. In her crises of delirium Esperance talked and talked....

"Albert, no, no, I do not love him ... I love the Duke.... Yes, he saved my life, but my father is going to tell him.... I cannot keep this collar.... It is cold, cold, it strangles me, I am stifling.... I am going to die.... Yes, Albert, you shall clasp the chain every morning ... and every evening.... No, my head is not too low, I can see the beauty of Perseus better. He is coming?... He is

Sarah Bernhardt

coming to cut off the long arms that hold me.... The blood, there, the blood running slowly!... No, Albert, do not die, I will love you, the Duke will go!..."

In spite of her trusting confidence, the poor mother must have come to wonder and perhaps to understand.

When Esperance regained consciousness the worst danger was over. Only Genevieve and Mlle. Frahender had heard the complete revelation.

Jeanette knew too, but Genevieve, who understood that she was there to keep the Duke informed, found her very docile and repentant and did not send her away. The Countess, to whom they had sent a daily bulletin for three weeks, found that Esperance, if not cured, was at least on the way to convalescence. She would still pass many hours when she failed to recognize people. A kind of coma took possession of her every now and then and kept her for days together in a kind of lethargy.

The season was getting late, and all the house guests had left. The Dowager Duchess did not wish to return to Paris, although her son, who had become a deputy as she wished, invited her to come and stay with him. The Prince de Bernecourt had had to once more take up his post, but his wife had stayed to keep her friend company, and because she loved the "little Darbois," as she called her. The Duke de Morlay was visiting friends whose Château was about an hour's journey away. He came every day for news from the Duchess, and from his goddaughter Jeanette.

A month went by. The young girl, now convalescent, was strong enough to be moved.

"We will take her to Penhouet for a month," said François Darbois's note to the Countess, "and when she is quite cured we will send her to you in Brussels."

The Duke was in despair at the idea of hearing that Esperance was to go away. He complained to Maurice whom he saw every day, "Can I not see Esperance?"

"Yes, but only for a few seconds," said the young painter. "I believe that you will have to wait several months before you can renew your love. She is convalescent, but not cured. Here is a proposal for you: I am going to marry Mlle. Hardouin in two months. Come to our wedding. Your presence will seem quite natural, for you have treated me as a friend. I am very much attached to you and I am sure that my cousin will be very happy with you when you are married."

"But will she be well in two months?"

"The Doctor assures us that she will be quite herself, and it is by his advice that we have set that date for our marriage."

"Do you think Mlle. Hardouin would accept me as a witness?"

She will be delighted, and I thank you. Genevieve has no relations except her elder sister, who brought her up."

"I hope that this marriage will recall Esperance's promise to her. Meantime I shall go to Italy for about the two months. Will you see if I may say good-bye to her?"

Sarah Bernhardt

"I will go now."

He was soon back again.

"My cousin expects you."

It was more than a month since the Duke had seen Esperance. He was painfully shocked by the change in her pretty face. She looked hardly real. Her eyes were enormous. Genevieve and Mlle. Frahender were with her.

"Here is the Duke de Morlay-La-Branche who has come to say good-bye to you."

Esperance turned her eyes towards the Duke.

"It is a long time since I have seen you," she said simply.

And her voice sounded like the tone of a distant harp.

"You have been very ill!"

"I have been very ill, I believe, but I cannot remember very well. I feel as if I had had heavy blows in my brain; sometimes I hear dreadful calls and then everything is quiet again. And then sometimes I see a piece of a picture, no beginning, no end, sometimes horrible, sometimes lovely. Why, now I remember," she spoke gently with a charming smile, "that you are part of all my visions, but I do not know any more how, or why.... And Albert, where is he? Why does he not come? He must come and undo the collar.... Ah! my God, my God, I am wandering you see, nothing is clear yet."

She raised her arms.

"My God, my God, have pity on me or take me at once. I do not want to lose my mind!"

She took the Duke's hand.

"Say you are not sorry that you loved me?"

"I love you always!"

She clapped her hands with a silvery laugh, "Genevieve, Genevieve, he loves me still."

And she hid her head on the young girl's arm. Maurice led the Duke away, overcome. He looked questioningly at the painter.

"No, she will not be light-headed long, the Doctors all agree about that, but her memory will have to come back by degrees a little at a time. She recognized you. She remembered her love and yours. That is a great step. Her youth, her love, and time will be, I believe, certain restorers."

The Duke left soon after they had taken Esperance away.

In Belgium the Countess had prepared for her beloved daughter. This beautiful woman of forty, so charming, so handsome in her mauve mourning, had already become an old woman whose movements were ever slow and sad. Her back was bent, from constantly kneeling beside her son's grave. Her black clothes reflected the deeper gloom of her expression. And to those who had seen her a few months before, she was

Sarah Bernhardt

almost unrecognizable.

Poor little Esperance regained her health very slowly. Her mind seemed entirely clear only on one subject, the theatre. Little by little she remembered everything connected with her art. She repeated with Genevieve and Jean Perliez the scenes they had given at the Competition. She worked hard on Musset's *On ne badine pas avec l'amour*; then busied herself with preparations for her friend's marriage. She did not know that the Duke was to be a witness.

"But," she would often object, "you must have two witnesses, and you have only one."

"I have two," said Genevieve, "but you must guess the name of the second."

CHAPTER XXX

The wedding, solemnized in the little church of Sauzen, at Belle-Isle-en-Mer, was very private. Maurice had for witnesses his uncle, François Darbois, and the Marquis de Montagnac, with whom he had become great friends. Doctor Potain and the Duke de Morlay-La-Branche were witnesses for Genevieve. The Dowager Duchess and the Princess de Bernecourt were present. The Countess Styvens had been ill for a month and could not leave Brussels. She sent a magnificent present of diamonds and pearls to Genevieve, who was filled with joy. The Duchess gave the young bride a splendid silver service, and the Princess brought with her some beautiful lace. Genevieve had attached herself very strongly to the first of these sweet women, and Maurice had made a conquest of the Princess by painting her an admirable portrait.

The sight of the Duke made the invalid exuberant with joy. She constantly forgot her duties as maid of honour to draw near the loved being.

Doctor Potain watched her closely, and made a thorough examination. He knew nothing of her love for the Duke, but when the latter questioned him about her health, he said, "There is only one chance of restoring her health. She must go back on the stage."

The Duke jumped. "Impossible!" he said.

"Why impossible? Her fiancé is dead."

The Duke spoke to the man of science. "Listen to me, Doctor, I am passionately in love with this girl who loved me, but only remembers that at intervals.... I cannot, indeed...."

"Approve of her going on the stage? Urge her yourself, and you will save her. When she is cured if she loves you, as you believe, she will leave everything to follow you; but now neurasthenia or madness await her. She must be roused to work outside herself. Do as I tell you and you will invite me to your wedding."

The Duke went straight to find François Darbois. Maurice would have retired. "No," said the Duke to him, "I want you to stay," and he told them word for word what the Doctor had said.

"Well, what do you think?" François Darbois asked him.

"I think that the most important thing in all the world is to save her! I will wait...."

François pressed his hand, and there was taken between these two men, who were so different in every way, a silent pledge that both were determined to keep at all costs.

From that instant each one strained every nerve to revive in Esperance her dearest desire.

Several days after this visit, Esperance received a letter

from the Comedie-Française, asking her to come to the office. She turned pink. Her lovely forehead brightened for the first time in many months. She handed the letter to her father, who knew what it contained, and had been watching his child's surprise very closely.

"We must go back to Paris, father, I feel entirely well."

"Good, Mademoiselle, we will obey your orders," he said tenderly.

She kissed her father as she used to do, and began to tease him a little.

"How nice it is to have such an agreeable papa! You have plenty of cause to be severe, for I give you endless trouble."

"So you are to make your début at the Comedie-Française?"

"My God!" said the young girl, starting up, "that might cost you your election!"

François Darbois began to laugh, for his joy returned to him when his daughter's memory came back to her.

"Leave my election alone. They won't even nominate me, and I shall not worry."

Mme. Darbois came in and François pretended to disclose the news to her. She assumed surprise. To hide her emotion, she took her daughter in a long embrace.

Maurice had taken his young wife to Italy, to show her

in its most harmonious setting the most beautiful aspirations of art towards the ideal. The Duke de Morlay travelled there with them, adoring Italy as does every devotee of art. There was not a corner of this rare country that he did not know.

The sojourn of the young couple in Italy was pure enchantment. Maurice was constantly surprised by the intellectual strength of his companion. Like most artists he had an indulgent scorn for what so many call and think the worldly class. When he originally met the Duke he had recognized his cultivation, and found that his eclecticism was exact, profound, and not the superficial veneer he had at first supposed. He realized that men of the world do not vaunt their knowledge, though it is often far deeper than that of certain artists who never go below the depths of but one art: their own.

Almost every day Maurice received a letter or telegram giving him news of his cousin. The advice of Doctor Potain seemed to be justifying itself. Every day Esperance began to recover her health and spirits. She was rehearsing at the Comedie, and her début in *On ne badine pas avec l'amour* was announced for the next month.

The travellers had intended to spend another ten days in Italy. But a letter to Genevieve alarmed them. She read it aloud.

"My darling, I am just now the happiest girl in the world. First because my dear cousin is seeing so many beautiful things that shine through her letters and show her so enchanted with life that I feel the stimulus myself, and long to live to go myself to breathe the divine air of Italy, and admire the masterpieces there. Tell the Duke de Morlay that no day passes without my thoughts flying to him. Only one thing worries me. I can confide it to you, Genevieve, you who are so perfectly happy. Why does the theatre draw me so that I am willing to sacrifice for it even those I love? I see the Countess Styvens every day. She seems a light ready to flicker out. Sometimes she looks at me as if she saw me far, very far away, and murmurs, 'Poor little thing, it is not her fault!' Then I shiver. What is not my fault? Albert's death. Dear Albert, who frightened me so much sometimes, that I felt my teeth chattering! Do you know how he died? Nobody seems to know! Genevieve dear, the pearl collar strangles me sometimes. I promised not to take it off, but I must take it off to play *'Camille'* in Musset's play. Mustn't I? She cannot wear pearls at the convent? When I promised that, I did not expect ever to appear on the stage any more; but now! Besides, when I am on the stage I am not myself at all. Esperance stays behind in the dressing-room and *'Camille'* comes forth. Then the collar? Ask the Duke, without telling him that I asked you, what I should do. This collar seems to me such a heavy chain, so heavy and sometimes so cold. I must stop this letter, for you see the confusion is coming back again. I am a little frightened! I must be trembling, does it not show in my writing? It is little Mademoiselle's pen. I embrace you with all the strength of my joy in your happiness. - Esperance."

The writing changed.

"I must make Esperance stop. She has been wandering again as she writes. Her pulse is very quick. I must tell her father. *Au revoir,* dear girl, and come back soon; for you are the brightness and peace she longs for. My regards to your husband. - Eleanore Frahender."

This letter made Maurice, his wife and the Duke very anxious.

"She must in some way be prevented from seeing the Countess Styvens," said Genevieve, "but how are we to manage that?"

They decided to shorten their stay in Italy by five days.

Esperance was to appear on the twentieth of December, about fifteen days after her letter reached them. All the elegant world of Paris, artistic, sensation-hunting, was waiting with delight for the appearance of the little heroine, the idol of the public. Count Styvens's death in a duel, slain by a well-known admirer of Esperance, had caused a great deal of ink to be spilled. But the devotion of the Countess towards the girl who would have been her daughter, the denials of the witnesses to the most intimate friends, asking if ... really ... between ourselves ... was not there something? ... deceived the most suspicious. All these "fors" and "againsts" had kindled the curiosity of the public, and the general sympathy was strongly in favour of the unconscious cause of the great modern mystery. The notice, announcing the first appearance of Esperance Darbois in *On ne badine pas avec l'amour* drew an enormous crowd. The house was entirely sold out several days in advance. Many who could not get admission waited outside the theatre to get news during the intervals. The corridors were full of French and foreign reporters.

Behind the scenes Esperance stood looking at herself in the mirror. It was almost time for the curtain to go up. Dressed in the convent robe, the strings of pearls was still about her neck. Should she unclasp it, should she not? If they went with her on the stage would she not be betraying her art; would they not clutch and strangle her, strangle "*Camille*," until Esperance had to come back in her place? And if she cast it aside, her loyalty, her promise? Must she wear fetters to keep faith? Oh, Albert, Albert! Oh, these dark shadows, these groping dark confusions where she so often strayed. Where was rest? Or peace? And joy, the joy of the theatre, would that, too, be taken away? She swayed a little and longed with all her strength for a force not her own to enter in. She was too weak to fight against her own Destiny.

She found it. A hint of it came first in the scent of gardenia flowers, sweet and strong and penetrating, compelling and agreeable to the senses. Then the Duke's strong arms were about her, and she sank gladly back as if she were falling into a flood of light.

But his swift words brought her back.

"Esperance, my darling, we have no time to lose. Come with me. The Countess Styvens is dying. She would not send for you, she would not spoil your triumph. But she can absolve you. She can loose the pearls. You can remember the other request Albert made you then, his dying wish, my living one. Come with me, be her daughter to the last, and then, my love, to Italy, where we will find you health and strength, and give you new life for your future as my wife."

Choose from Thousands of 1stWorldLibrary Classics By

Adolphus WilliamWard
Aesop
Agatha Christie
Alexander Aaronsohn
Alexander Kielland
Alexandre Dumas
Alfred Gatty
Alfred Ollivant
Alice Duer Miller
Alice Turner Curtis
Alice Dunbar
Ambrose Bierce
Amelia E. Barr
Andrew Lang
Andrew McFarland Davis
Anna Sewell
Annie Besant
Annie Hamilton Donnell
Annie Payson Call
Anton Chekhov
Arnold Bennett
Arthur Conan Doyle
Arthur Ransome
Atticus
B. M. Bower
Basil King
Bayard Taylor
Ben Macomber
Booth Tarkington
Bram Stoker
C. Collodi
C. E. Orr
C. M. Ingleby
Carolyn Wells
Catherine Parr Traill
Charles A. Eastman
Charles Dickens
Charles Dudley Warner
Charles Farrar Browne
Charles Ives
Charles Kingsley
Charles Lathrop Pack
Charles Whibley
Charles Willing Beale
Charlotte M. Braeme
Charlotte M.Yonge
Clair W. Hayes
Clarence Day Jr.
Clarence E. Mulford

Clemence Housman
Confucius
Cornelis DeWitt Wilcox
Cyril Burleigh
D. H. Lawrence
Daniel Defoe
David Garnett
Don Carlos Janes
Donald Keyhole
Dorothy Kilner
Dougan Clark
E. Nesbit
E.P.Roe
E. Phillips Oppenheim
Edgar Allan Poe
Edgar Rice Burroughs
Edith Wharton
Edward J. O'Biren
John Cournos
Edwin L. Arnold
Eleanor Atkins
Elizabeth Cleghorn
Gaskell
Elizabeth Von Arnim
Ellem Key
Emily Dickinson
Erasmus W. Jones
Ernie Howard Pie
Ethel Turner
Ethel Watts.Mumford
Eugenie Foa
Eugene Wood
Evelyn Everett-Green
Everard Cotes
F. J. Cross
Federick Austin Ogg
Ferdinand Ossendowski
Francis Bacon
Francis Darwin
Frances Hodgson Burnett
Frank Gee Patchin
Frank Harris
Frank Jewett Mather
Frank L. Packard
Frederick Trevor Hill
Frederick Winslow Taylor
Friedrich Kerst
Friedrich Nietzsche
Fyodor Dostoyevsky

Gabrielle E. Jackson
Garrett P. Serviss
Gaston Leroux
George Ade
Geroge Bernard Shaw
George Ebers
George Eliot
George MacDonald
George Orwell
George Tucker
George W. Cable
George Wharton James
Gertrude Atherton
Grace E. King
Grant Allen
Guillermo A. Sherwell
Gulielma Zollinger
Gustav Flaubert
H. A. Cody
H. B. Irving
H. G. Wells
H. H. Munro
H. Irving Hancock
H. Rider Haggard
H. W. C. Davis
Hamilton Wright Mabie
Hans Christian Andersen
Harold Avery
Harold McGrath
Harriet Beecher Stowe
Harry Houidini
Helent Hunt Jackson
Helen Nicolay
Hendy David Thoreau
Henrik Ibsen
Henry Adams
Henry Ford
Henry Frost
Henry James
Henry Jones Ford
Henry Seton Merriman
Henry Wadsworth
Longfellow
Henry W Longfellow
Herbert A. Giles
Herbert N. Casson
Herman Hesse
Homer
Honore De Balzac

Horace Walpole
Horatio Alger, Jr.
Howard Pyle
Howard R. Garis
Hugh Lofting
Hugh Walpole
Humphry Ward
Ian Maclaren
Israel Abrahams
J.G.Austin
J. Henri Fabre
J. M. Barrie
J. Macdonald Oxley
J. S. Knowles
J. Storer Clouston
Jack London
Jacob Abbott
James Allen
James Lane Allen
James Andrews
James Baldwin
James DeMille
James Joyce
James Oliver Curwood
James Oppenheim
James Otis
Jane Austen
Jens Peter Jacobsen
Jerome K. Jerome
John Burroughs
John F. Kennedy
John Gay
John Glasworthy
John Habberton
John Joy Bell
John Milton
John Philip Sousa
Jonathan Swift
Joseph Carey
Joseph Conrad
Joseph Jacobs
Julian Hawthrone
Julies Vernes
Justin Huntly McCarthy
Kakuzo Okakura
Kenneth Grahame
Kate Langley Bosher
L. A. Abbot
L. T. Meade
L. Frank Baum
Laura Lee Hope

Laurence Housman
Leo Tolstoy
Leonid Andreyev
Lewis Carroll
Lilian Bell
Lloyd Osbourne
Louis Tracy
Louisa May Alcott
Lucy Fitch Perkins
Lucy Maud Montgomery
Lydia Miller Middleton
Lyndon Orr
M. H. Adams
Margaret E. Sangster
Margaret Vandercook
Maria Edgeworth
Maria Thompson Daviess
Mariano Azuela
Marion Polk Angellotti
Mark Overton
Mark Twain
Mary Austin
Mary Cole
Mary Rowlandson
Mary Wollstonecraft
Shelley
Max Beerbohm
Myra Kelly
Nathaniel Hawthrone
O. F. Walton
Oscar Wilde
Owen Johnson
P.G.Wodehouse
Paul and Mable Thorn
Paul G. Tomlinson
Paul Severing
Peter B. Kyne
Plato
R. Derby Holmes
R. L. Stevenson
Rabindranath Tagore
Rahul Alvares
Ralph Waldo Emmerson
Rene Descartes
Rex E. Beach
Richard Harding Davis
Richard Jefferies
Robert Barr
Robert Frost
Robert Gordon Anderson
Robert L. Drake

Robert Lansing
Robert Michael Ballantyne
Robert W. Chambers
Rosa Nouchette Carey
Ross Kay
Rudyard Kipling
Samuel B. Allison
Samuel Hopkins Adams
Sarah Bernhardt
Selma Lagerlof
Sherwood Anderson
Sigmund Freud
Standish O'Grady
Stanley Weyman
Stella Benson
Stephen Crane
Stewart Edward White
Stijn Streuvels
Swami Abhedananda
Swami Parmananda
T. S. Ackland
The Princess Der Ling
Thomas A. Janvier
Thomas A Kempis
Thomas Anderton
Thomas Bailey Aldrich
Thomas Bulfinch
Thomas De Quincey
Thomas H. Huxley
Thomas Hardy
Thomas More
Thornton W. Burgess
U. S. Grant
Valentine Williams
Victor Appleton
Virginia Woolf
Walter Scott
Washington Irving
Wilbur Lawton
Wilkie Collins
Willa Cather
Willard F. Baker
William Makepeace
Thackeray
William W. Walter
Winston Churchill
Yei Theodora Ozaki
Young E. Allison
Zane Grey